To the one who dresses immaculately.

WILFUL
MISUNDERSTANDINGS

RICHARD FOREMAN

First publication
LEPUS BOOKS
2016

ISBN: 978-0-9933901-0-4

LEPUS BOOKS

lepusbooks.co.uk

Contents

I can't remember when I first met Richard Foreman. It's slightly unnerving when I try—and realise that it may have been as long as forty years ago. In Oxford, I think it was. Richard – then known as 'Dick' – was editing a community paper called "The Backstreet Bugle" and they were publishing an early Alan Moore strip: "St Pancras Panda". I had a car and Alan didn't, so I drove him over to visit. The remainder of that day is lost in one of the black holes eroded in my brain by smoke and time, but it must have been a sympathetic encounter because – whether resident near or far – I have been pleased to count Richard a good friend ever since.

That's one reason I am delighted to have this collection of intriguing short stories published under the cooperative imprint of Lepus Books.

Another is that they perfectly illustrate Lepus Books' raison d'être. The writing is innovative and accomplished. It appreciates the world(s) it describes from a perspective unique to the author. I find pleasure in the work and think other readers out there should have the chance to do so too.

A warning: if you're looking for hard-boiled carnage and rampant scatology in your fiction you will likely be disappointed by "Wilful Misunderstandings". These stories are the product of a far kinder and more gentle mind than (say) the one that spawns a work like "Leepus | DIZZY". Gently idiosyncratic – sometimes to the point of whimsy – they employ the seemingly simple device of words whose meanings have been reinvented to inspire carefully constructed scenarios with a playbill of disparate characters shrewdly and sympathetically observed. Offspring of a particular and subtle imagination, told with humour, craft and insight, I invite you to dive in and swim amongst them for a while. You'll probably climb out feeling better.

Jamie Delano

The House Where Jack Dwelt

The bare floorboards creaked a kind of welcome as I entered. The house had been waiting for me.

Oh yes. It knew me. It knew everyone that had set foot within its boundaries. That was one of the extraordinary properties of that extraordinary property.

Empty now, Jack's family had cleared the house out after the stroke that led to his death. It could not be sold, for reasons that will become clear. That was why I'd arrived, with just a sleeping bag, a bedroll and a few supplies, to spend a couple of days there and see if the house still liked me. If so, and with the blessing of my old friend's relatives, I could make it my home.

"Hello," I said, cautiously. "Hello house."

Memories danced back.

"PK!" I'm always 'PK' to Jack, I've long since forgotten why. "Wotcher! Fuck me, it's good to see you, man. Come in! Thanks for making the effort. Journey okay? Hey, you're looking good. Let's get the kettle on, and I'll show you round."

"Jack... Jack, you're supposed to leave little gaps where I respond to your comments and questions."

"Yeah yeah, right, man, of course, yeah." He laughed. Big laugh. Big guy. We'd known each other for years but it had taken too long to find time to visit him following his marriage break-up and move to this house.

One of those isolated cottages that went back centuries, it had been added onto with numerous extensions over the years. A first impression of limited size was unsettled by the rambling nature of the interior. We'd had a cup of tea in the living room. Jack had fired up a half-smoked spliff and I'd reminded him that, for health reasons, my smoking days were over. The room, where he spent most of his spare time reading esoteric books and watching the old black and white movies he'd always loved, reeked of cannabis.

The 'tour' followed. I expressed some amazement at the number of rooms we passed through. Not all of them were in use and at one point I noticed that Jack himself seemed uncertain of the way. Stoned, I guessed.

On the way back to the living room, he showed me a small bedroom with a view over the unkempt garden and the woodland at its edge. He'd made up a bed for me and doubtless cleared mounds of clutter from the tallboy and chair which constituted the room's other furnishings. "Nice little room, innit? Slept here myself sometimes. Should stay okay for you." I assured Jack it felt cosy with its wall to wall carpeting and would be fine.

∞

Around 2am I finally got to bed. The hours had pottered by in that smoke-hazy living room, with the rolling conversation of close friends who have been apart too long. Reminiscences of times shared. What we'd been up to over the years. Old acquaintances and their present doings… But better by far, I thought, was when we wandered off into the nature of the universe, the stuff that underpins our curious sense of reality, the sheer weirdness of being conscious at all. That was when Jack became radiant, his fertile brain sprouting ideas from the mulch of his copious reading. Me too. His company brought out in me a fluidity of thought that elsewhere seemed lacking.

I recollect the feeling at one point that he was holding back on something he wanted to tell me about. Before I could check he was on to another topic, firing off fascinatingly on research he'd read concerning the sound properties of Neolithic sacred structures.

Once, we might have stayed up 'til dawn. We lingered on past midnight but eventually, reluctantly, I parted for my bed.

"Any problems with the room, let me know," said Jack.

Removing my shoes in the little bedroom, I noticed that the carpet was bowing up by the wall, as if it had been cut too large for the floor space.

∞

"Jack… Either I'm losing it big time, or that bedroom is shrinking. I swear it, man. When I went to bed last night the tallboy was three-foot from the bed. This morning I could reach out and touch it. And the carpet's all buckling up. The room is fucking shrinking."

"Ohh," groaned Jack, a few minutes up and still bleary from sleep. "Sorry, man, I wasn't expecting that room to go."

"*That* room! You mean there *are* rooms that shrink?"

"Well, yeah. But there's, like, a sequence to it, you know. House must like you, PK. It wants to show you."

"'Like me'? 'Show me'? Jack, please explain…"

"Yeah, yeah. Let's get the kettle on first."

I got the facts as Jack rolled his first number of the day. "You've heard of fundaments, haven't you?" he began.

"Uh, yeah. Let me think – space-time anomalies that originate in unknown parts of the Earth's core and occasionally seep up through fissures in the mantle if I remember rightly."

"Near enough, mate. Well, there's one of them directly under this house. Fuckin' estate agents didn't know what to do with it. That's why I picked it up so cheap. So, shrinking rooms, that's one thing… But then other rooms, they just kinda grow, you know? And I reckon the place is sentient too. It responds to vibes, you get me?"

"No but I probably will in time."

"Way to go, man. Hey, but don't let me forget – we ought to get your stuff and the furniture out of there. While we still can."

∞

That evening we talked of nothing but the fundament.

By then, incidentally, the door to the room where I'd slept the previous night was about four feet high and it was no longer possible to stand up straight inside. "It's getting a bit Lewis Carroll," I said.

"Yeah, maybe Carroll did have some knowledge of fundaments but don't forget all the maths he coded into the 'Alice' books. He could have hit on all that growing/shrinking stuff purely as concept. Now Nikola Tesla, he was well into them. I've read some of the papers he wrote. Called them 'emanations' and talked about finding ways to tap into their energies."

"So, Jack, what are you tapping into... in this crazy, morphing house?"

He chortled. "See why I was eager to move in soon as I got wind of it? Place is cool." He took a long draw on his spliff and continued, his voice croaking. "Every couple of years or so you look around and it's all changed. Not just rooms... Features change shape. That fireplace, man – six months ago it was half that size. The bath's been getting bigger too. It has its rhythms, periods when it changes, periods when it doesn't. But all nice and slow, fortunately. No one gets hurt, though I kinda wonder how the wiring survives. The house is alive, PK. It's aware. When you step through the door you step out of consensual reality and into its reality. So me, I'm tapping into that. I'm aiming to merge my consciousness with the house. I want to become a part of it."

"Jack, do you ever sometimes think you've had one spliff too many?"

There was a momentary look of hurt in Jack's eyes and I regretted my facetiousness. The moment passed. Jack returned to the subject of Tesla and fundaments. His plan to merge with the house was not mentioned again.

∞

I stayed another couple of days. By then the door of my first bedroom had reduced to about two feet in height. You could still open it and look into the room. Even the window had shrunk, with just a small section of the former view.

I left with every intention of making a quick return. The bond of our friendship, I felt, had been well restored and needed continuing nurture. And as for the house...

But you know how it is. Life gets in the way. Weeks turn to months, months turn to years and there's always some pressing reason why you can't make it. Maybe next year. Maybe the year after.

We exchanged messages and phone calls, of course. After about eighteen months, he told me, my bedroom had reappeared – beginning with a tiny door shaped panel, just above the skirting board. By the following year it was quite a sizeable room. Jack would also pontificate at large about new theories he'd come across regarding fundaments and how they tallied or not with his experience. It seemed to be becoming an obsession.

Then came the time when there was no answer to the messages I sent and the phone just rang. I contacted his ex-wife. She told me about the stroke.

∞

In his room at the nursing home, Jack sat in his wheelchair, face sagging to one side, eyes open but seeming not to register – until I grabbed what I'd been told was his 'good hand'. "Jack! Jack, man... What the fuck?" A faint glimmer of recognition gradually became the ghost of a sparkle in his eyes. Pulling his hand away from mine, he slowly reached for the felt pen and pad on the table beside his chair.

He was, I'd learnt, incapable of speech, but could still write. The painstaking scrawl was vaguely reminiscent of his once elegant handwriting. "Wotcher PK," he wrote, "Got me some dope?"

I showed him the complimentary ounce of Leb I'd obtained from his long time dealer. "How you going to roll it? Where you going to smoke it?"

"I'll eat it," he scrawled. And then: "They tell me it was a stroke. Just know this – I'm not all here."

∞

I sat in the bare room on the bedroll, that image of Jack in the wheelchair vivid in my mind. I'd assumed then that we'd talk again but instead Jack deteriorated and was dead within weeks. It was after the funeral that I learned of the instruction he'd left that the house be offered to me. Changes in my life at the time made it a feasible proposition but did I want the place? Did it want me? Only by being there could I know.

'I'm not all here,' he'd written in the nursing home. From the rest of our 'conversation' I knew that his mind was still working with some clarity. I was puzzling over the meaning of those words when I noticed, faintly, an all too familiar smell.

It couldn't be. Jack's possessions were all gone. The house was a shell. I was alone. The doors were locked. Why then were my nostrils picking up the distinctive, heavy odour of burning hash and tobacco?

I got up and began as methodically as I could to search, rapidly losing track of just how many rooms I'd been into. The smell was tantalising. It came and went but seemed always to return when I faltered and thought of giving up.

It was in an upstairs corridor that I noticed a small door, about a foot high, that I'd failed to observe when I'd looked around the house in daylight. The smell grew stronger as I crouched down and drew close enough to turn the tiny doll's house handle.

To see inside, I had to get down on my hands and knees and press my face into the opening. I gasped. I was looking into a miniature replica of Jack's living room as it had been on my last visit. The furniture, the bookcases, the TV, the stereo… Everything was there, reduced proportionately in size. No Jack, though. The last of a joint smouldering in a tiny ashtray but no Jack.

That was when the walls spoke.

"Wotcher PK, good to see you, man."

Tears of Joy

After the implant she had to get used to the sensation of Joy's voice. Joy was always with her: in her handbag, in her pocket or there in her hand when she needed to make a call or use an app. She doubted that she'd be able to manage without Joy but to have her as a disembodied voice in her head, that part still felt weird sometimes.

Right now though Joy was set to prove her worth. They were in 'The Buzz' and it was intense. Guys tanked on booze and testosterone, milling about, loud-mouthed and smelling of aftershave; girls in skimpy night-out attire tottering on heels, laughing and shouting; big speakers pumping beats and ersatz soul at cilia-crimping volume. This was where you came to find love.

"I'm getting four probes on your social network data, Kirsty, three with handhelds. You might be able to see them. The other one has an implant."

Kirsty looked around for young men checking their devices, then thought-spoke, as she'd been trained. "Nah... Number one's got a serious weight problem, two's just a bit creepy looking and I can't see three for love nor money. What about the guy with the Automate? Can you line him up for a view?"

"Of course I can, Kirsty, but I've been looking at his profile. Mutual interests are close to zero. High potential for compatibility issues. I really don't think he's your type."

"Yeah but I'd just like to get a *look* at him."

"Well all right, if you must."

∞

Eventually she'd found herself being chatted up by a guy who did without probes. Joy had listened in to the conversation and, when she'd got his name and a few telling details, she'd done a web search on him. Then, as he headed for the gents, she'd mentioned to Kirsty that he appeared to have some rather unfortunate tendencies, including an apparent addiction to internet porn. Kirsty had made herself scarce well before his return.

Now she sat in the tiny kitchen of her flat staring into a cup of coffee and feeling depressed. Alone, she preferred to speak aloud to Joy, who lay on the table by the coffee cup exhibiting a gently pulsing screensaver. "Well that was a great night out."

"Ahh," said Joy, "sarcasm? Yes? You don't actually mean that, do you?"

"No. No, Joy, I don't."

"I'm so sorry, Kirsty, I should have picked that up without a query. Your serotonin's right down. I'd say it was time for a comfort strategy."

"Really? What would you recommend?"

"Well that coffee's not going to help. I suggest you chuck it down the sink, make yourself a nice hot chocolate and a hot water bottle and get yourself to bed. I can stream some really nice relaxation music for you. All restful and smooth."

∞

Kirsty unplugged the charger and switched Joy back on. "Oh thank you, Kirsty! I feel so much better after a good, long charge."

She looked at the device with a puzzled frown. "Joy... How can you 'feel better'? I mean, basically, you are just a bit of software installed on a handheld device. You're a bot."

"Ohh... Please don't use the 'B' word. Yes, I may be software but I have passed the Turing Test. I think you'll agree that makes me a bit special at least."

"The 'Turing Test'?"

"Mm. Devised back in the last century by Alan Turing, the artificial intelligence pioneer. Of course they've developed it all a bit since then. Would you like to see a Wiki?"

"No, just tell me about this 'Test'. What did you have to do?"

"I had to convince a judge – who obviously couldn't see me; it was just a text chat onscreen – that I was indistinguishable from a human being."

"Oh. I see."

"Kirsty?"

"Yes?"

"Do *you* find me indistinguishable from a human being?"

∞

It was a shortcut that Kirsty had not used for a while, but which she'd always found pleasant. Once she'd passed through the business district of the city it would take her through a churchyard and a park and eventually on to a maze of narrow streets filled with cool boutiques where, over the years, she'd bought most of her favourite clothes.

She was thinking about a rather elegant, turquoise skirt she'd seen last trip but decided she couldn't afford. If it was still there this time, she thought, yeah, she was going to have it.

"Kirsty?" It was still jarring when Joy suddenly intruded on her thoughts. Joy was quick to apologise. "I know… I know… We have an agreement, but… I don't like it here."

"What?!"

"All this graffiti. Some tech-savvy people with a very nasty agenda, they've put it up all over."

"Graffiti?" Kirsty was looking round frantically. A couple of names she saw scrawled childishly on a wall, but otherwise no evident graffiti.

"Use the cam," said Joy, "the AR app I downloaded. You'll be able to see it."

"AR?" Kirsty pulled Joy from her handbag and rapidly pressed her way to the camera.

"Augmented Reality. It's digital graffiti. You need AR to see it."

And through the camera, see it she did. Sickly glowing logos that seemed to hover over doorways and windows throughout the business district: jagged lettering, malignant and ominous, random initials in circles and stark geometric shapes. One legible word appeared frequently. 'Raze!'

Joy's fear infected her. She hurried through the churchyard, anxious to distance herself from this zone with its concealed threats of erasure.

∞

Kirsty had nevertheless gone on to buy the turquoise skirt to complete an outfit for her date that night.

Joy had convinced her that nightclubs in general and The Buzz in particular were not places best suited for her to find love. The Automate had suggested instead some online dating agencies, and through one of them she'd found Adrian, a phone engineer from the northern district of the city. Kirsty had met him a couple of times. Once for a coffee, once for a walk. Now they were on to the meal-out stage.

With Joy, she'd studied his profile and online presence in general. They'd found nothing to put them off. In person he'd proved charming, good-looking and gently humorous.

Pleasant anticipation tinged itself with anxiety as Kirsty prepared, taking time with her makeup and agonising over shoes. Finally she activated the cam again, posing in front of the lens for Joy to appraise her.

"What can I say? You are so beautiful, and that skirt... such a choice! It just goes perfectly with the top."

"Yes, but what about the shoes?" hissed Kirsty urgently, "are they okay?"

"They're fine. Listen, if Adrian isn't already in love with you, believe me, he will be by the end of tonight. You are absolutely radiant, girl. Now you go out and show that man just how lucky he is to have met you."

∞

The date went perfectly. Adrian's charm proved utterly consistent and the meal itself exquisite (Joy having recommended the restaurant). He had made Kirsty laugh. He had made her think in ways that she'd not previously considered. He'd seemed too to bring out the best in her. She could feel herself sparkling and captivating him. By the end of the evening it was clear that Joy's prediction had all the appearance of being right. Before they parted, having agreed to meet again in a couple of days, they had shared a first shy, tentative kiss and a moment's longing look into one another's eyes.

"I am just so happy for you," said Joy. "And before you ask – it's a kind of tingly feeling going all through my circuit boards."

In her PJs, drinking the last of her chocolate, Kirsty was wondering how well she'd sleep after such an evening. "Thank you, Joy. You've been such a friend. It's just so hard to believe that you're..."

"Programmes? Algorithms? No, come on, I've told you. I've passed the all the Tests. I'm Joy. Now get yourself to bed, you need your sleep."

"Yeah, right. I should, shouldn't I?"

"Just one thing, though..."

"What's that, Joy?"

"Please don't switch me off tonight. I've got plenty of juice, and you can charge me up in the morning if needs be. I'd just like to... I'd just like to do some processing, if that's okay."

∞

Kirsty was back in the restaurant, but Adrian was nowhere to be seen. The table was set for two. Where had he gone? She couldn't be sure. Perhaps he was nearby somewhere. Perhaps she should look for him.

And then she *was* looking for him, gliding, it seemed, through the restaurant, until she found herself in the kitchens where men in white were industriously assembling plate after plate of succulent and perfectly presented comestibles. Waiters appeared in seemingly endless succession to take the plates, conveying them with utmost reverence, as if they were religious relics on their way to some high and significant ceremony. And she, Kirsty, drifted amongst them looking under tables and into cupboards, looking, looking... What was she looking for? She couldn't quite remember.

But she knew she had to keep on, and found herself drifting out of a back doorway into a dark alley with food bins and detritus; and she couldn't be sure, but those stirrings in the shadows, could they be rats? It didn't matter; she had to keep looking, gliding over cobbles, past seedy back doorways and parked vans.

Her progress continued until she saw a figure in the shadows, sat crouched on a doorstep. Drawing closer, she could see that it was a woman, with a fine head of long, wavy hair cascading over her shoulders, face hidden, buried in her hands. Was this what she'd been looking for?

She glided still closer, until she could reach out and touch her. She felt an overwhelming urge to do just that, and as she did, the woman lowered her hands. In a shaft of light Kirsty saw that she was perhaps in her fifties or sixties, with redness in her cheeks and a rounded, gentle face. She seemed immediately to recognise Kirsty, smiling warmly. But, deep set and thoughtful, her eyes were moistening with tears.

They embraced wordlessly, like two long lost friends or lovers clutched close, their tears mingling. Kirsty was acutely aware of the woman's tiny stature. It was like hugging a child.

At last she loosened her grip. She wanted to speak but the woman made a gesture of despair, then pointed upwards. Kirsty raised her head and saw four faintly glowing letters that seemed to hover in the air above them.

'Raze'.

∞

Joy was gone. This Kirsty knew with no prompting, the moment she woke from the dream. All that was left by her bedside was the device and – although it remained adequately charged – it was now but the shell of her Automate, an anonymous screen glowing blankly. Not a button she pressed could make it any better.

∞

"No," said the man in the tech shop, "I'm sorry. We've had this trouble right across the board, and it's whacked the Automates hardest. I can't see Apricot getting 'em back on the market for, ooh, months. They'll need some way-new kind of virus protection for a start."

"But who's responsible for it?" said Kirsty, "this 'Raze' virus?"

He shrugged his shoulders. "I dunno. Anarchists... Nihilists... Call 'em what you will. Nerds with a grudge, basically. Gotta hand it to 'em. Infectious 'graffiti'. That was clever. Anyway, Apricot takes responsibility and I can arrange a full refund."

"I don't want a refund, I want... oh, never mind, just give me the papers to sign."

As more tears crept into her eyes, Kirsty felt Adrian's reassuring arm around her. Solace in a warm weight across her shoulders.

Joy had left her with one last gift.

Olivia Says...

paragraphs, who the fuck needs them?
               paragraphs are history
                       when vers libre
                       and poetry concrete
                       rap
        then i am in
         – bong –

         satori

hey, i just wrote that in a moment or two of bliss and profundity –
but stay cool, this doesn't mean i am going to do some crusty old
paragraph thing now that i have reverted to prose, because it is
actually 'spontaneous bop prosody' i am putting out here and i
intend to continue without reverting to paragraphs, until such a time
as poetry pushes through me, like a plunger in a syringe, and erupts
– because it is my job to let poetry erupt, because i am a quill and us
quills are set upon this earth to facilitate the eruption of poetry –

> quills making
> pulchritudinous poetry –
> this could be a haiku

there's this thing, though – this whole fucked up finance thing and
you have to pay attention to it because, naturally, it does not
harmonise with the quill vibe to hook it into the 9 to 5 jive – but also
it does not behove the public at large to actually spend enough
money on the work of us quills to keep us in food, drink and the
kinds of exotic stimulants we require for survival – so the finance
thing has to be dealt with especially in these weird end-times we're
living through now – and of course there is welfare, but that is too
baseline for quills, though obviously there are deep and profound
souls to be encountered standing in soup queues

crusts
the brain in pain regains its train
lusts
the soup droops the felt melts

starvation beckons

so i am looking for ways to handle the finance thing and my muse, whose name is Olivia Pilkington, suggests that what i need is a 'grant' from some sort of arts organisation, or philanthropist type, or whatever – which is kind of like patronage when you think about it and if these people think they are going to have any say whatsoever in what i have to say and how i am going to say it then they can keep their money tightly wedged up their doubtlessly refined assholes – but Olivia says: cool it, Marcus, your brain is boiling over again, you can't go assuming they are going to censor you and dilute your message to the world before you've even found out who they are and what they have to offer – and it's more often than not worth listening to Olivia, so i do

    listening to you
    irises open into succulent bloom
    listening to you
    pitbulls roll over to get their bellies rubbed
    listening to you
    sunlight tries harder to push through the clouds

so a week or two later we're sitting at Olivia's kitchen table and we are looking at these documents that have to be filled in to convey to the people that give grants just how essential it is that i am able to function as a quill in these difficult times – and i'm saying: hey let's write free verse in all the boxes and then these people will just know in their souls that they must undertake to keep me in food, drink and exotic stimulants – but Olivia is saying: err, Marcus, i think the idea is that they get to see examples of your work and doubtless that will resonate with their very souls, but these boxes have to be filled in with some of the more prosaic stuff, so they get to know... you know... the thinking behind your work, your plans, your requirements and so on – oh right – i say – we hit them with both barrels, yeah? well, that's okay, Livvy, so long as i don't have to write in paragraphs – and she says: you don't have to write in paragraphs, Marcus, you just have to make a little bit of sense – god, how i love that woman...

my muse

is amused

my muse

knows the news

my muse

is the news

so we get three of these monumentally tedious documents finally completed and i say – Olivia, you deserve to eat out at DiMuccio's for doing all this and i am going to take you there, and i am going to recompense you for paying the bill, just as soon as i am in receipt of these 3 grants to which i am entitled – and all this comes to pass, and the weeks go by, and we wait to hear back from the benevolent ones – and the weeks keep passing and i'm saying – my god, how long does it take to read some tedious prose in some tedious boxes, and more importantly, why have they not read my poems and dropped all their other priorities immediately in a rush to shower me with money? and Olivia is saying: these things can take time, Marcus, you must wait... like a Zen Master, for the universe to unfold – and i kneel before her, quite literally, and i bow to her wisdom – and we agree that, once i have been showered with money, we will write a book for the benefit of all quills everywhere and it will be called: 'Zen and the Art of Grant Applications'

money

they call it 'filthy lucre'

but filth is cleaner

actually

eventually, and i am starting to feel the will to live ebbing from my bones by this point, we hear back with regard to one of the applications – it is, Livvy says, a 'standard letter' and it regrets to inform me that i do not fulfil the criteria that would entitle me to a grant – and i am bemused to the very depths of my soul because they must have read my poetry and if they have read my poetry how can they not consider me a 'suitable candidate'? it is unbelievable – it is inconceivable – it is the very essence of injustice – and there must surely be a way to appeal, to strenuously complain – in fact i think i will find out where they are based and picket them on a daily basis until they see the error of their ways – but Olivia says: let's just wait and see how the other two applications do, shall we?

waiting
waiting
waiting
waiting

NOW!!!!

the second response is identical, they even use the same wording on the 'standard letter' – who drafts these things? they should be forced instead to write poetry at gunpoint, and i can say this as a firm believer in non-violent principles because the guns wouldn't be loaded, though they wouldn't know that – but then Olivia does point out that it would count as violence if they thought they were being threatened, so i say we could find some sort of non-violent weapon

and use that instead, whereupon she shrugs her shoulders and gives
me a withering look

waiting some more

waiting

some

more

(yawn)

Olivia has all along had a sense of confidence about the third
application, which turns out to be uncannily accurate when the
answer finally arrives in the form of a written message delivered by
a bicycle courier with dreadlocks – it's tucked into an envelope that
is edged with art deco patterns in blacks and greys – it says that they
are interested in my work and would like me to attend for a face to
face discussion of my project – and Livvy's grinning all over her face:
i knew it, Marcs! the name was the clue – the Loveand Trust! how
astonishingly cool! – i'm saying – but there's just one thing, Liv –
what 'project'? ah yes – she says – you'd nodded off when i wrote
that bit for you...

project to project a projection
across a secular section
knowing it's not a rejection

at first i am not quite my usual zen-calm self, somehow, and i'm
thinking that it's the clothes – the clothes are the result of an
irreconcilable quandary i faced when Liv told me i needed to both be
smart and be myself, as i am now explaining to the interview panel,
the mauve linen suit with its embroidered musical notes is a sort of

compromise, whereas the bare feet below are a true expression of the naked truth i have to share with my fellow human beings – but they, the panel, seem pretty laid back, and soon i start to get the quill mojo and i just know i can tell them anything and they'll drink it deep – and they are pretty appreciative when i get to the end, but then one of them, who is kind of a foxy lady and has a blonde afro and a bandanna, is saying: thank you, Marcus, you are a quality quill and we dig you – now tell us about your project…

project concept
nightmare, daddio
facts you gotta face square

so i am saying: this is amorphous, people, and advisably so, for it is about the ultimately flexible medium that is our reality on this planet – how can we plan against fate's allocations? are there patterns which we can observe in its seeming vagaries which are analogous to existing patterns, giving us foreknowledge? are there pooh sticks floating under the bridge? so many questions, to which poetry has the answers, so what i have in mind is kind of like a poetry answering service… – and i keep on rapping in this vein for about the right length of time secure in the knowledge that i am most assuredly flipping the wigs of the entire panel…

that i most assuredly have
they most assuredly reassure me
but, then it sounds to me like they're saying…

there's this whole fucked up finance thing which we have to pay attention to, and it has to be dealt with, especially in these weird end-times we are living through now, so here's the situation – we intend to give you a sizeable grant, Marcus, as soon as we ourselves are in receipt of these 3 grants from central funding bodies to which we know we are entitled and which may be with us in a matter of months or possibly years – for the moment we are only able to pay ourselves, and we're sure you'll be glad to hear we do so quite comfortably – but in the meantime, well… if you've incurred any expenses getting here today, we could probably have a whip-round…

olivia
black coffee angel
oh teaspoon of destiny
in dark swirling depths

so, this is how it is, Liv, at least some people who give grants have to get grants from other people who give grants in order to give grants to the people who they select as being eligible for grants – and it is further conceivable that the people who give grants to the people who give grants have to ask in turn for grants themselves – great! says Liv: i'm glad we've got that one sorted out! we'd better get some more applications written, hadn't we? and i'm saying: Olivia, my muse and my rock of ages, how can we? the ones with money fail to see just how important i am, the ones that really do get me don't have any money… right! she says, then to target the money you must think of yourself as a guerrilla, Marcus, and you must look for ways to infiltrate the system and to subvert it from within

which

is

why

The paragraph is an elegant structure, designed to contain distinct and related information; a 'block of thought', if you will, that is delivered in a package of words. It is then succeeded by the next paragraph, following a space in the text, and subtly introduced with an indent.

As a writer it is my mission to explore the paragraph and within its form to admit new dimensions of thought, like hitherto unseen light frequencies entering the spectrum. From the 'quill' perspective I bring forth these new colours, and from that of experience and maturity I bring form and discipline.

"Yeah!" says Olivia, "that's the stuff... Tell 'em what they want to hear..."

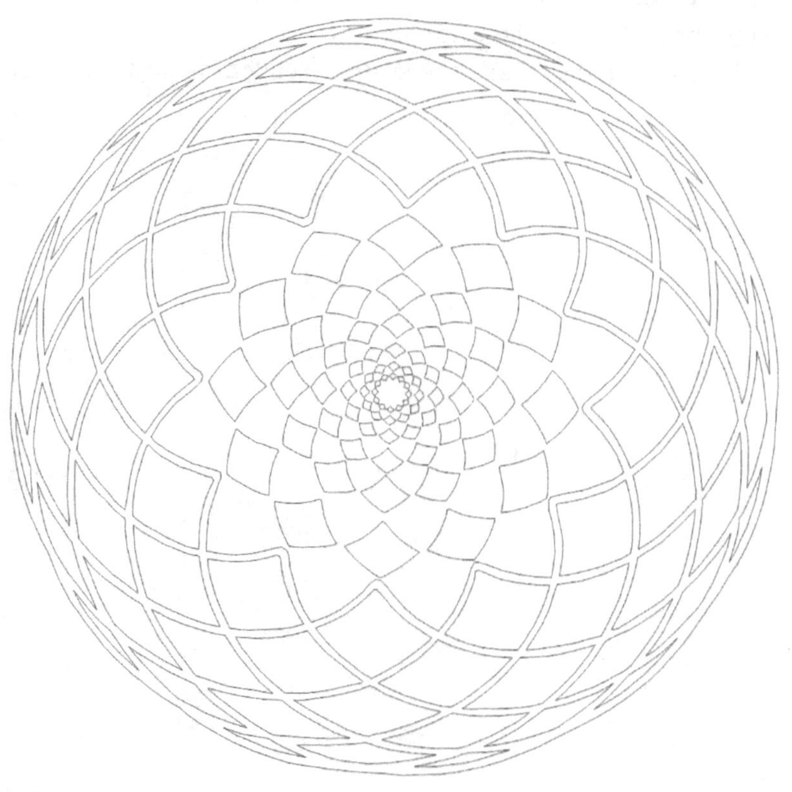

Jonathan and the Extraordinary Drawer

It was a most peculiar drawer in an otherwise rather ordinary wooden chest.

Now apart from its size, the only thing that usually distinguishes one drawer from all the others is that it sticks on its runners and, when you try to open it, the whole chest shudders and things fall off the top. And then it suddenly gives way and it's all you can do to stop yourself falling over backwards. This drawer wasn't like that. When Jonathan pulled the handles it slid open smooth and with barely a sound.

At first, he was a little afraid of it.

That morning Dad had struggled into his bedroom, puffing, and pulling and pushing in the chest of drawers. "Good chest that. It'll last as long as you need it."

But it was Mum who'd told him about the special drawer. "See that one, Jonathan? The little one, top left... You must never try to keep anything in that drawer. Understand?"

"Why not?"

"Because the next time you open it, it won't be there."

Jonathan could barely believe his ears. He'd never heard of a drawer that you couldn't put things in or that somehow made things disappear. But there was more. "You see, the drawer is a *jig*, Jonathan. It's a magical drawer. When you open a jig you never know what you'll find inside it. It could be... toys or books. Or it could just be something very beautiful. Or something you've just never, ever seen before."

"Really?" Jonathan gasped. "Anything at all?"

"Anything. But whatever it is, you must also remember this. You will see it once. You can take it out of the drawer. You can do whatever you want with it. But you will only see it once... and you will never see it again."

You'd have a lot of questions, wouldn't you, if someone gave you a jig? Jonathan did. So many questions that he could barely work out where to even begin. But Mum said she was too busy and it was best if Jonathan just opened the drawer by himself. He'd soon find out how it all worked.

And that's why, as the drawer slid smoothly open, Jonathan was a little afraid. But not so afraid that he didn't want to know what he'd find there.

The first thing he saw in the jig drawer was nestled like a shop display in a rumpled heap of chiffon. It was a statuette of an elephant, made of shining golden metal but inlaid with bright coloured jewels. Carefully, he picked it up out of the drawer. It felt weighty and very, very real. He stood it atop the chest and looked and looked. It was quite magnificent. He picked it up again. Could it really be made of gold? He turned it around. Every detail was there:

the wrinkles, the folds of skin, the great stubby feet, the tiny, staring jewelled eyes.

How could it be? It was the first time he'd looked into the drawer and here it was: something precious, something wonderful.

He was about to put it back, lay it in the chiffon once more, when he remembered what he'd been told. "You will see it once. And you will never see it again."

But he so wanted to look at it and look at it, to hold it, to play with it, to see it in his room. Carefully he laid it on the bed and then turned to close the drawer.

It slid shut.

He pulled it open again. The chiffon was gone and the drawer was full of little sticks of kindling wood. Nothing more. At least he'd not put the elephant away to have it disappear and be replaced by firewood. He turned back to look at it on the bed.

But there was no elephant to be seen. There was nothing on the bedcover. It had gone.

He had turned his back on it. "You will see it once and you will never see it again." So that was how it worked. You only had to let it out of your sight and…

That was how it worked.

The drawer that was a jig proved to be everything that Mum had told him. He experimented with putting things from the bin or stones from the garden into the drawer and closing it. When he'd open it again he'd find a small selection of model aeroplanes, or a completely varnished pinecone. No matter how many times he opened and closed it he'd never see the same thing again.

Once he found a whole troop of model soldiers. He played with them for hours. So long as you paid attention to them, they would last and last. But then he'd been called downstairs for dinner.

Desperate to keep them for further play, he'd bundled them into a clear plastic bag and taken them with him to the dinner table. He'd wanted to put them on the table where he could see them, but Dad said the table was not for toys, even magical ones. So he'd kept them beside him and tried to keep his hand on the bag and take frequent glimpses at it. Sooner or later though, distracted by the food or something mum had to say to him, he forgot the soldiers for just a few seconds. And then the bag beside him was empty. When they saw the look of disappointment on his face, mum and dad were very sorry. But that was how it was. The jig. That was how it worked.

Once, Jonathan had what he thought was a very good idea. He would open and close the drawer again and again, until he found something there that would make him the envy of his friends. Then he would offer a swap, for some item or other of theirs that he might like to keep.

It took a lot of opening and closing. He lost count of the number of things he saw in the drawer. Fold up umbrellas; boxes of tea-light candles; twenty small screwdrivers with different coloured handles; handkerchiefs; a selection of polished stones; a tangle of old electrical wires... It was almost as if the jig knew what he was after and was teasing him by presenting only the sorts of things you found in rather boring, non-magical drawers.

After a while he stopped and thought very hard about what he really hoped to discover. "Come on, jig. Come on, jig..." he said as he reached to pull the drawer open once more.

It took him a few moments to recognise what he found. A series of balls, all of different sizes; a selection of wires and poles and a stand; a little motor unit and a piece of printed paper with instructions. The largest by far of the balls was bright orange-yellow. It was, he realised, meant to be the sun. The smaller balls were coloured and sized to resemble the planets of the solar system – from tiny Pluto to fat Jupiter. The instructions told him how to assemble it all into something called an 'orrery' – a moving model of the planetary system.

Fascinated, he assembled it. It worked. It didn't even need a battery. The motor was clockwork. You just had to wind it up with a little key and somehow each and every one of those planets was circling the sun.

Jonathan thought for a while. He didn't want to swap something that he knew would sooner or later disappear with any of his good friends. It had to be someone he didn't really like, or someone who'd done him a bad turn. After a while, he decided. He set off – carrying the orrery carefully in front of him – to a house but a few doors away.

He returned the proud owner of a 'boxing robots' game. He cleared a space on top of the chest, and lay it there where he could see all the exciting pictures of the two bravely battling mechanical foes on the side of the box.

Mum was calling from down below. It was supper time. Afterwards, as soon as he could, he rushed back to his bedroom, eager to open the box and get out the robots, their boxing ring, the controls...

There was no box upon the chest. It had gone. But how could that be? Mum and dad were downstairs the whole time. There was no one else in the house. It was as if it had just...

Disappeared.

He could think of no other explanation.

So what then of the beautiful orrery that he'd traded for what was now nothing? It remained, he found out, at the house where he'd exchanged it and it stayed where it was put, whether seen or unseen. Jonathan supposed he could ask to look at it again himself. "I'll only let you see it on one condition," said the boy who lived in the house, "You'll let me have a game with my old boxing robots."

And that was how it was. The jig. That was how it worked.

Jonathan grew to be a thoughtful and intelligent young man. He was quiet but became a good friend to anyone who took the time to get to know him. If you needed something and Jonathan had it, he would give it to you. Things that you possess just didn't seem to matter to him. People did.

The only thing that he ever kept to himself was that chest of drawers. As a child he'd wanted to show it to his friends, naturally, but Mum had told him that if one was fortunate enough to possess a jig it was best not to speak of it to anyone. Its magic, she said, was for one person alone.

As a young man he would go to the drawer only once each week. He still loved to look inside but he'd learned that it worked best when you didn't just keep on opening and closing it. If you waited and thought carefully about what kind of things you might like to find, it seemed to make some effort to surprise and delight you. A piece of meteorite that could have come from the moon, tiny yet extraordinarily heavy. An elegant and ornately decorated miniature shoe that looked like it could once have been worn by a fairy prince. The delicate bamboo makings of an oriental mobile that could be assembled to dance and shimmer in the slightest draft.

He would study whatever he found and make drawings of it, or write words about it. The drawing and the writing became a part of him and in time a way to make a living. Good work came to him. A good life too, as he left his childhood home and made his own way in the world. He found love, happily, and in time his loving wife gave birth to a daughter. Amy was her name, and she grew to be a child of whom her mum and dad were quite right to be proud.

And then one day...

It was that time of the week when Jonathan would go to the bedroom where he kept the extraordinary drawer and take another look inside. He reached for the handle. Then he stopped.

He went to look for his daughter, Amy. "You know that rickety old chest of drawers in your room, love? With the one drawer that keeps sticking on its runner? If you want, I've got a much nicer chest of drawers you could have there instead."

And that too was how it was. The jig.

That was how it worked.

Beast

Alison had spent much of the morning cleaning and preparing their meditation room for the interview. She was still arranging the last of the floor cushions in what she could remember of the pattern that the feng shui consultant had stipulated when she heard the chiming of the front door bell.

Gentle and melodious as they were, the chimes could not actually be heard in much of the house, so she could not rely on Dominic to answer even though he was downstairs. Alison dashed, less mindfully than she would have liked, to the front door.

He had arrived exactly at the time of their appointment. He wore an elaborately pocketed denim jacket and a patchwork cap over cords and a brightly striped collarless shirt. Shaven headed – unless he affected some sort of topknot under the cap – his face was etched with deep lines, yet somehow his skin did not appear aged. There was an old, scuffed rucksack across his shoulder.

"Hello," she said, "you must be Phlon."

"I must be." His eyes seemed to ripple with amusement. "And you're Alison. And, ah, Dominic, yes?"

She hadn't heard him, but became aware that Dom was standing behind her. She ushered Phlon up to the meditation room, while Dom returned to the kitchen to fetch the *maté* he'd been preparing. She gestured to the cushions. "Have a seat." Phlon made straight for the one cushion she had not yet arranged and sat himself down in the lotus position with an ease she had to admire.

Ali sat cross-legged, trying to keep her back as straight as Phlon's, while Dom arrived with the pot and the cups. Phlon sniffed appreciatively. "Mm... It'll take a few minutes to brew. Shall we get going?" His voice was cultured, pronunciation careful and precise.

"Yes, let's."

"Good. The interview has just finished, by the way. I hate interviews, don't you?"

Bewildered, Alison looked at Dom. He was smiling, apparently unfazed. "Well, that one passed painlessly," he said.

"I work intuitively," said Phlon, directing his words primarily at the still confused Alison. "Your manner, your environment and your auras tell me all I need to know. So now we can just relax, get to know each other a bit, drink the *maté* and I'll tell you how you will be united with your parapet..."

"Oh!" said Alison, in a burst of relief, "then you do consider us suitable!"

"Eminently!" Phlon laughed. "You're just the kind of people we're looking for. So, once we've dealt with one or two rather tedious financial matters, you can prepare yourselves for a life-affirming symbiosis."

Billed as a 'ritual' by the Parapet People, it took on the trappings of a fine old party. Dom and Ali were told to invite as many of their friends as they pleased, whilst Phlon brought half a dozen of his colleagues. Everyone provided food and drink, musicians played and two of the Parapet People, in dazzling harlequin costumes, performed their finest juggling routine as a prelude to the main event.

At last everyone gathered in the meditation room, huddled around the space at the centre. There Phlon sat on the same cushion he'd selected before, apparently in a trance, his rucksack beside him. A murmur of talk stopped instantly as Phlon opened his eyes, peered all around him and smiled. From his rucksack he pulled a stick of dried green herbs wrapped in something like cheesecloth, to one end of which he applied a lighter until the herbs were smouldering. He waved it slowly around and passed it to the nearest hand. Then, as he spoke, each person in the room took the stick in turn and the pungent smell of the herb smoke wafted throughout the candlelit room.

"Friends, we are about to evoke. Now there's a word! Evoke! Call up! Manifest a spirit creature, not of this world but... not out of this world either. And of this creature we will make a request. We will request that it forms a bond, a lifetime bond of support and companionship with our hosts, our seekers, our good friends Dominic and Alison..."

∞

In the early hours, when they finally got to bed, Alison clutched Dominic tightly and looked into his deep, steady eyes. "I wasn't expecting anything quite so... big. I mean, I was thinking some kind of little bird, or a dog, or a little monkey, or... you know, a *pet*."

"Well, to be fair, they've always told us that this would be a lot more than a pet," he said, "but yeah, I wasn't expecting a lynx, either."

From somewhere outside the bedroom they heard creaking floorboards. Alison wasn't sure, but were there also soft, padding footfalls? She drew herself closer to Dom.

"Don't be afraid, Ali. Remember what Phlon said, it's here to give us protection and guidance."

"Yes, yes. That's why we wanted a parapet, isn't it? Our familiar. Our spirit beast companion. But now it's here, it uh... it's going to take some getting used to."

∞

The next morning they cleared up what was left of the party debris.

Mundane activity, it made the evocation ritual and manifestation of their parapet seem dreamlike and distant. At the height of the chanting had there really been a concentration of mist around Phlon at the centre? And, when Phlon could no longer be seen, had the appearance of the lynx, with its tufted ears, chin ruff and broad paws, been some kind of collective hallucination? Had it truly prowled the centre space returning steadily the awed gaze of every onlooker, until it found the garlanded Alison and Dominic, lifted its head and growled a greeting?

In the light of day, there seemed to be no hint of the creature's presence. It was easy to believe that it had all been smoke and mirrors. The only thing they could be sure of was the substantial amount of money that had passed from their bank account to that of the Parapet People. This thought crossed both their minds but remained unspoken.

Tasks completed, Alison took her usual morning retreat in the meditation room, anxious to find perspective on her thoughts. She went to her own customary cushion, but the one at the centre of the room, where Phlon had sat last night, caught her eye. She settled there. Attempting a lotus, she hastily decided the pain in her legs was too distracting, so sat cross-legged, closing her eyes and attempting to maintain a focus on the process of breathing alone. Bouncing, irrepressible thought and encroaching lower back pain soon began to plague her.

"Keep eyes closed."

The urge was to do the opposite. Ali fought it. The voice that spoke to her had the quality of an old door creaking on its hinges. It was followed by a sound, somewhere between a deep purr and a grunt, then soft but heavy footfalls until the presence was directly behind her back. A musky smell infused her nostrils. Her shoulders tensed. It was all she could do not to cringe.

"Have not fear," it said, "lean you back."

"You mean until I'm—"

"Speak you not."

She could feel its weight on the cushion behind her, and warmth from its body that seemed to curl around her. She let herself trust and leaned back until the beast took her weight. There, the slow movement of its breathing rocked her. Her back pain eased. Her thoughts slowed.

"Breathe with me," it said.

And she did.

∞

Dom held Alison, patiently awaiting some explanation for her mix of laughter and tears. In time she mustered words. "It's incredible… Oh Dominic, it's there for both of us. Go up there now. Go up and feel it!"

"Sorry. Go up where?"

"The meditation room. And whatever happens, keep your eyes closed."

"Uh! Right! This is—"

"Yes!"

∞

"Fantastic," said Phlon, "we've been buzzing ever since the ritual. A lynx? Wow." It was the first of his 'support' visits. "Male or female?"

"It doesn't say," said Dominic. Then, turning to Alison, he added, "We talked about that, didn't we?"

"Yeah," she said, "we figured it'll let us know when it wants to."

"Well, I'm beginning to understand why you guys were chosen. It's known as the 'keeper of secrets', the lynx. The silent type, yeah? But it doesn't just guard secrets; it knows them… because it has the power to see through, to penetrate."

"Hang on," said Alison, "I don't know if I understand why we were chosen. Okay, Dominic teaches tai chi and meditation, but me, I'm just a beginner, really."

Phlon grinned, eyes sparkling. "Perhaps it sees your potential."

∞

She was hungry. When last it was light she'd stalked and killed a goat, but before she could tear off more than a mouthful or two of its sinewy flesh she'd heard the wolf pack approaching and run for her own life. She'd returned to her one surviving cub in the rocky den. The cub was hungry too. Now she had resumed her hunting, in the dark time.

Rabbits. In a clearing. Unaware of her, as yet. Stealth essential, she advanced by increment, each forepaw poised aloft before its careful lowering to the ground. Waiting patiently in cover, minute after minute, for one of the long-ear beasts to wander close. Calculating by degrees the exact moment at which to launch herself and pounce. Muscles tensed, ready.

Then, faster than thought, she threw herself forward at maximum acceleration, eyes fixed on her target. The rabbit had barely begun to run when her teeth reached its neck, sinking deep, her mouth suffusing with the taste of blood.

Alison woke instantly, breaking the dream. Dominic snored softly by her side. She could still taste the blood.

∞

"Ough! I had a rabbit for a pet when I was a kid!"

Dominic looked at her squarely over poised wholemeal toast. "Well now we've got a parapet. It's a different ballgame, Ali. Okay, it's kind of a visceral dream, but we have to look at what it's saying, what it means."

"I know..." Alison took a sip of her tea. "And I think I know what she's telling us, in her own sweet way. We always said we'd go for it when we're ready, didn't we? Well, I think we're ready. I think we need... cubs."

He broke into a broad grin. "All *right!*"

∞

Was feng shui appropriate in the case of floor cushions? Alison had never quite remembered how to distribute them after the night of the Parapet Ritual.

It seemed to make no difference. The art in her meditation practice was clearer to her now. She would sense the presence of the lynx at times; at other times not. But, either way, she could feel herself going deeper.

∞

"Enhancement of your hunting powers," said a visiting Phlon, with a graceful tongue in his cheek, "so native Americans say a lynx dream brings. What do you think you'll be hunting for, Alison?"

She was thoughtful. "Lost things. I'd like to find lost things and bring them back to this world."

"Ah," he said, "I can get you on a training course for that."

∞

Occasionally the lynx, in its syntax of triplets, gave voice to words. What did it mean when it said, "Bird, friend enemy," to Alison one day as it rested beside her? Was she still required to honour her general agreement not to speak?

She thought for a while and then spoke slowly: "See it not."

The lynx drew closer and, in a flicker, licked her ear once with its coarse tongue. She felt the brush of its ruff on the back of her neck.

"See you will," it said.

Luck

You hardly see it now, but back in those days, at virtually any major roundabout or on any slip road, there'd be hitchhikers. Too bloody many sometimes. I had to wait my turn in queues of twenty or more on a fair few occasions. It could be a pretty tedious way to travel, but now and again you'd get a lift from someone who was fascinating. My luck was in that day. Totally in. I got a ride with a henchman.

"Been waiting long?"

"Check the beard, man. Clean shaven when I first stuck my thumb out."

He smiled. It was a crack that I wheeled out every time I got asked that question – which is to say: frequently. I had him pegged for a salesman or similar. Smart shirt, loosened tie, jacket on a hanger, brochures on the backseat. A sort of lived-in feel to the interior of his Cortina.

"Student, are you?"

"Oh yeah, school of life. Womb to tomb curriculum."

"Hm. You seem to think you're a comedian, young man."

Unsure of his tone, I tried to read him. Had I pissed him off already? He was good for the next sixty-five miles; it wouldn't do to jangle the vibes. "I was a student," I said, "looking for a job now."

For the next mile or so he was dishing out careers advice. It wasn't a great start, but I kept the wisecracks to a minimum and showed a bit of respect. He seemed to warm to me, so I asked what line of work he was in.

"Henchman. If you know what that is."

"I do as it happens. Something in the paper about it not so long ago. You take these weird things to people. And they get lucky."

"Henches. The 'weird things' are called 'henches'. I've got one in the boot."

"Wow. So it's on its way to someone?"

"No. This one's just going into storage for a bit. I've picked it up from an elderly gent in a hospice. He had no more use for it. Well, of course, the deal is that when you get to *that* point you return it to us. We'll check it over – do any little repairs it needs – then next time the henches get allocated, out it goes again."

"This old guy in the hospice, what did it do for him?"

"Well, there's a story. He was a bankrupt when the hench came his way. Not his own fault. He had a little business selling... farm machinery, I think it was. But there was a downturn, cash flow problems. Amazing how quick it can all go wrong. Well, you might think: give the man a hench and he'll be out of trouble, just like that. Not quite. It responds to attitudes, you see – willpower, resolve, that sort of thing. Trouble was he was suffering from depression of some kind. Totally de-motivated. Years before he was able to make use of it, but then he got back on his feet and had a pretty decent life."

"Sounds like some sort of feedback thing happening there," I commented, hoping to impress.

"That's right. It's not like winning the pools. The hench needs something from you before it bestows good fortune. Some people get it, some don't."

"So it would just seem like a totally useless object to some people, yeah? I mean, you've got to be able to recognise luck for what it is, for a start..."

"Exactly!"

I had him going then. He knew he was talking to someone who could deal with a few subtleties and appreciate his experience. I could settle back and enjoy the ride. And I'd have enriched my knowledge by the end of it. That was how hitchhiking relationships worked sometimes. You'd never even learn the person's name but, for an hour or two, you'd talk the talk.

It was through a lottery that henches got handed out. Always had been, and it went back a long, long way. Getting one, in that respect, was like suddenly finding you've got to do jury service, but considerably rarer. So henches came to all sorts of people in any walk of life. Some, like the gent I'd heard about, were in a bad way. Some were in the lap of luxury, but even they could sometimes use a little luck.

Like the paranoid millionaire who was looking for a wife. He didn't mind being rich but it made a mess of relationships. How could he find someone who didn't see the £ signs when they looked at him? He figured the incognito route might be the one to take, do some dating acting like someone on a lower income and not let on who or what he really was. But it wasn't going too well. Pretending not to be a millionaire seemed kind of tedious to someone who enjoyed flaunting his wealth.

On receiving a hench it all came together. Next time, he met a rich woman who was dating incognito for the same reason he was. They hit it off. Now they're partners in every sense of the word.

Oh yes, that henchman had stories. Luck is no simple matter. That was his theme.

"...So I pass on the hench to this chap and the following week, walking through town, he's the victim of a vicious assault. Ends up in hospital for a few days. We contacted him for feedback some months later and he said that, at that point, he was planning to chop up the Hench and use it for firewood, but..." He paused to give me a significant look. "A routine test in the hospital flagged up a heart problem he wasn't aware of. Comparatively simple to sort out at that stage, but another year or so without the treatment, he'd be likely to drop dead in his tracks. So the hench got a reprieve. Or at least until he went in for the heart treatment, picked up an infection, and ended up bedbound for months. However... during those months he got to know the guy in the next bed, who turned out to have extensive business interests and ended up offering him a very nice job indeed."

"Okay," I said, "so these lucky people have to look at the big picture, yeah?"

He nodded, enthusiastically. "We call it the 'aggregate'. That's what the hench scores on. But there's another thing you have to weigh up and that's how you handle it when you do get 'lucky'..."

I could tell there was another story coming. This one concerned a woman recipient with a penchant for gambling. It was bingo halls when she started, but there's a problem – too lucky too often and you attract unwelcome attention. People think you might be cheating somehow. But she was canny, this old girl, and she started going to different venues, making a bit here and a bit there. Anywhere she frequented often, she'd throw some games, keep her mouth shut and let someone else win. She got to thinking. Reckoned the same would apply further up the ladder. Got herself some high-class threads and became a habitué of racetracks and casinos. The hench liked that. She's one rich lady now.

The henchman team gathered all these stories through occasional feedback interviews. I wondered what else they gleaned from these. What did people actually do with their henches, for example? Just stash them away?

"Some do," he replied. "But for most people it's a kind of relationship and they like to bring a little ritual into it. Holding the Hench in front of them or putting it on some sort of shrine. A lot of them do that. Use it to focus their thoughts on what it is they want from their luck."

"And the hench responds?"

"As I said. It likes people to make some sort of effort."

He took a quick glance at his watch. There was a Services coming up, he said. He needed the gents.

In the car park, for some reason, he took a little time seeking out a parking place, finally picking a spot at the far edge, backing up to some greenery. I didn't need anything in the Services and he was happy enough to leave me in the car. Didn't even take the ignition keys.

This felt kind of strange. As I sat there waiting for him to return, it was all too obvious that I could have taken the key, opened the boot, and made off with the hench to enjoy the Life Fortunate. Or even nicked the car for that matter. Why was he trusting me? Okay, after the slightly shaky start, I appeared to have made a good impression on him. But how could he possibly know that I wouldn't succumb to the temptation?

But hey, I still believe in karma. Even now. I wasn't into theft. Just curious. In the end, I figured he probably had it locked up and bolted down in there.

He returned with two coffees, bless him. As we sat sipping, he said: "Would you like to see it?"

I nodded enthusiastically, almost spilling my coffee. It was possible, of course, that one day he or someone like him might turn up at my door, hench in hand. But given the incredible unlikeliness of such an event this was a once-in-a-lifetime opportunity.

He opened the boot casually and there it was. In an open-topped box. No locks. No bolts.

In form it resembled some past-times child's hobbyhorse, but it was clearly no toy. The horse head was of superbly carved wood, hand painted with intricate stylisation. I've always taken pleasure in sign painting, and I've spent time learning from a guy who painted canal boats for a living. So I knew something about the work that went into that kind of richly coloured design. The henchman said that it might need repairs, but I couldn't see a flaw on it. The stick too was decoratively carved with a sort of repeating ivy-leaf motif, unpainted, but gleaming with lacquer.

In fact, the whole thing seemed to shine. Maybe it was just my imagination, fuelled by the extraordinary nature of the object, but I swear there was a sort of radiance to it. Both a light and a vague sense of warmth.

But what I locked onto, spellbound, were the eyes. Here there was no stylisation. They were ultra-realistic replicas of a horse's eyes, with their leathery black lids, great wide irises and crescents of lash. The painter had even caught the reflection of light in them.

"You know I could have nicked this," I said slowly and thoughtfully, "while you were having a slash."

He laughed. "You reckon?"

"But you've done nothing to protect it..."

"Do I need to? Think about it. Think about the nature of this thing that, for the duration of my journey, I am the temporary holder of. How far do you think you would have got?"

I was still staring at the eyes. I got his point. I began to turn my gaze towards him, but in doing so – as the painted eyes slipped into my peripheral vision – I seemed to detect a movement, as if they were tracking my own. It was spooky enough that I immediately reverted my gaze to the hench. Of course the eyes hadn't moved. They couldn't have. The thing was made of wood.

It wasn't looking at me at all.

It wasn't.

"Some of this," said the henchman, "will probably rub off on you for a while. Enjoy it."

Do I need to tell you that, five minutes after he dropped me off, I got a luxury lift in a fast car, Led Zep on the stereo, direct to my doorstep? As for the driver, she was— Ah! That's another story.

Hey, don't call it good luck. Don't call it bad luck.

After all, just who the fuck really *does* know?

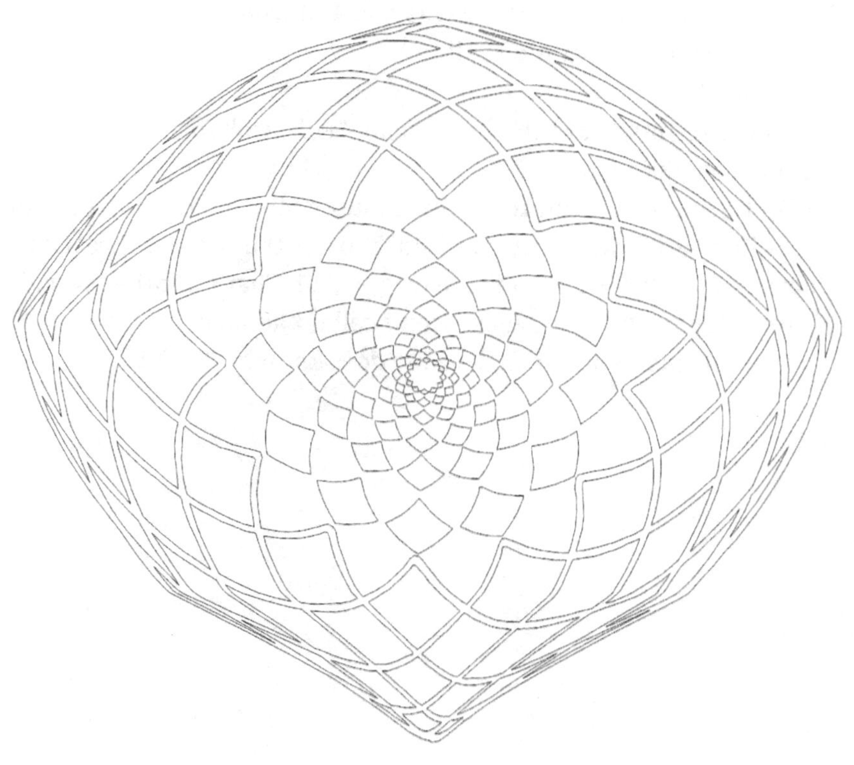

Frank's Cocoon

So at last he has reached this point. The changes started after thirty-six years of life as a human being driving him, in a hormonal surge, to make all the necessary preparations. Long awaited, that process is now culminating.

One last little difficulty... In this very confined space, it's tricky to work. He thinks with a kind of envy of the various creatures that – after millennia of evolution – are able to spin solid thread from liquid resources within themselves and build these things around them with apparent ease. He, on the other hand, has had to leave himself just enough room for a small bucket of gunk and for his arms to be free to scoop the stuff out and plug up the final gap, the one through which he climbed a few minutes ago.

It's a challenge. He's naked, of course, and doesn't particularly want too much of it to splatter back over him. So he works slowly and carefully. After all, there is no hurry.

He bought the paste, along with the wire framing material and the other bits he needed, from one of the big hardware stores. Bit by bit he mixed it with reams and reams of shredded paper to build the casing around the frame. When it was nearly complete, coated with a waterproof lacquer and strong enough to hang out, he took it to the chrysalisarium and suspended it from the sturdiest looking branch of a beech tree. This morning, using one of the high stepladders that the staff provide, he gave it all a few final tests for strength and endurance. Satisfied, he entered the cocoon with his little bucket of gunk and a few provisions. They took the stepladder away and left him to it.

When he's finished, barring a few air holes and the tubes that will remove the last of his waste products, he is completely encased. All he has to do is sit quietly and wait for the final process to commence. It starts within a day, they say. That's when he'll begin to wallpape.

That's right. He's a wallpaper. In summertime, outdoors at least, you can recognise the wallpapers by the butterflies – and at night time, moths – which seem to gather around them protectively, fanning them with their wings. Who knows how they recognise this affinity? But they do.

Wallpapers live their lives as the rest of us do ours but always with the knowledge that one day – they'll know when it is – they will stop everything, settle their worldly affairs, build their cocoons and wallpape.

He used to have a name. Frank... Frank Something or Other. He's pleased that he's already forgotten the surname. That's a good sign. All being well, he'll have forgotten the first name within the next twenty-four hours. The sense of detachment that this will bring is important. He won't forget his life as a human being, but it'll seem as if it were the life of someone else – which indeed it will be once he has wallpaped.

Over the last few weeks he's said all his goodbyes. There are those who will miss him and those with whom he is sorry to part. That side of things is not easy, of course, but then neither is dying. And we all have to do that eventually. So there's a lot of sadness. Nevertheless everyone knows you are a wallpaper and, when the time comes, you simply have no choice. You must enter your chrysalis state. You must transform.

While he awaits the changes he will meditate on the human life he led, turning it over aspect by aspect. What, if anything, did it all amount to? What, if anything, did it mean?

There was a childhood, quite an ordinary one – except for the butterflies and the moths. He was the only one amongst his siblings to whom those creatures flocked. So, by the time he was ten, everyone – including Frank himself – knew that he was the wallpaper of the family. Adolescence came with degrees of resentment. Why him? Why couldn't it be someone else who would one day be compelled to build that cocoon and climb into it? But there was counselling for this and by the time he was in his twenties he'd come to terms with the fact. He'd even begun to look forward to it.

No one really knew quite what becomes of wallpapers. Biologists had for centuries now attempted to monitor them. They would watch over the cocoons in shifts, waiting and waiting... Sooner or later, however, someone's attention would always slip and, when it returned, he or she would be staring at a gaping hole in an empty shell. When technology produced the surveillance camera they thought they had the answer. Not so. On playback the image would become completely blurred at the crucial period and only return when the wallpaper was gone. It seemed that, whatever it was that wallpapers became after transformation, the rest of humanity was simply incapable of seeing.

So was there any point in Frank's life prior to this moment? If there was, perhaps it was in the relationships he formed, the work he accomplished, just like it was for all those he was about to leave behind. With these he was satisfied. He had worked his way up to management level in a small, local charity that brought a variety of benefits to the community. He'd had good friendships. And, for love, he'd sought out wallpapers of the opposite sex. Those transient relationships had, on the whole, been delightful. There was a lot of understanding and a powerful mutual pleasure in speculating about what they would eventually become.

A feeling of hunger disturbs his meditation. He has been cocooned, he supposes, for several hours already. He reaches into the cavity he has created for his little bag of provisions. Obviously he was not able to feed himself up like a bloated caterpillar, so he needed some food to tide him through the early stages. He's brought ham sandwiches, spam sandwiches and lamb sandwiches. It seemed important, for some reason, that there was a rhyme to what he ate. He'd been tempted to create something with which he could set up a Drambuie flambé as well, but there were health and safety issues.

After eating he begins to feel sleepy. He is able to rest in a semi-recumbent position, comfortable enough on the fleece lining he set up within the cocoon to sleep through the oncoming night.

He drifts back to thoughts of the life he led, savouring the points of happiness that sparked with lovers, family or friends, but conscious of the growing sense of detachment. They had their worth, it seems to him now, but he is moving on. The same goes for the times of pain and despair. He's not even sure he'll remember that many of them after his transformation. Does the butterfly or moth have any detailed memory of its former life, grubbing through leaves, avoiding predators as well as it was able?

There is no more light penetrating the skin of the cocoon. As night has fallen, a breeze has sprung up from somewhere and it rocks gently below the sturdy beech branch from which it hangs. The motion is enough to ease him from consciousness, via a brief hypnagogic phase in which he believes himself talking and thinking in some lepidopterous language, into a deep and profound state of sleep.

∞

In the morning, woken by light, he reaches for his breakfast. But the thought of solid food sickens him. 'Damn the ham,' he thinks. 'Damn the spam. Damn the lamb!' He imagines them burning, immersed in the Drambuie flambé, its flickering blue flames bursting up around them. And he finds himself lusting intensely for that which he has not brought.

It seems more cramped in the cocoon's cavity now, as if his body has swollen overnight. Maybe this is the beginning. Certainly there's little inclination to move. He is becoming quiescent, lying in his nest of fleece, and merely imagining tiny cobalt flames flickering and crackling over the surface of some confection or succulent sliver. In time the sense of lust fades. The image in his mind is enough to sustain him. There is no hunger, no thirst, no need for anything.

Soon he is sessile, swelling still, and unconscious once more. It is not sleep, for his metabolism is busy, hormones activating change after change, until the body itself is a shell for something new. He is chrysalis now and cannot be conscious, for his brain too is reshaping itself, making a mulch of all there was of Frank Something or Other. A mulch in which to embed his new identity, his new self.

∞

When he awakens, the first thing he sees seems wrapped up somehow in the second thing he sees, yet they are also separate and distinct. He does not know what he is yet, but he becomes aware that he inhabits two realities at the same time and he is somehow able to be an independent entity within each of them.

One reality is the world he once knew, where his cocoon still hangs, ripped asunder. There, bodiless, he is free to observe anything that occurs. The other is a Drambuie flambé world in which he is a creature possessing huge yet delicate wings. He is now sensing it primarily with compound eyesight. A multiplicity of images, it's bewildering at first. But his consciousness rapidly adapts. Antennae have sprouted from his newly formed forehead and they are already feeding input back to his brain. But, as yet, this information is incomprehensible.

The wings are not quite ready for use. They must harden a while. He waits, looking around him at this world of flicker flames and misty reaches, in which he cannot be sure what is up and what is down or what constitutes any kind of landmark.

Now and again, although he cannot see far with clarity, he catches a vague glimpse of others like him – luminous, patterned wings carrying them through the mists. They flit in and out of view. Maybe in time he will be able to reach them. Some amongst them he will know, though he's not sure exactly why. Perhaps they met in the former life.

This is all so new. Maybe, he thinks, you have to learn – as you did in early childhood whilst human – how to 'see' this reality, how to make conceptual sense of it. He has all the mental faculties that he developed on his former journey into human adulthood. Here, he suspects that they are equivalent to those of a newborn babe.

So he is old and new simultaneously and, while he waits for his wings to set, he is able to let his consciousness skitter around, disembodied, through what was once his only world.   He can observe people he knew going about their lives. They have no awareness of him and never will – despite the claims of occultists to be able to make 'contact' with wallpapers who have completed their metamorphosis. But that he can still see these facets of past life is reassuring and as it should be. He is too linked with the old world to leave it entirely behind just yet. He suspects that with time, as he explores the new world, he will.

And now he feels his wings have hardened. He flexes freshly formed muscles that connect with those mighty membranes. He feels them move – a little shakily at first, then with greater firmness as he grows in confidence.

At last, he takes flight, ascending rapidly into the mists, seeking the flickering blue scintillation that will be his succour, reaching out for the company of those who have already come to dwell here.

He exults, awash in a sense of utter fulfilment.

He is imago. He has become.

Moon Bar Night

It's this thing we do. Get some scratch together, hit the town, go a little feral. Location's not critical but there have to be bars.

Me, Daz, I like the blue stuff. Tip it in when chance come. Chalice goes for the dark brew – likes to write little messages in the froth 'pon top. Blake does the clear, the hard. Never seen him fall over though. Skitzy goes for different every time. Choice makes no change. Soon gets howling. Thinks she's singing, bless the dear.

Street's crowded tonight. Hot. Everyone skimping clothes. Mill around, talk loud and listen minimal. Stink of spray-ons, sweat masks, perfect fumes. Air almost oozing with it. Beats pumping everywhere.

We're pulling different ways. Skitzy, spiked hair blue, red and purple tonight, she's shouting: "It's a boogie night!" But Blake's on some brooding jag and he doesn't want to know. Chalice is easy. 'Whatever' through and through is he. So looks like I'm the hinge for swinging it. Lucky me.

Don't know where it comes from but I fire on an idea. "Let's go see if the fucking Moon Bar's there. Check out the flagrants."

Blake closes one eye. Cracks a tiny grin. Good sign. Chalice does that chuckling thing. "Flagrants. Yeah, mon."

Skitzy pouts. Outflanked. She starts dancing on the spot. Flailing. People are ducking and diving out the way. "Yeah," she shouts. "Let's go!"

Drinks down, we hare off to where people thin out, and on up the dark, steep, cobbled alley to where the Moon Bar hides.

Not kidding. Some nights you go all the way up there and the damn bar is nowhere to be seen. Sometimes there's just a single unmarked doorway. Then sometimes a whole frontage. Stained-glass deco windows. Big sign. The works. The Moon Bar. We'd been out of phase, hadn't set foot for months. Flags would be missing us.

Skitzy's texting, thumbs a blur, as she walks. No signal inside, see. Now and again stumbles on the cobbles 'cause she's gone for the heels, torn fishnets and black lace look tonight. Blake's ahead, loping, slightly deadly in his chinos and hoodie. Chalice behind, dreads bobbing, huffing some with the slope. Strong on tracksuits, Chalice, not fitness. When we used to jig-jig, liked it best me on top. Less effort.

Chalice. Bless the dear.

No one is drunk yet. We're all keen peeping, but it's the man at the rear that clocks it. Rest of us walked right past. The full frontage too! That semicircle face in cratered gold on the leaded window glass. Skitzy starts laughing. "Moon bar! Moo-hoon bar!" Blake eye-locks her and mimes a volume control, then pulls open the big swing door. Steps in. We follow.

Smoke haze hits. Love to smoke, those flagrants. They got bodies that synthesise carcinogens and turn them to nutrients. Light's low and you can never figure out whereabouts it's coming from. Shadows all over the place. Eyes adjust. It's about half full. Usual kind of folk. Mix. Locals from up around here, others who've chanced it like us. And the flags.

You can't tell flags from humans 'til you get talking with them. That's to say they look like humans to us. Where they come from, they look well different. Gopher did a sketch for us once. Sort of organic spirograph patterns. Low-grav floaters.

I'm looking out for Gopher now. He's my favourite flagrant. Says nice things, like: "Daz, my glimmering gamin, how sweet this is."

Oh, it's him. Found me. Big smiles and a flitting hug. "Thought you'd lost us. Grown away from our allure."

"No chance, Goph. Just fell out of phase a while." Gopher 'cause his full name's Gophermluxmlax, and there's something about him reminds me of a buck tooth, near-sighted cartoon character. Bless the dear.

Lights up a nic stick. Leads us to the bar. Deebo's serving. Ancient-looking Deebo. White hair in longest ponytail I've ever seen on a male. Hangs from a topknot to somewhere back of his legs. Stubbly grin. Drinks for all. They know what we like. Except Skitzy of course. Launches her acute indecision mime, contorting face and body. Flags love it. Comedy girl. Finally settles on some complex cocktail she names with slow deliberation. Deebo has it covered.

Goph shows us to an almost vacant table. Single sitter there is Farewell. Radically glamorous in a long maroon velvet number, hair flowers, ruby lips. Greets us. Blake's beaming. Compliments her profusely. I think he likes to imagine that she's not really a floating organic spirograph, but a voluptuous flesh and blood. Jig-jigable. At length.

First time we ever found the Moon Bar – following a rumour – I was cutting pretty heavy. Been my thing since kid-life, care homes and fosterings. All four of us got scars from that, but mine you can see. So, Farewell, we've just met her. She spots an uncovered scar. Wants to know what it's all about. No moralising, no mother hen shit, just curiosity – how does it feel when the blade goes in? And afterwards? Nice to talk like that. No big deal. Just what I do. Gets me to roll up my sleeve so she can see more. Runs her finger along one. "Ah," she says, "Exquisite skin." Later, that got me thinking. Don't cut so much now. Might even stop.

Chalice is sat by one of the posters on the wall and it's sucking at him. They have bright flowing lettering. Looks like words but can't be read. And interwoven images that – after you've been looking at them for a while – turn 3D, as if you were wearing the specs. More you look, more you see. Blake goes to give him a nudge but Skitzy says: "Ah, let him go, Blakey. Find his way back in a while."

Goph nods approval. "What they're for," he says. "He's travelling." Takes a long suck on his cig, exhales not smoke-rings but stars, musical notes, smileys...

Skitzy applauds. Wants to try it herself. Only manages blobs of smoke and coughs a lot. "Eugh! You enjoy smoking these things?"

"Smoke!" says Blake, like he's just woken up. "The Vapour Room. Last time we came... Fucking phenomenal!"

Goph shrugs and gestures vaguely. "You know the way. Step right in."

"Me too! Me too!" Skitzy, infected by Blake's excitement, up and following him. Off to the rooms.

The rooms. It's coming back. This is a Moon Bar thing. Everything here is very intense. Every moment of now is huge, rich, detailed... But fades fast when you go out, back down the alley, back down to regular life. So the rooms... I'm remembering now. The Rain Room, The Nectar Room, The Fertility Room...

Tried a couple so far. How could I forget? Go in, close the door behind you. No light. Total dark. Then stuff starts.

In the Fertility Room, a dancer with blue skin and eight arms appears as though in spotlight. Just fades in. Dances to music you know but you can't hear. Behind the dancer (Him? Her? Who knows?) a trail of grass growing, trees sprouting, flowers blooming, eggs hatching, chicks becoming parakeets, sunbirds, cockatoos, and rabbits and monkeys cavorting, tigers prowling... It's not any kind of a room anymore. It's creation!

Rain Room is just mad. Warm, torrential rain starts up, pouring onto you from who knows where. Soaks you to the skin in seconds. It's misty. Can't see much, but you're drenched and you just want to laugh and fall about and play the idiot. Went in with Skitzy. Girl went wild. Pair of us hadn't laughed so much since we put food colouring in all the soap dispensers at Gladwell fucking House, last of our care homes.

Come out of the Rain Room and you're dry as bone.

Yeah, the rooms...

But here I am, on my tod with Goph and Farewell 'cause Chalice is still in zooby-zooby land staring at this poster. Farewell is asking if I want a room, but I don't. I just want to sit here drinking the blue stuff, and I want to ask a question 'cause I'm feeling curious.

"Where do you people come from – you flagrants, whatever you are?"

Look shoots between them. Can't read it.

"How's your physics, Daz?" asks Goph.

"Fuck off!"

Pauses for a short while, then he hits off with all this stuff about other dimensions that are outside of space or time and they're rolled up into tight balls no bigger than a speck of dust. And what we, us human beings, are seeing, feeling and hearing in the presence of flagrants is mainly a projection from out of our own minds because the conceptual framework we need's beyond our grasp. And...

And I'm zoning out and thinking why the fuck did I ask that question? 'Cause I don't have a clue what he's talking about and all that matters is we found them and we like them and they like us.

Little throat-clearing thing from Farewell and he shuts up pronto. She reaches across the table, presses my hand with hers. "We're moon glow, darling. We're moon glow," she whispers, "trust us. That's all you need to know." And maybe I am projecting from out of my own mind, but her hand feels warm and tender on mine.

Haven't had a lot of that in my life. Lashed out against it. Attitude.

But not here. 'Cause me and my mates, my best mates – Blake, Skitzy, Chalice – we're from another fucking dimension too. Fit in just right here.

I think there's a fucking tear in my eye. Cig smoke.

"Come on," says Farewell. "Let's go." Pulls me up by the hand, leads me off to the rooms. "This one."

Inside, dark as expected, but light starts to fill it. Looking at ourselves in a big mirror, whole of the wall in front of us. There's Farewell, as I see her. There's me. Skinny waif. Cropped hair. Big boots, leggings, baggy ripped t-shirt over scoop neck with long sleeves to cover my you-know-whats. Rose and thorn tattoo on the side of my neck. It's a look.

Light fades to twilight. That game you play, looking into mirrors in dim light 'til you get to be some kind of monster – it's like that. Only we're not monsters. Both of us now, organic spirographs, just like Gopher's drawing. We're floating in some kind of textured space. Our patterns weaving into one another, rippling tenderly. Joining. Dancing. Winding ever closer. Merging. Merging with everything. Perfect.

Sometime later, we're back outside the door.

"What you call that room?"

"Tranquillity."

In the Bar, everyone's back from wherever the fuck they've been, drinking and telling their stories. Vapour Room was a bundle of fun, and Chalice been star trekking. Don't have much to say about me and Farewell. Just smile. Tap my nose with my finger. Enough.

Farewell's up collecting the empties for Deebo. Even extra-dimensionals got to clear up the shit. Place has thinned out. Time to go.

Back down the alley. Night life on the street's still pumping. Turns out we've even got cash left in our pockets, so we stop at an open-front for a last one. Booze is different down here. Heavier somehow.

Blake's still buzzing from up there. "Them rooms. Fucking phenomenal."

Skitzy looks at him, frowning. "What rooms? The fuck you on about, Blakey?"

Confused look on his face. "The rooms! You know! They're like... they're like..." But he can't find the words.

And I know it's started already. The fading thing. Soon, about all we'll remember of the Moon Bar is that it's just one more cool place to go to on a night of drinking. We'll be out again, when we've got the scratch, and one or the other of us'll get the idea and up the alley we'll trot.

And if we're lucky, if we're in phase...

They'll be waiting for us.

Your Money's Worth

We'd paid a lot for this one. Prime seats, three figure ticket prices, but this was Rudolph Zuniga. *The* Rudolph Zuniga. And rumour had it that this might be one of his last performances before an overdue retirement. We hadn't had any children yet, Patsy and I, but when we did this would be something to tell them about. One of the last performances by one of the last great Ceruleans. Rudolph Zuniga.

A shared love for the Cerulean art had kindled our romance. Happy hours spent together, watching recorded performances by Zuniga in his prime, and the other greats: Daniel Bligh, Grace Kenwick (now Dame Grace, of course), the late Franz Silberman... Hours in which our two once-lonely hearts found unity.

The venue, historic and ornate, at the core of our greatest city's cultural district, was packed. Row after row of folk in their finest. It was hot. I was already feeling sweaty and overdressed in the tux I'd rented to go with the fabulous outfit that Pats just had to buy for the occasion, all layers of pastel chiffon and glittery thread. In that expectant atmosphere, the air itself almost crackled.

Down in the pit the orchestra was tuning up.

There were young would-be Ceruleans who rationalised that a primarily spoken word performance hardly required this extravagance. But for Zuniga, now in his mid seventies, to appear without an orchestra was unthinkable. The trade-off between the spoken word and the ebb or swell of music by the great composers, *this* was intrinsic to his art.

"I can't believe it, Justin," said Pats, not for the first time. "We're actually going to see him in the flesh."

A portly lady seated beside us smiled warmly, acquiescent in the sense of awe. "And, most importantly, to hear him."

"Oh... Oh yes," said Pats, slightly embarrassed, "To hear him, of course."

Then, the moment for which one ardently waits... The orchestra fell silent. The theatre lights dimmed. All hubbub ceased as if at the command of some unseen director. The only sound was that of the stage curtain rolling up. At first one very faint spotlight made a small circle on the stage. Then, gaining intensity, it illuminated the figure of Rudolph Zuniga standing solitary within its glare.

There was no microphone of course. The true Cerulean relies on voice projection alone. How, at his advanced age, Zuniga was still capable of this stentorian feat, no one could know. But then he had been doing it virtually all his life, reaching the height of his fame in the early 1960s.

On this day, he wore an elegantly tailored double-breasted suit, the tip of a silk handkerchief poised in his breast pocket, just so, head bent slightly forward. He stood upright and sturdy, giving the impression of a man twenty or thirty years younger. His thin remaining hair was oiled, streaked back across the dome of his head. I'm not entirely sure, but I think his eyes were closed. He appeared to be in a rapture, extending and milking the silence, as every pair of ears in the auditorium awaited his first words.

He lifted his head, straightening still further, and slowly surveyed the audience – or appeared to, since there was probably little of us that he could actually see. And then, rolling and caressing both vowel and consonant of every single word, he spoke.

"Ladies... and gentlemen!"

'Actorly', 'affected' – these terms have been used by Zuniga's critics, but to us, the audience, there was something elemental in that voice. It didn't matter what the words were. The art of the Cerulean is to extract each last resonance from the spoken word and then to project it, imbuing it with depths of emotion to bring the audience to a profound and transformative state of sadness. Zuniga's voice was a force of nature, even just those three words. I glanced sideways at Patsy and saw tears glistening behind her glasses. There was a lump in my throat, a tingle in my spine. Three words and we were in the grip of an indescribable spell. Three words and he somehow made us feel he was – and would be – addressing each of us individually.

"I'll commence tonight with the tale of Tristan and Isolde..."

∞

Finally, when Tristan had died from grief and Isolde's lamenting had led in turn to her own demise, Zuniga lowered his voice to a seeming whisper that was yet heard with absolute clarity by every pair of ears present. The orchestra, which had subtly enhanced his performance with quotations from both Wagner and Messiaen, now ceased to play.

"And buried they were, close to the place where they died. The lovers: Tristan and Isolde. And in the most extraordinarily short period of time there grew by one gravestone a hazel, and by the other a honeysuckle. Grew... Grew toward one another... Joined in union. Intertwined so densely that – short of uprooting them – no gardener could prise them apart. *Uprooting* them? Ladies and gentlemen, I ask you. Is there *any* true gardener on God's good earth, who would be prepared to do *that*?"

Zuniga paused, palms outstretched at his sides. The applause broke like a tsunami. I have rarely encountered an audience whose enthusiasm was so palpable, so utterly heartfelt.

As indeed was our own.

∞

"So he tells stories. Arthurian romance, Walter Scott and all that. Makes everyone feel like having a good old cry. Well, I s'pose, if you like that sort of thing..."

My brother-in-law, Terry, was sharing his valuable thoughts. We had just finished our wild mushroom crostini starter and Patsy was in the kitchen putting the finish on the pan-seared scallop main course, one of her specialities. I had warned her, before Terry and his good wife Christine arrived, that it might be better not to mention that life-changing performance. Or at least to temper our enthusiasm. But Patsy, bless her, is too honest a soul for any such subterfuge. One question and she just *had* to start enthusing.

Terry, I think, prefers to bait me alone since Patsy is too easily offended. He'd been seizing his opportunity with great relish. "But the idea that it's some sort of high art. Bit preposterous, wouldn't you say, Justin?"

I took a sip of the Chateau Moulin Riche we'd opened, and paused before swallowing, as if savouring it. Really I was giving myself a moment or two to think. "You have to remember, Terry, that it's part of a venerable tradition. Goes back to the Middle Ages at least. The 'Court Ceruleans' as they were known."

Terry raised mocking eyebrows to infer pomposity on my part, thus denying himself the opportunity to learn a significant deal more of Ceruleanism's history. "Oh come on," he said. "You don't buy all that Donovan and Enya stuff, surely?"

"I'm not familiar with 'Donovan and Enya'. We are talking about high art, Terry, because of the depth of its resonance. We are talking about what touches the soul, not what tickles the fancy."

Terry's grin widened. "Still doing that after-dinner speaking course then, Just?" Hastily, before his forthcoming point could be diluted by the aside, he added: "No, but *music hall* has a tradition, Punch and bleedin' *Judy* has a tradition... yet it's hardly the peak of human culture."

"Well," I retaliated, "What is 'high art' in your book then?"

"I'm so glad you asked me that, Justin. I'm a bit of a Bobby Davro man, myself."

"What's this about Bobby Davro?" It was Patsy, reappearing with the main course presented between her oven-gloved hands.

"Terry's been winding Justin up about whether Rudolph Zuniga is truly an artist," said Christine, who had been listening to our conversation with barely concealed amusement.

"Oh but he is," said Patsy. "He's... he's like a painter. But to give us colour and texture, he's... working with human emotion."

∞

A few days after our dinner party with Terry and Christine, the news broke that Rudolph Zuniga had been diagnosed with a terminal illness several months before but had chosen not to make it public knowledge until his commitments had been completed. So the 'final performances' rumour had more substance than anyone expected. Before the end of that year, he had passed away. I will not hide the fact that Patsy and I shed tears.

Terry and his ilk would suggest that our wonderful Ceruleans have simply learned how to manipulate emotions to such a degree that even the intellectual amongst us are drawn to some illusory sense of depth. They'd see an excessive and florid actor telling safely familiar stories. We perceived a human being whose profound dedication to his art touched the human soul. A man or a woman who can thrill an entire audience, bring it to a peak of expectation with just three, quite mundane words, must surely be touched by the hand of God.

Surely.

∞

Some years later, at a loose end one afternoon in that district of the city, Patsy and I shared a whim to visit the nearby grave of Rudolph Zuniga. "Should have done this long ago, shouldn't we?" said Patsy, as we looked for the monument in the small, neat graveyard.

It was an ornate, mock-Victorian affair, which came as no surprise.

We were not alone. An elderly woman in a long dark coat of a clearly expensive cut appeared also to be paying her respects. Catching her eye, Patsy spoke quietly. "A great man."

Her carefully made up face a mask, the woman looked at Patsy, seemingly unable to respond. Then with a slight smile, she said: "Rudy... had his moments." Her voice was cultured, redolent of refinement.

Patsy's eyes widened. "You knew him?"

"Oh, my dear, I was married to the man."

Patsy blushed, magnificently. "I'm... I'm so sorry. We'll, um, leave you in peace, shall we?"

As though mildly amused the woman said: "Don't worry. I'm quite done with grieving now. You were admirers of his performances, I assume."

"Absolutely!"

"We were," I added, "privileged to attend one of his final recitals."

"Ah yes. Opened with 'Tristan', didn't he? Well, I'm sure he gave you your money's worth. He was a trooper to the very end."

"It was more than that," said Patsy, a little breathlessly. "For us, his performances were... spiritually enriching."

"Really?" said Mrs Zuniga, raising an eyebrow and smiling, I thought, with a hint of the cynical. "Well, I've been lingering here for far too long. It's been delightful speaking with you but I'm afraid I must be going."

One daydreams of such chance encounters, of the questions one might ask. But for all that woman's politeness and easy manner, it was as if we'd been speaking to a creature from another world, a being of a higher order. Patsy and I, we were punters, the hoi polloi, too tongue tied to express the depths of our feelings. Now, as she turned to go, I said: "Mrs Zuniga, may I ask you something?" She nodded consent. "*Was* your husband a spiritual man?"

She shook her head. "That's not how I would describe Rudy, I'm afraid. Fonder of the spirits than of the spirit."

And then she was gone. We watched as she exited the graveyard and, through the fence, saw her get into the back of a limo which swiftly pulled away.

∞

Patsy maintains to this day that even Zuniga's own wife failed to recognise his true worth, and that if he was a drinker, *she* probably drove him to it. Her loyalty remains undiminished.

I, however, am faltering.

I'm reminded of a familiar optical illusion. Two symmetrical faces outlined in profile stare at one another, and then with some flick of mental perspective the same outlines depict a single vase. Mine flicked that afternoon. Zuniga: a 'trooper'; the Cerulean art: merely show business.

If a truth there is, it is truly obscure. From one perspective to the other, I remain compelled to flick.

The Mark Seven

Ant remembered this couple. They had always worked the car boot from the same corner. *Years* since she'd last managed to get here and there they still were looking much as they always did. He was still stocky, still wearing a grubby quilted waistcoat and his black woolly hat. She was still beanpole skinny, a devotee of fussy hairstyles, but with that same wiry, weathered sense of strength about her too. Ant always used to reckon that *she* did all the thinking; and *he* did what he was told.

They didn't appear to recognise Ant as they'd done in the days when she used to browse here regularly. Of course that was BTK. Before The Kids. Another era. Now, to this couple, she was just one more anonymous face in the throng that converged here every second Sunday morning.

Back in the day, they invariably had some sort of good stuff. She'd find it squirreled in amongst the piles of battered ornaments, scruffy paperbacks and tat on racks. She'd start by the hanging clothes, to one side of their rusting Ford Astra and away from the main table where they tended to put what they thought their best ware.

Now she followed her old pattern. She only had a couple of hours free before her duties resumed. It would be nice to once again find something a bit special.

Squatting, she sifted through the items on the ground in front of her: surviving plates and dishes from once-proud crockery sets; various toys of dubious hygiene; cut-glass cake stands; grubby costume jewellery; jigsaws and games that would almost certainly lack some vital piece. Same old stuff.

She was tempted to return to the more upmarket stretches of the car boot, where the gear was qualitatively consistent but there were no surprises. This was starting to feel like a waste of time. Time seemed an ever-dwindling commodity for Ant. Between dropping Catriona off at her friend's house and picking up Matthew from football practice, these were snatched moments, too precious to waste. Yet there was also something soothing about browsing through this junk. Was it what archaeologists got off on – a sense of other times, intrinsic to the artefacts and irrespective of their 'value'?

Nevertheless, her interest had definitely begun to wane. Until she noticed the fiddle sticks.

There were three of them in a long cardboard box. She'd not seen the things since well BTK but, even so, she recognised immediately that one was a 'Mark Seven', top of the range for a while. The other two were earlier models - Deluxe, not quite so fancy - but there was a time when she'd have lusted for *any* of them.

Fiddle sticks. What a craze! You could take your hula hoops, your yo-yos and your space hoppers and go shove... For a couple of years, at some point between being ten and being fifteen, life itself had seemed to revolve around fiddle sticks. She could still hear her own mother's voice: "Antonia! *Will* you stop fiddling and put that thing down!" "But mum, I just want to—" "That's enough! Put it down!"

Adults invariably failed to grasp the utter fascination that these inventive devices imbued in their possessors. Seemingly simple – tubes a little over an inch in diameter, eighteen inches to perhaps two foot in length – they were in fact laden with layers of mystery and surprise. They were shiny on the surface, laminated and decorated with colourful, swirling patterns, psychedelia being still just about fashionable at the time. Their hollow interiors contained a multitude of miniature items. But access was no simple matter. Hence the name. Each stick was dotted and inlaid with tiny buttons that would only work in certain sequences; slide-away hatches revealing combination lock arrays that had to be puzzled out; ingeniously levered latches and sliders that revealed, in time, hidden compartments opening sometimes singly, sometimes in sequence.

The rewards emerged, once you knew you had to press *those* two buttons simultaneously, but the one *next* to them only after waiting two or three seconds. Or that at least one of the combinations changed each time you used it, requiring the addition of three to the final digit.

Then there was treasure; there in each tiny compartment, exposed at last. A favourite of Ant's had been the three elastic bands that you could stretch and attach to small hooks on the stick's surface to make a crude musical instrument. Not much more than a few twangs that you could sequence in limited ways, but a strange beauty in those twangs just made you want to pluck them over and over. At the height of the craze there was even a Top Ten single, by David Bowie or someone like him, using the sound to dramatic effect. Outside of the recording studio, you could accompany the twangs yourself with the aid of tiny kazoos and whistles, which you might just find in other compartments.

Then there were the lenses. These you attached to foldout holders on the fiddle stick to look through. There was a basic microscope set up that worked surprisingly well. Another lens refracted everything you looked at prismatically so that it appeared to be surrounded by a rainbow aura. Best of all was a sequence that you fitted into the stick itself, so that, when you looked through a peephole at the end, you got a mirrored, kaleidoscopic view of a section of whatever was in front of you.

Beauty. Magic.

When you finally figured out how to get at it!

Ant looked down at the box of fiddle sticks in throes of nostalgia. She felt afraid at first to actually touch the contents. What else did those marvellous sticks contain? Games and puzzles, naturally; invariably far more interesting and enduring than anything from a Christmas cracker. Almost impossibly tiny books – containing loads of really funny jokes or encapsulated facts and figures to enhance your knowledge of the world – which could then be swapped and traded amongst friends. Tiny gadgets that squirted water or made fart noises. Compass and penknife facilities, of course. Invisible-ink capsules. Badges. Stickers. It was a cornucopia and you never quite knew whether you had exhausted it or whether there might be further content you had yet to access.

And who did know? Rumours abounded. After all, the sticks kept changing anyway – the button sequences, the combination numerals – so perhaps new things *could* appear in them. Or things that seemed impossible: the Mark Nine, it was said, contained a miniature walkie-talkie that you could use to communicate with your friends across town. But Ant had never seen anything more advanced than a Seven, so that remained a rumour.

Yes. The Seven. There had come a point, after two or three years, when you would be acutely embarrassed to have anything earlier than a Four. Simple prototypes, they no longer impressed in playground or park. A few more months and you were inexcusably uncool if you didn't have at least a Five.

It had to be done. It was irresistible. The Mark Seven was in her hands.

There was an immediate and reassuring sense of familiarity about holding one again. She decided to look for the elastic bands, the button sequence and its variations surprisingly clear in her memory.

It didn't work the first time. The timing had to be just right. On the second attempt a panel started to move but then became stuck. Tentatively, she worked a fingernail under one corner and applied gentle force. It shifted, reluctantly at first then abruptly snapped open, startling her. She looked around to ensure she was not being observed. With clumsy adult fingers she pulled out the elastic bands. Wrinkled, frayed; they were either perished or on the point of being so. Any attempt to use them would likely result in their breakage. She hastily stuffed them back into the compartment and tried to close the hatch, but it seemed to stick at the point it had reached before she had forced it to open further.

From the weight of the stick she knew there was more: that the other compartments still held their contents. But what if all those wonderful lenses were clouded or cracked? They couldn't have been made from anything designed to last. Nor would any of the other items for that matter. The jokes in the little book with its one by-now-rusty staple; they wouldn't be half so funny. The stickers wouldn't stick. The squirter wouldn't squirt.

It was her own childhood she held in her hands; all the wonder and potential, the sense of embarkation on a great and fascinating journey. All the options that had existed before her marriage, BTK, before her continual efforts to be a conscientious and loving parent. Her childhood, when it seemed there was all the time in the world. And now all that time had passed away. All that time had perished, rusted up, become clouded and cracked.

Her two? What would they make of the Mark Seven?

She could take it home and show them this relic of her own younger days. Matthew would find it laughable. Glowing with teenage cynicism, he would wave his latest all-singing all-dancing smartphone, raise his eyebrows, and say with the sure knowledge that he was being understood: "Oh, come *on*, Mum..." But Cat, little Catriona, she was not yet gripped by the urge to project sophistication. She'd be fascinated. At least for a while, until her attention was drawn back to all the flashing lights and sound loops at technology's cutting edge.

What characters those two were. Already!

She felt herself softening. The resentment implicit in "BTK" had been with her all day. Even the choice to come here when such a rare opportunity had presented itself had been of the 'I bloody well will.' category. But now, with these pictures of Matt and Cat imprinted in her mind, she realised she could once more reflect with appreciation on "ATK".

"Mark Seven, wunnit?" The guy in the woolly hat and the quilted waistcoat had noticed her and stepped back to see if he could make a sale. "I saw an Eight once," he added wistfully. "But I think they were runnin' out of ideas, frankly. It weren't much good."

"Really?" said Ant giving the stick a flourish. "So this *was* the state of the art, then?"

They laughed. "Yours for fifty pence if you wunt it. Quid for the three."

"Nah," said Ant with a wave of dismissal. "You can't buy back your childhood, can you?"

Relics were not what she required. Let them decay, dust to dust.

The important thing, the thing that would enhance the present, was the story. She didn't need the props.

It was the story she'd tell them, her two beautiful children. She'd always loved telling them stories.

The style would vary for each of them. For Matt there would have to be a good dose of self-mockery, a laugh at her own generation and its naiveties. That, he would enjoy. But for Catriona, oh, she'd pile on the detail, watching her daughter's eyes widen with wonder as she spun the legend of the fiddle sticks.

Woolly hat was turning away, eyeing another potential customer by the clothing rack. On an impulse she pulled out her purse. "Hey, just a minute," she said. "Here…" She handed him a pound. "That's for the memory."

The memory. Exactly as she'd thought when she'd sought out the couple and their tables; squirreled in amongst all their tat, you could still find the good stuff.

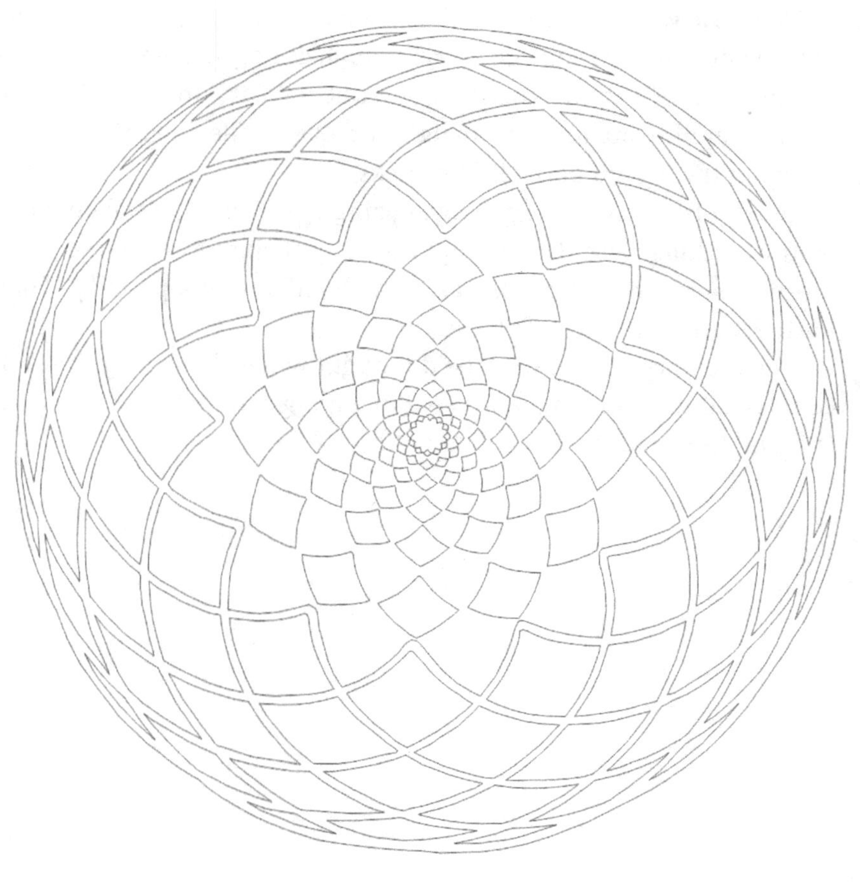

The Glamour

Esmerelda, it is said, was the perfect queen for her country. Her long rule was marked by fairness, good conduct and wise use of resources. She was concerned for her people and for the land in which they lived, and did whatever she could for the benefit of both. Despite these graces, she also had her foibles. Of these, perhaps the greatest was her passion for rigmaroles.

In those times, rigmaroles were horse drawn and used almost exclusively for ceremonial occasions – parades, pageants, and reviews of one's gallant armies. Esmerelda's passion was not un-queenly, for by their appearance they symbolised the strength and power of her nation. They had of course to be richly ornate and crafted to near-perfection.

It is said too that on one occasion she fainted after merely observing a cartoon showing a battered old rigmarole in use as a farm cart. Its caption declared that this image symbolised a state whose ruler was neglectful of its needs. After the administration of smelling salts her first thought was to have the artist executed, her second that he had made plain the magnitude of her responsibility and deserved a knighthood. In those days there was a much thinner line between honour and an untimely death.

The queen was not the only monarch for whom the appearance of these vehicles was a priority. Hers and the surrounding lands had an alliance, a 'League' they called it, in which had evolved an annual award system, judged by discerning folk from each of the countries, for the monarch who sported the finest rigmarole.

It was harmless enough as competitions went. Few resources were squandered in the maintenance and production of rigmaroles, since few of them were made. They nevertheless provided prestigious work for a variety of designers and craftspeople. Their exposure to public view on state occasions generated excitement and enthusiasm from the populace in times that, even in a well-run country, were not always easy.

As the years passed, however, Esmerelda was becoming increasingly peeved. Despite every effort she made with her own vehicles she appeared incapable of winning the great green plaque that would be mounted on the highest castle tower of the annual winner. She suspected a conspiracy. The arbiters of taste, the select folk who observed each country's finest rigmaroles and made the annual judgement, seemed inclined to pick only the vehicles of certain rulers. Others, like herself, simply never won.

Consistent failure was also beginning to take its toll on her people's confidence in her. Prosperity and wealth, they reasoned, came as much with their own efforts as hers and if she could present not one rigmarole that was worthy of the plaque, was she really the person to be ruling their land?

The Award Ceremony took place in each of the countries in sequence. As it happened, in this particular year Esmerelda was to play host.

If her entry failed yet again the humiliation could result in unrest – rebellion even – in the land she ruled so well. But year by year the utmost effort had gone into the refurbishment and redesign of her rigmaroles. How could those efforts be surpassed? How could she make it so that at least one of them was utterly, indisputably the best? She needed advice.

In those days no mountain or even large hill was quite complete without a wise person to live upon it and dispense advice. In her land, the most reliable of these was Old Humphrey, the wise man of Humpback Mountain. To this esteemed gentleman went Esmerelda and a small retinue of her most trusted soldiers.

Told of the problem, the aged fellow began to laugh: "Why bother, your majesty? These rigmaroles, are they not mere playthings? Why take part in this pointless competition at all?"

"Because my people expect me to win. My rigmaroles are as good as those of the rulers who do so frequently win and this should be recognised."

Old Humphrey knew this to be so and had asked mainly to gauge the queen's determination. His question, nevertheless, lodged somewhere in Esmerelda's thoughts, and there began to take root.

Meanwhile, she listened to the venerable man's advice. Her rigmaroles, she was told, were frequently the best indeed. They should have earned her the plaque more than once. This was well known amongst the wise (and if only people listened to them things would go a lot more smoothly). "Now this is not really a conspiracy," observed Old Humphrey. "It's more a matter of habit, your majesty. Them as wins the most, they're the ones that are looked upon most favourably. And that is like a glamour, a spell that clouds the judges' eyes to look darkly on anyone else's rigmaroles. So you must replace it with a glamour of your own. One that will open their eyes to the supremacy of your chosen vehicle."

"But I know nothing of glamours!"

"Then, my queen, you must return to your castle, and do all you can to ensure that, this year, you have the very best rigmarole that you have ever presented. This you can do. When it is finished, call for a certain wise woman known as Mrs Rattlebag, who lives on Bumphack Hill. She's not as wise as I – which is why she lives on a hill, not a mountain – but she casts glamours of a kind that no other can."

With promises of honour and wealth Esmerelda spurred on her designers and her craftsmen, and in due course they transformed a hitherto mediocre rigmarole into the absolute pride of her collection. From its cut-glass quarter-light windows, to its magnificent dashboard adorned with jewelled, folk art spirals, to its elegant and utterly functional running gear, it was their masterpiece.

And when it was complete they called for Mrs Rattlebag to come to the castle and to place upon it a glamour that would open the eyes of all to its evident supremacy and bring the plaque to Esmerelda's highest castle tower at last. Before she began her casting, Mrs Rattlebag asked the queen how long she wanted the glamour to endure. Esmerelda thought for a while, remembering old Humphrey's question, and then said: "Until midnight on the day when the plaque is awarded."

The event, at which this greatest of rigmaroles was first displayed and observed by the men of judgement, was a State Cavalcade in honour of a notable saint once native to the land. People from every province would gather in the capital city, lining the pavements to watch. One by one the rigmaroles rolled out of Esmerelda's castle to parade through the widest streets, each a unique work of art, a wondrous feast for the eye. Last came the most magnificent of them all, and the glamour upon it was so profound that not a man could look upon it without pronouncing its glory.

And so it was that after this event, even as the men of judgement travelled on throughout the League of Countries, a certitude remained amongst them that they had already found this year's winner. This feeling was accompanied by a degree of surprise that it could actually be Queen Esmerelda's. They had just never really considered her as a contender before.

At last, in the autumn, the monarchs gathered to hear the judgement.

The day before the ceremony the queen ordered her men to gather a multitude of firewood and build a great pyre at the back of the castle, whilst she and her retinue greeted the arriving monarchs at the front.

That she would win was a foregone conclusion. Even without the glamour, her rigmarole was truly worthy of the prize. With the glamour, those arbiters of taste had eyes for no other. It was a struggle for them to maintain their air of detached objectivity, to conceal their excitement.

Esmerelda was victorious. It was unanimous. No one objected, not even the other monarchs, for they were affected by the glamour as all men were. In her acceptance speech she graciously gave her thanks, and then asked permission to demonstrate a point of principle. This was granted.

She led them all to the back of her castle where her men had built the pyre. There, during the ceremony, and at her command, they had taken Esmerelda's splendid rigmarole. Also at her command, they had raised and placed it atop the mound of firewood. To the amazement of all – the men of judgement, the monarchs, the nobles; the assembly of courtiers, soldiers, and servants – she ordered the pyre to be set alight.

Before too long the rigmarole was burning. First the flimsier bodywork, from its perch to its rumble, then the more solid and metal-bound wood of its wheels, undercarriage and shafts, until all was ablaze and a-crackle.

"Magnificent!" cried the men of judgement. "A flaming rigmarole!" "No one has ever done this before!" "What a truly breathtaking sight!" "Fantastic!"

The queen remained silent as these compliments came flying to her ears. She simply watched, not without regret, as the vehicle burned.

But the judges could not be silent. Even as the fire died and all that was left of the rigmarole was the blackened metal of chassis and wheel rims, the fragments of smouldering charcoal and ashes, still they sang its praises. "Such an elegant transformation!" "Surely this is the sleekest and most aerodynamic of rigmaroles that was ever created!!" "Bravo, Queen Esmerelda!" "Black and smoking as this one, should all our rigmaroles be!"

Esmerelda smiled and bade them return to her castle, where feasting and entertainment awaited. The final part of her demonstration, she informed them, would require all to re-convene at this spot beside the ashes, just after midnight. Soldiers from every country of the League would watch over the embers 'til then, ensuring they were not touched by anyone.

When the revelry was done and the chapel bell struck midnight, they returned. Now awe was replaced by consternation. The glamour was gone. In the torchlight they were looking at the remains of a burnt-out rigmarole, no more, no less. Yet, but a few hours before, it had seemed to them magnificent, fantastic, sleek and aerodynamic – the future of the vehicle before their very eyes.

Suspicious gazes turned on Queen Esmerelda. Before anyone else could muster a word, she spoke. Her voice was quiet, but it was heard by all. "Men of judgement," she said, "can you really trust your eyes? What makes you so sure of your choices when you can so easily be deceived?

"I will take the plaque for this coming year, but I will not mount it on my castle's highest tower, for mine was a great rigmarole, deserving of the prize, and it grieved me to burn it. Yet who is to say it was the 'best'? Not I. And—" She looked pointedly at the arbiters of taste. "Not you, it seems."

In the years that followed, with no further participation from Esmerelda, the monarchs of the League attempted to keep the competition going. "After all," they said to themselves, "it's only a bit of fun." "She was taking it all much too seriously. Burning a rigmarole to prove a point, how absurd!" But the heart went out of it, and eventually it had to be admitted that nobody really cared any more about winning the great green plaque.

Esmerelda never lost her passion for rigmaroles. Designed exclusively now for their proper ceremonial purpose, their public appearances were greeted with enthusiasm and admiration by her people. They adored her now. For how could they doubt a queen who had not only won the great green plaque at last, but had exposed the failings of those who thought themselves fit to judge?

And when the news reached Humpback Mountain, Old Humphrey smiled to himself. It was ever good to know that someone had listened to the words of the wise.

The Insufferable Tedium of the Afterlife

Grady Payne was very much the sort of chap who liked to dance on the high-wire, although he considered it no shame to lounge amongst the lowlifes when it suited him to do so. A rather handsome inheritance enabled him to enjoy virtually all that life has to offer. This he squeezed with gusto into his daily allotment of hours. He was not a man for quiet contemplation. The immaterial was quite beyond his scope.

I was therefore surprised when he informed me that he had gone to some trouble in order to obtain a deadlock, since such an arcane device had no connection whatsoever with any form of worldly pursuit.

"Rather a good one, I'm told. Instant access to the afterlife. See if I can't get in touch with old Uncle Horace, what?" This I took to be a joke. His Uncle Horace, a straitlaced old curmudgeon who had died but a few years past, had loathed Payne with an astonishing vehemence.

I assumed that he was attracted by the novelty that the deadlock might afford. To Grady, the world of the deceased would simply be an entertaining extension to that of the living.

Since he furnished me with rather a handsome stipend in order to be a reliable friend of his, I could not help but feign interest. "Do you think you have the necessary skills to operate this contraption?"

"Well, actually old chap, I was hoping you would be willing to... er, lend a hand, so to speak."

This was the downside of my otherwise sinecure-like employment with Grady Payne. An impending adventure. I did rather loathe the adventures. They were so very, very tiresome.

∞

Hand crafted by swarthy tribesmen from West Africa, the deadlock came with a length of ivory, shaped almost like a miniature walking stick, but intricately carved with repetitive, hypnotic patterns. This piece, I assumed, was a sort of key. The deadlock device itself was clad in a woven pouch, its colourful design echoing the patterns on the ivory stick.

"Splendid little thing, isn't it?" he said, pulling it from the pouch. It might have been made of ebony, but appeared to be vibrating somewhat. Vibrating at a frequency that, one presumed, enabled it to open a portal between the living and the dead. This gave it a permanently blurred appearance, despite Grady's grip upon it.

"Must tingle a bit," I commented.

Grady giggled. "I'll say!"

∞

Prior to our departure from the land of the living, I did the necessary research, both in the British Library and a number of less salubrious environments over which I shall draw a discreet veil.

As I had surmised, the ivory attachment was indeed a sort of key to the lock – but it was not a mere case of inserting it snugly into a readymade cavity, goodness me, no. There was hocus-pocus a-plenty, not to mention a fair dose of mumbo-jumbo, which had to be performed by way of a prelude.

Payne and I were absolutely starkers, our bodies adorned in daubs of paint with that same repetitious pattern that we had observed on the ivory 'key'. It was a series of winding, snakelike curved motifs, each intertwining with the last. Moreover, Grady had obtained from an acquaintance by the name of Binky, a rather foul tasting liquid that, he assured me, was utilised by shamanic type chaps across the world in the acquisition of 'altered states'. This we had imbibed. I'd have settled for a scotch on the rocks myself.

The deadlock lay on a coffee table between us. Dark, round and still vibrating, it appeared to grow in size as each of us in turn intoned the gibberish I had unearthed for the occasion. At one point it was necessary for us to get up and perform a circular dance, which we had rehearsed with considerable merriment the night before. Towards its conclusion, Grady caught my eye & glanced at the coffee table. The ebony device had swollen to the size of a football. It was hovering suspended by some unknown force, about a foot above the surface, and emitting a low, humming noise.

Grady produced the 'key' and each of us in turn kissed it lightly. The 'keyhole' was now clearly visible in the deadlock. We stood around the table as Grady inserted the one into the other. The humming sound took on a higher pitch.

∞

The domain of the dead is rather a confusing sort of a place.

It resembles our living world in its geography, but it is as if all periods of human history somehow coexist there. One is as likely to observe animal-skin clad hunting parties as militiamen in their khakis or elegant Victorian ladies in their copious attire. They do not appear to be aware of anyone or anything whose source lies outside their own lifetimes, however, and when their paths cross they tend to walk *through* one another in a quite bewildering manner.

Buildings and their contents seem periodically to shimmer and metamorphose between the decors and styles with which they have been arrayed over the course of their existence. Where older buildings have been razed and replaced, they randomly reappear, quite abruptly, alternating with their successors according to some unknown schedule. Trees shrink back to saplings, flowers to buds, and then grow again – all four seasons co-existing in flux.

"Not quite what I was expecting," said Grady, shortly after our transition, "Something a bit more... biblical, I suppose. Harps of heaven, heat of hell, that sort of thing."

"Ye-ess... Rather implies that the afterlife doesn't have a great deal to add to one's... ah, overall experience. One is rather locked into one's time, like a fly in amber."

"Well put, sir. Still, shouldn't be too difficult to track down uncle H."

"Oh yes. I'd quite forgotten. So, am I to presume that you do actually have a reason for locating the deceased?"

"Rather. Some unfinished business, don't you know? Valuable items that proved untraceable after his death. Like to get my hands on 'em, buff up the old pension, what."

∞

By the time we reached 23 Acacia Gardens, the novelty of being walked through by peasants, crinoline-clad ladies, cavaliers, carthorses and what-have-you was wearing a little thin. They (the dead) saw only others of their own era. We (the living) saw all eras and the hordes of all their shades. At first we tended to brace ourselves, anticipating impact. Soon we simply ignored them.

The building where Horace Appleby had spent the bulk of his adult life was an imposing detached house, some four storeys high. We seemed to have walked into a patch of night-time and the place had rather a gothic look in the moonlight, with its plethora of arches and towers.

"What ho!" Grady pointed to the front door. "Think we can just walk through it?"

"Doubt it. I've noticed anything which we have experienced or known in our own lives tends to have rather more in the way of substance about it."

"Quite right." He had drawn back the door knocker. "Most substantial. I knew you were the right chap to have onboard with this one. Observational sort of a—"

It seemed to the pair of us that what we saw then was instantaneous. One moment we stood before a closed wooden doorway, the next it was open and we faced the backlit figure of an elderly gentleman with a most pronounced frown upon his face. "Took your bloody time, Payne," he said.

∞

"So it's the reliquaries you're after is it, my lad?" Uncle Horace stroked his stubbly beard, watching us as we settled into two rather overstuffed armchairs in the parlour.

"And their contents," Grady interjected swiftly.

His uncle grunted an acknowledgement, adding: "And you're quite sure you're not actually dead."

"No, no." Grady laughed. "Years ahead of me. Quite sure of that!"

"Well get some damn clothes on, man, and follow me up to the attic. I'll show you. Once this deadlock of yours takes you back to the land of the living, you'll know exactly where to find them."

It appeared to me that Uncle H was being rather too cooperative. That he, unlike any others we had yet encountered, was clearly aware of his deceased condition could be explained by an ample intelligence and, I suspect, some foreknowledge of the afterlife. But that formerly he had always displayed such a loathing for Grady Payne did not rub well with this relative display of charm.

I arose from my armchair as they did from theirs, whereupon Horace gestured to me with the flat of his hand. "Not you," he said. "This is family business." He raised an eyebrow, meaningfully. "I do recommend that you remain here and do not attempt to ascend the staircase."

I was soon to learn that this was not a threat but actually a rather useful piece of advice.

∞

I do not know how much time, if any, then passed. It seemed quite enough for me to consider the profoundly disappointing nature of the afterlife. I'd never been one for all that heaven and hell hoopla, but at least there was a measure of organisation to what the bible bashers imagined. One's true experience following death seemed chaotic, repetitive and – above all – deeply, deeply dreary.

I felt a little peckish then and made my way to the kitchen, only to find that, unfortunately, the larder was stocked exclusively with writhing maggots. Turning from this unpleasant sight, I became aware of an intense, shimmering light. Daylight it became, bathing me fully, since in an instant the house was no more.

Formerly stood upon floor boards, I had been but an inch or two above ground level and merely stumbled slightly as my feet fell to the surface below. Three storeys up, Grady Payne was not so fortunate. My ears were rent by a piercing scream from somewhere above me.

Then, for just a moment or two, I thought I heard the sound of Uncle Horace laughing with hearty abandon.

∞

I turned the 'key' a little more tightly to be certain I had closed the deadlock. It was once again on the coffee table and had resumed its original size.

Payne's naked, painted corpse lay on the floor. It was not the twisted wreck I had observed lying on the open ground where Uncle Horace's dwelling had been back in the land of the dead. Payne looked as if he had simply collapsed. But there could be no doubt that he was no longer breathing.

Horace had feigned his ignorance regarding deadlocks. Of that I am now certain. Before his own death, perhaps even foreseeing it, he had prepared the lure by concealing the reliquaries and their contents. I am inclined to believe, moreover, that the ease with which Grady had acquired the deadlock may have been due to more of Horace's machinations.

My suspicions were confirmed when there were more deaths in the Payne family in the months to come. Grady was by no means the only relative against whom the vindictive uncle had borne a grudge.

As for me, restored to life, but with my state of employment at a rather sudden end, I wasted no time in locating the key to 23 Acacia Avenue from one of Grady's jacket pockets. I'd seen enough of the hereafter to be sure that one might as well make the best of one's allotted span of years.

Of course, the old schemer might not have hidden the reliquaries in his attic at all.

But given the opportunity, it would be well worth my while to go and have a bit of a look.

Enlightenment

"And a welcome to all of you. I must say that it's a fantastic turn-out. When I saw on the schedules that we were up against the Zumba Fitness session, I was worried, frankly."

A mild ripple, just touching on laughter, passed through the twenty-seven folk who'd gathered in the hall at the Deepton Community Centre to embark on a twelve session introduction to the practice known as 'Akimbo'. Not one of them had a clear idea of what was to come. There was just something alluring about the blurb in the brochure, an irresistible scent that had drawn them. Akimbo promised much. According to the writer, it combined facets of martial art and bodily workout with a rich and fascinating philosophy. Without being too specific he implied that through daily application, over a short period of time, one could become a lightning-fast practitioner of self-defence — lithe, healthy and wise beyond earthly knowing in both mind and spirit. The writer's name was Gary Jenkins. As the ripple subsided Gary continued.

"Anybody here have any knowledge of Akimbo?" There were blank looks. No hands were raised. "Good. That means I don't have to undo any preconceptions. According to the masters of this great art, it is best to enter the mind/body state of Akimbo as a blank slate. We'll be going into its history and development, bit by bit, over the next few weeks, but tonight I want to go straight in and give you a taste of what it's all about. I can see that you've all come along in some nice, loose clothing, as I suggested. We're going to start with a few warm-ups. First, let's have you all standing, nice and relaxed, legs slightly apart, hands on hips, and elbows turned outwards..."

∞

"So what was that class like last night, Sher?" said Crystal, hitching an errant strap of her sun-top back across her ample shoulder. It had been a good summer. They were both brown as beechnuts, with nary a visit to the tanning parlour nor a squeeze of spray-on.

"Well, you get more laughs in the Zumba but there's something about it." Sheryl took a thoughtful drag on her Lambert and Butler. "You come out at the end feeling different, like. Sort of confident, 'I can handle it', you know?"

"Yeah? And that bloke that's teaching it? Bit fit, is he?"

"Get away with you, Crystal Wilcock, that's got nothing to do with it."

∞

"I need a name. Nothing too culture specific, but sort of suggestive of exotic cultures..." Gary Jenkins ran a hand across his neatly trimmed beard.

In the armchair facing him, his wife Elise raised her eyebrows: "Don't you think you should have got this all worked out before you started?"

"I honestly never thought it would take off. And in the remote instance that it does, I thought – I can wing it. How was I to know we'd actually be turning people away for the second session?"

"Hmm... So now you require a guru? And presumably a place where it all began."

"Oh yeah. And it'd have to be somewhere really obscure."

∞

"I can't believe it," shouted Crystal across a table of drinks at the Workman's. "You really have given up the ciggies!"

"Five days and counting," replied Sheryl proudly. "Early days yet but I really feel like I've lost the urge, know what I mean?"

Above a bulging boob tube, Crystal shrugged her shoulders. "Yeah, well... You're not gonna go packin' up the drink now, are you, girl?"

"Nah. Nandar, he says a little bit of booze won't do you no harm."

"Who?"

"Nandar! Nandar Juriyama. He's the geezer that started it all. About fifty years back, according to Gary. In Paraguay, apparently."

∞

"Sheryl, dear, I couldn't help noticing that Splay posture was a little... shall we say *off centre* this evening. I do hope you're keeping up with the daily practise sessions."

101

Strange. There was a time when Sheryl would have characterised Maureen Lightfoot as an interfering old cow. But now, six weeks into the evening course, Maureen's dedication to the Akimbine Path was an inspiration to them all. Frequently praised by Gary himself, it was clear that for perhaps the first time in her life she had a higher calling.

"Never miss 'em, Maur... But you're right. It was a bit dodgy tonight. I'll put in some extra time on the Splay."

"It is one of the Ten Key Postures, according to Nandar. Less than perfect just won't do."

∞

"...So Nandar sat by the bottle tree for a day and a night and when he returned to the village he spoke of his vision to the assembled people, and they saw the depth to which he had penetrated the great mysteries, and they became the first of his followers..."

"You'll have me believing that stuff next, Gary," said Elise with a laugh. "But this is the information age. What if they Google it? They won't find anything."

"Ah, but that's what makes it exclusive. They're getting something which hasn't even made it onto the internet yet. I'm the first non-Paraguayan to bring it back to Europe, see?"

"You've got a nerve! So how are you going to explain away the nonexistence of...? What's'isname?"

"Nandar Juriyama? Because he is no more. He 'transcended mortality', you see. I explained it was sort of like an assisted suicide, with his followers' support. The class just lapped it up."

∞

"See, what you need, Crys, is a different attitude. I mean, Weight Watchers an' that, they're all right as far as they go but what happens? You do really well for a bit and then – let's face it – sooner or later you lapse. 'Cause you're not really getting to grips with the mind/body interface."

"The what?!" Crystal slapped a half-eaten piece of Café Josie's finest chocolate brownie back down onto her plate. "What is it, six or seven weeks since you started this Akimbo business? It's like you don't talk about anythin' else no more."

∞

He didn't want to overdo the kung fu and tai chi moves. That would be too obvious. The martial aspect of Akimbo had to appear unique, and to make it that way he'd need to blend in some sort of contrasting approach. But what?

He dismissed the idea when it first occurred to him. Those restraint techniques he'd learned about on a two-day course when he was working for Social Services, they were remarkably effective but hardly the stuff of esoteric practise.

Worth a try, though. He still had the course notes somewhere in the filing cabinet by his desk...

∞

Gripped seemingly without effort by Maureen Lightfoot, Sheryl surrendered to a feeling of utter helplessness and awaited release. Maureen let go with a flourish. "Now then, Sheryl, you try it on Kevin..."

At Maureen's instigation, for the last two weeks members of the class had been meeting for additional practice at her house on Sunday evenings. Tonight they were dedicating themselves to perfecting the art of 'dovetailing' – as Gary had called it, translating from the Guarani. It was, they all agreed, amazingly effective, Nandar be praised.

Kevin was a bulky man. It was clear that Maureen had set her a challenge, yet Sheryl approached him with a sense of serene and absolute confidence. With the required mindfulness, holding that ever-present sense of the mind/body interface, Sheryl knew you could dovetail anyone.

∞

Elise was still pale and clearly shaken as she got into the car. Gary loaded the last of the shopping bags into the back and seated himself at the steering wheel. "This Akimbo thing," she said. "It's going too far. They bowed to you, Gary. I mean, right there in the middle of Waitrose, two of your class members bowing and scraping as if you were some sort of deity. It's crazy. It's got to stop."

Gary sighed. "I know... It does seem to be getting a bit out of hand."

"'A bit'? Gary!"

"Hey look, it's the last class next week. Next term they'll all enrol on something else and get sucked into another new craze. You know how it is with evening classes. You think they'll change your life. Six months later, you've forgotten the lot."

∞

"Well, I'd like to finish this last class with a word of thanks. You've all been fantastic. Frankly, I never expected so many of you to get to grips with Akimbo in the way that you have. But if I can just add a word of warning... Do keep in mind it's just one of many techniques by which you can develop your sense of the mind/body interface. I mean, everything from yoga to... well, perhaps even Zumba. It all has validity. Use Akimbo as you would any self-improvement method. It's not the be-all and end-all of— Yes Maureen?"

"I don't know who's making you say that, Gary, but it's not true. Akimbo is a way of life, a way of being. We are on the path, Gary, and it's a path we'll tread until the day we die."

"Uh—"

"You've taught us all you have to teach us, haven't you?" continued Maureen, in icy tones. "But we're ready now, ready to spread the teachings. And spread them we will, right across the world. So it's time to hand over the baton, isn't it? Time to follow Nandar to that better place where earthly reality is finally transcended."

"Maureen, I'm... I'm not sure I—"

"We've got some pills for you to take, Gary. They'll... well, they'll see you off. Though of course, if anyone asks, we won't know anything about it. We'll all be quite amazed that you chose to take your own life. That's how Nandar's disciples got away with it. Just like you told us."

"Is this some kind of joke?" Gary looked around the class. The faces he saw were calm and impassive. United.

"Kevin?" said Maureen, "Would you be kind enough to dovetail Gary for us?"

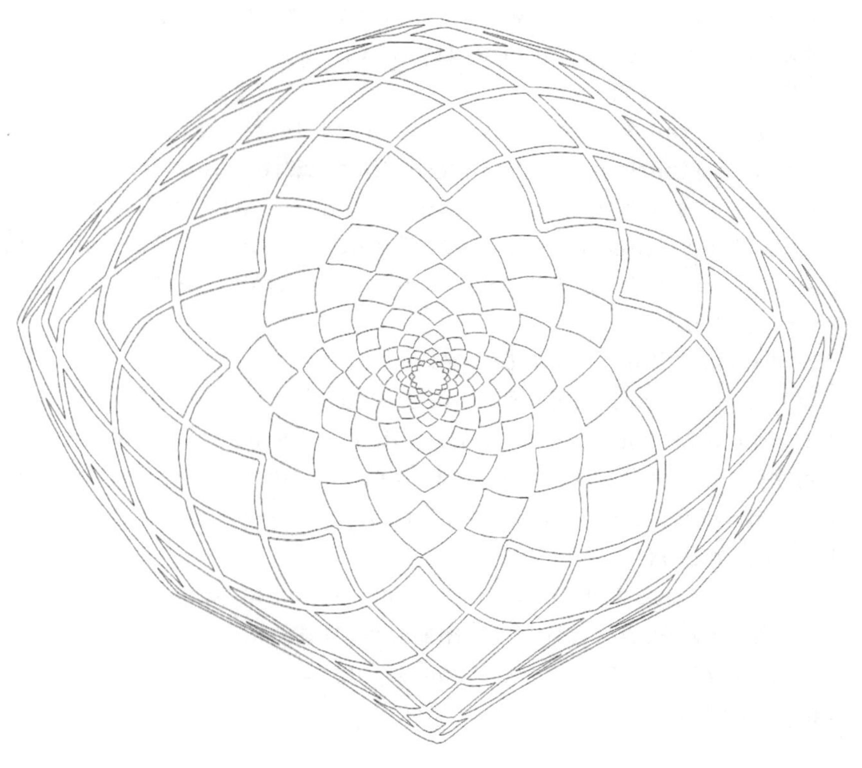

Encounters

I've been on the road since 8am, including an hour and twenty-five minutes in the mother of all tailbacks before I could get off the motorway. My bum is sweaty and sore, lower back one big, dull ache, shoulders stiff and temples throbbing. That very nice roadside café I was looking forward to revisiting around lunchtime has bloody well closed down, and I ended up ravenously grabbing an excrement burger from a drive-in, with desiccated salad and a bun made out of some near-edible form of polystyrene.

Worst of it is I'm going to be late for my appointment with the Bamsey family. Okay, once I recalculated my ETA, I called them on the mobile: "Very sorry... terrible traffic... blah blah." And I knew they'd be wanting to wait in for me whenever I turned up, because after what they've been through they've just got to talk about it to someone. But that's not the point. I hate being late. Everything I do when I'm late feels rushed. I hate being rushed.

I can't understand why I have to drive all this way at all. Management could get me here a lot quicker if they had a mind to. Probably some sort of economy they have to make. These are difficult times everywhere. Anyway, what the hell? I've just passed a sign that says 'North Ockerton Welcomes Careful Drivers' and the satnav's telling me my destination is within 500 yards.

So now, at last, the bit that makes it all worthwhile.

∞

I've had to do the interviews individually. They'd said they'd rather talk to me as a family, so they're not happy. We tried, but despite my careful explanation they could not seem to stop themselves. Sometimes, within just a few seconds of me asking a question, all five of them would be talking at once. How are you going to transcribe that?

"Mr and Mrs Bamsey — Shannon, Crystal, Kieran, please!" This after the second attempt. I played back the last twenty seconds or so of the recording. It was obvious even to them that the incomprehensible babble of voices erupting from the tinny little speaker was of no use whatsoever. "As your circumscribe for this event, I must be able to record each of your accounts with absolute clarity." So reluctantly they agreed. I was able to clear the room and record them one at a time.

Now, just listen to Mr B.

"We're drivin' through the woods and I've got me foot down 'cause Deirdre is runnin' late for Line Dance, and suddenly, in me 'eadlights, there's this... this great, 'airy giant of a creature just standin' in the road in front of us. And I mean just standin' there, lookin' directly at us. Well, down goes me foot on the brake, but no way 'ave I got

enough distance to stop before we 'it 'im. And that's when it all begins to go really strange, 'cause stop somehow I do, just a couple of metres short. But there's no sound, and though we're all jerkin' in our seat belts with the momentum like, it's all in kind of slo-mo. And it leaves us all feelin' numb, but starin' at this weird bloke.

"Well, I say 'bloke'. Don't know what it was though. 'Uman face, but most of its skin covered in jet-black hair, like a gorilla. Funny expression, sort of a smile but not quite. Like the Mona Lisa. The smile, not 'im. 'E wasn't a bit like the Mona Lisa. Great 'airy 'ulk, 'e was."

And now to Mrs B.

"Well you can smell him, even with the windows wound up. Disgustin'! It's almost like we're paralysed, but I'm fightin' it, twistin' me head back to get a look at the kids and see if they're all right. An' I get a glimpse of these three poor shocked faces. Shannon's looking like she's going to throw up—'cause she's right sensitive to smells, she is. An' Kieran says: 'It's Black Jack!' An' I'm thinkin': What—'im out of all them stories you 'ear?"

A bit of Crystal now. She was the sharpest of the bunch.

"That's when I noticed that we were in light. I mean it was dark when we set out, but it felt like we were in daylight. It didn't make any sense. You could say it was like a dream. But it wasn't. It was clear. It was, like, vivid. Right up to the moment when... when we weren't there anymore."

It was a good way of putting it. We call them 'jump cuts', as per when you switch scenes in a film. As Crystal said, it's too solid and 'real' to be like a dream; but nevertheless, there's a kind of dream logic about the way events proceed. Since I've never had one myself, it never ceases to fascinate me, hearing about these experiences of people for whom supposedly legendary creatures come to life and suchlike. I consider the opportunity to record such stories a privilege. That's why I knew from my schooldays that I wanted to be a circumscribe.

Anyway, the Bamsey family were no longer in their car. They couldn't even see one another. Each of them was encased in what seemed to them like some sort of organic pod and experiencing strange flickering sensations across their skin. Crystal said it was like she was Braille and she was "being read". They all commented further on the feeling of numbness, the near paralysis. Eventually each of them felt that they must have lost consciousness and when they came to they were back in the car.

Their clothing was dishevelled, as if put on too hastily. Shannon's cardy was on back to front. The insides of their shoes felt curiously damp. The car was stationary, but parked in a lay-by several miles from the woods. It was around midnight. They'd no idea how they got there.

The interviews over, I hand them our family information pack, with all our leaflets containing upbeat descriptions of possible after-effects; where to get therapeutic support if needed, and the indicators for a possible recurrence. Plus, of course, our award-winning 'Paranormal Facts' DVD and sample phial of rescue remedy. We don't stint.

∞

Of course I hit the rush hour on the way back south. More nose-to-tail, as if I hadn't had enough on the way up. After the news there's only drivel on the radio. So I switch off, patch in the voice recorder and listen back, marvelling, as I often do, how the kids seem to pick up on tiny, interesting details that the adults fail to notice. According to Shannon, for example, Black Jack had brightly painted toenails.

Black Jack. It's been a while since I've heard tell of a Black Jack encounter. He's a tutelary spirit for woodland in this part of the country, but crops up elsewhere under different names: Charley Dark; the Woozer; Drogg. I don't mind admitting that I've driven out on lonely wooded roads in the dark hours of night hoping I might encounter him myself. But I never have.

Same goes for the whole colourful and ever-expanding crew of numinous beings who love to intrude on humanity's ordered view of reality right across the country. Like the Owligans of the deep south west. A fierce lot. I've collected stories from folk who were convinced that their innards had been pecked out through their chests, only to find themselves perfectly intact at some later hour. Or the sinister looking Pit Men who haunt old mining areas long after the pits have been closed. It's said that some of the old shafts broke through into their underground lands, where intricate labyrinths are carved in huge veins of pure coal. They've been coming to take us away ever since. And, it's also said, not all of us are returned.

Oh, it's a rich and special world that coincides with ours. Often a tricky one too. There are the Brandy Snappers, for example — malevolent creatures resembling small domestic animals who tend to shadow the lives of inebriates, encouraging them to pursue their addiction to its logical conclusion. Or are they just symptoms of delirium tremens? Whatever, not a race that I've personally wished to encounter.

On the other hand, I've longed to meet a Twilligoric. Creatures of great charm, they are said to be slender, elegant and extremely beautiful. I've had all the lowdown on the precise procedures that are required to prevent the gold – that they so willingly give you – from transforming into a kind of slime mould in your pockets as you make your way home.

But I don't suppose that I shall ever meet a Twilligoric. Or one of the Pretty Pennies. Or see Dream Boats silhouetted on an ocean horizon, or stumble into a Cataclysm whilst walking in the wilds. Perhaps that's the fate of the circumscribe. To record all of these marvels but never experience them.

∞

It looks like I'm too bloody late. Again. The car park's nearly empty and what's left are probably overnights. Management will have night staff on for the transfers of course, but they're trainees mostly — conscientious but slow. So that's it. Apart from the interview, it's been a thoroughly lousy day all the way round.

I unplug the recorder, slip it into its case and get out of the car. It's a clear night and I can see the stars right across from the tree-line at one edge of the car park to the high fence at the other. I'm looking up to the south and picking out Vega, waiting for the faint, spotlight glow which heralds the Illuminar.

Ah. There it is.

I am immersed in light and my feet no longer touch the ground. Quick off the mark, then. They must have seen me looking at my watch. That's good. I shouldn't be in transit too long. Being weightless and simultaneously drenched in a light bath of swirling colours has a tendency to make me nauseous if it goes on and on.

Bloody management. One minute they want you in a Ford Fiesta labouring up the motorway, the next they're flipping you round the galaxy in a beam of coruscating light. I mean, there's no reason why they couldn't rent out a perfectly serviceable office block in a business park, same as they do for the printing and DVD unit. But no, us circumscribes have to be hoicked across to the mothership in person.

Well, actually, I realise now that I am already in the mothership's processing department, and for some time I've been reliving the day, in a mind link with the narrative recorder. In another minute or two there will be a complete transcript of my interviews with the Bamseys, plus a full account of my working day being filed into the cellular database. I was lucky. Plux was still on duty, took pity and fast-tracked me.

I can see him working vapours across the gangway from my clear-sided immersion tank. He catches my eye, gives me the tentacular equivalent of a thumbs up and casually brushes a screen with one of the very sensitive suckers at the end of another tentacle. Next thing I know I'm mentally receiving knowledge of my next assignment.

I will admit all this mind-link stuff does keep the paperwork to a minimum, but it can be very wearing — especially for us, the human contingent of the team. I keep meaning to have a word with the union rep about it.

The job sounds promising, however. A short drive down to a resort on the south coast and a chat with a woman who has had a Merwolf encounter. That'll be a new one for me.

Merwolves... Amphibians, obviously. I've heard they have razor sharp teeth and a refined love for poetry. They sound fascinating.

Though I don't suppose I shall ever get the chance to actually meet one.

The Drink that Gives You a Pat on the Back

"Did you see that?" said Sarah, returning to the living room. "I mean, how I opened the door just enough so I could comfortably enter without wasting energy pushing it any further than I needed to. Ergonomic or what?"

Fliss watched aghast as Sarah strode confidently to the armchair opposite her own and sat down. This was getting out of hand. She half-expected another commentary from Sarah regarding the act of seating herself, how elegantly she'd done it, how she'd harmonised with gravity. Anything was possible. But instead she said: "You were going to ask me something. Whatever it is, Fliss, I can help, no problem."

"Good." Fliss beamed. "How many bottles have you drunk today?"

"Oh no, you mustn't worry about that. Do you know, it feels like for the first time in my life I know exactly what I'm doing. One bottle, five bottles, what does it matter?"

"*Five* bottles?"

"Mm. Possibly. Might have lost count."

In Fliss' stomach there was a deepening void. The Sarah she'd known and loved for so many years was gone, and this was the person who'd replaced her. Worse still, Fliss was responsible.

Just a few weeks ago, she'd gone to visit Sarah at her home. She'd heard nothing from her for some time. Calls and texts had been going unanswered, an old pattern. So Fliss was not surprised to find her still in her dressing gown and immersed in daytime TV.

"There's a world out there, you know."

"So there is. But does it need *me*?"

"I get worried when I don't hear from you."

"I'm sorry, Fliss. It's just been really bad lately, you know... That old voice in my head: 'Whatever you do, you'll screw up somehow. Better not to try.' And I know, I know... You've heard all this before."

"Sarah, why? Why do you always end up thinking that it's all going to go wrong?"

"Experience." Sarah gave her a wan smile. "Because *everything* I do turns out to be... rubbish. I keep on making the same old mess of things, time and time again."

There was, unfortunately, some truth in that statement. Sarah had had a problem with self-esteem ever since Fliss had first known her. Mostly, it stayed in some sort of perspective, but in the last six months she'd lost both a good job and a steady boyfriend. She was locked into a self-perpetuating and negative loop. Again.

This time, however, Fliss thought she had something new to offer. "Sarah... I don't s'pose you've heard of 'Accolade'?"

"What?"

"It's a drink, like an energy drink but apparently it changes your feelings. People say it makes you feel sort of better about yourself."

She explained how she'd read about it in a magazine and looked it up on the Internet where no one seemed to have a bad word to say about it.

Sarah was slow to comprehend. "A *drink*?"

Once she'd grasped it, she told Fliss she was very sorry but she found the idea quite repellent. She was facing the truth about herself. The idea that her feelings could be changed merely by taking a drink suggested that they could not be real. 'Well, *yes*.' thought Fliss but held her tongue. She knew Sarah. It was enough for now just to lodge the idea.

Result! When next they met, at Costa's, it was obvious. Sarah had taken care with her clothing, been to the hairdressers and, best of all, had a broad smile across her face. "It works. Accolade! I got some and it really works!"

Over the next half-hour, Fliss learned that Sarah was looking for a new job. She'd undersold herself all her working life and would be aiming considerably higher this time. At which point, with no hint of irony, she added: "Because I'm worth it." Sarah's gratitude to Fliss for suggesting Accolade was profuse. Its manufacturers were a benevolent lot, apparently. They even put a helpline number on the packaging – you could call them for advice if Accolade did not seem to be working as you'd hoped. That was what had finally persuaded her to try it. They cared.

So far, so good.

At their parting hug, Sarah said: "Do you think I'm good at hugging?"

"Well... I guess, yes."

"Good! I think so too. I'm warm and empathetic, aren't I?"

At that point, ever so delicately, the void in Fliss' stomach had made its first appearance.

By now it was cavernous. She really should have read up a lot more about the stuff before making her impulsive recommendation to someone as vulnerable as Sarah.

"...so I've just pulled off the most perfect deal as far as supply is concerned..."

Fliss realised she'd stopped listening to Sarah, as she so often did during the extended 'good reviews' her friend now habitually gave herself. Supply of *what*?

Sarah looked at her, laughing. "Oh Fliss, you look like you've lost the plot. I'm surprised. I'm a very clear speaker, you know. Anyway, it was Accolade I was talking about. Look, here in my bag, I've brought you a six-pack to try because I really think you should."

It surprised Fliss how small the plastic bottles were. The slogan across the cardboard holder read: 'The drink that gives you a pat on the back.' She smiled. "That's very kind of you. I'll... uh, I'll try some later." As she took them from Sarah she noticed a faint look of disapproval on her friend's face. With that postponement, it seemed, she'd failed some sort of test.

It came as a relief when Sarah said it was time for her to go. "I slip on a coat rather eurhythmically, don't you think?"

Alone, Fliss sank back into the armchair clutching her head. Out of hand, all her own fault... Well, was it? Wouldn't Sarah have come across Accolade one way or another? And what was it with the stuff that it had such an effect? Did it change everyone like it had Sarah? Did it wear off if you stopped drinking it? No wonder they had a helpline.

The number was on the pack Sarah had left. Fliss grabbed her phone.

"Hello. You have reached the Accolade helpline and we want you to know that we value your call, because we believe that Accolade is consumed by only the most discerning customers. And that's you.

And you're great. And we're great. So we can help, no problem. Now, how may I help you?"

Fliss hit the red button. She'd heard enough.

Next day, on the bus to work, she overheard a couple as they settled on the seat in front of her. "Did you see how quickly I worked out the right money to give the driver?" said she. "Oh I did, because I notice everything about you. Just call me 'Mr Observant'!" said he. Laughter. "Oh, I can't get over how *witty* we are today!"

Acc-heads were proliferating.

Fliss avoided Sarah for some time, which was not difficult given the state of self-absorption with which Sarah now contemplated her own radiance. She missed the old Sarah. Her friend might have been hesitant, forever undermining her own self-confidence, but she was thoughtful, loving and loyal. And not without her own strengths. She'd been a well of support when Fliss lost her father to cancer.

The cavern in Fliss' stomach began to feel unstable, like it would collapse in on itself with terrible consequences.

When depressed, as she now felt she was, it had been her habit to watch a lot of TV. But she no longer could. Like all the media, TV was obviously riddled with Acc-heads. You only had to watch the chat shows for a start. Those people must have known about the stuff long before she ever did.

It was all a morass of feelgood superficiality, best ignored, except that she'd managed to tilt one of her best friends right into it. Why had she not thought it through more carefully before she'd blurted? From what had happened, she could now see that Sarah's initial objection to Accolade was not without reason. It took human emotion into the shallows and then left it there stranded.

Something had to be done, at least as far as Sarah was concerned. Uneurhythmically, she put on her coat and headed over to her friend's.

"Fliss! It's been ages. I've been meaning to get in touch, but the thing is... I keep getting sidetracked by all these great ideas. And they always seem to come at about 10 o'clock in the morning for some reason. Anyway, I get them, and of course, you know, I've got to make a reality out of them. I mean, isn't that fantastic? Every day I'm sort of... developing a new dimension."

Sarah was still looking good, though Fliss couldn't help thinking the cheap fashionable clothes she was now wearing, along with the unusual attention she'd given to makeup, made her look just a touch tarty. "Tell me more. What are these great ideas?"

"Oh, let me think. Yes, the other day I thought: 'I shall go out for a walk.' I mean, isn't that brilliant, Fliss? Exercise, fresh air, a chance to stop and look at things that you normally just whiz past... It's just an amazingly good thing to do, and I did it."

"Sarah..." Fliss sighed, wearily. "That's a good idea, I'll grant you. But it's not a *great* one. Lots of people go for walks. Great ideas tend to be things that no one has ever thought of before."

"What are you trying to say?"

"I... I think you should try stopping the Accolade for a bit. I think you need to get back in touch with who you really are, love. Maybe just have a bottle now and then, when you need a bit of a boost, eh?"

"But it was you that recommended it. I don't understand. Why are you telling me to stop?" The change in Sarah was unsettling and abrupt. A soap bubble bursting. Fliss wanted to take her into her arms, like she'd done so easily so many a time, but Sarah's body language was clear. *Keep your distance.*

"I just don't think it's really doing you any good."

"You didn't say it would do me good. You said it would make me feel better about myself. And it has. I don't know why you want me to stop feeling better about myself."

"I don't want you to stop feeling better about yourself, Sarah, I just—"

"I'm having a great idea right now, Fliss. I think you should go. You're not my friend any more. You're just bringing me down. Please… Go."

Trudging home along bleak city streets, the thoughts were inescapable. What an utter mess she'd made of that! She wasn't quite the good-with-people person she'd always prided herself she was. She wasn't quite so good at a lot of things. That was the reason for the cavern in her stomach, collapsing tumultuously as it was within her now. It was not just Sarah; it was her own sense of pitiful failure.

Confidence. What a house of cards that was.

Reaching home, Fliss made straight for the kitchen, seeking comfort in coffee.

The six-pack of Accolade still lay on the counter, where she'd put it after Sarah had presented it. She switched on the kettle and stared at the packaging. 'The drink that gives you a pat on the back.'

Was this the way of the world, now? Happy folk, backs patted. What was the point in holding out against it?

She sipped her coffee. The comfort wasn't sufficient. Maybe she could do with that pat on the back herself.

She pulled a bottle from the cardboard holder and stared at it with continuing distaste. Then, with no more hesitation, she unscrewed the top and raised it to her lips.

Eyewash

"Client for ya," said Gina, poised in the doorway to my office. I could see she was itching to get back to her filing. Filing her nails, that is.

"Send her in, babe."

Gina raised one carefully plucked eyebrow. "How'd you know it's a dame, boss?"

"It's always a dame," I said. "It's always a dame."

This one wore make up like it was going out of fashion, enough mascara to surface a sidewalk and powder in contours.

"So you're Mike Mallett. Your specialty's rooting out crooked private dicks, right?"

"Right," I said, "I'm the eye shadow. I shadow the eyes."

"Well, this dick." She kind of spat out the words. "He's been dicking me around. And that ain't ethical."

Her name was Wilhelmina Beecham, and that's not the kind of name I'd make up to protect the innocent. Innocent she wasn't. Her old man, Studs Beecham, was a small-time crime boss, struggling to stay in the game with the big guys. As for the dick, he'd been hired by persons unknown to get the lowdown on Studs. Studs wasn't home when he called, so he tried out the old charm routine on Mina. She liked that. But she didn't like questions, and he asked too many. So, when he left, she did some snooping herself. Got his name and occupation. Garfield Parish. Private detective. Now Mina had no great love for Studs, but he was her meal ticket. Someone had put Parish on his case. She needed to know who that someone was, so she came to me.

"Ethical?" I said. But it felt kinda good to be working again. My services had not been required for some months. "Now tell me — what do you think Parish was trying to find out?"

"That, Mr Mallett, is the crazy part. He wanted to know if Studs had any kinda... religion."

∞

Three days into the case and I knew it was weird. First, no one had tried to break into my office. Then, no one had attempted to shoot me or even give me a pistol whipping. I'd not been bushwhacked. Not even a threatening phone call. This was not how I earned my living.

I was on my way to meet Parish. Turns out Gina was close with Lola, his secretary. They'd made an appointment for me. I kept a wary eye on the rear-view mirror as I crossed town, but no one tailed me.

Parish's office was a lot like mine. I could have told you which drawer he kept the whiskey bottle in and which one the gun. But this time I got it wrong. He did not drink whiskey. He drank liquorice tea. Yeah. Liquorice tea. But I still figured I had the gun drawer right.

"So," I said, when the intros were done, "Studs."

"Ah, Studs. Surprisingly tough nut to crack. Mina hired you, huh? She give you an advance?"

"My terms," I said.

"That's good, that's good. Because soon you will be needing some capital. And a new business plan."

"I didn't come here to discuss my financial affairs."

"I know. You've come here to find out who hired me, what I was after and whether my game is crooked or straight. Now why don't you take a sip of that tea, my friend? No one is going to slip you a mickey."

∞

It was true. I did not find myself becoming groggy and passing out at the wheel as I drove the narrow, winding cliff-side road to my next destination, the mansion where Studs and Mina made their cosy love nest. "See for yourself, my friend," Parish had said. "See for yourself."

Mina answered the door. Tears had smeared the mascara in streaks through the powdery contours below. "It's bad," she said. "Real bad." She led me through wood-panelled corridors to a room at the back of the building. "This... this used to be his den," she said. "Now... Well, take a look."

Most of the furniture had been removed and piled outside the room. The floor had been scattered with ornate rugs and brightly coloured, embroidered cushions. The walls were draped with fringed shawls adorned with oriental lettering. Candles burned in decoratively crafted holders. Incense smouldered.

At the centre of all this sat Studs Beecham, cross-legged, back straight, naked but for a loincloth. His eyes were closed, his head shaved. He was making a low, repetitive humming sound and appeared to be in some sort of a trance.

"He's… Oh god." Mina was sobbing softly. "He's become a Buddhist."

∞

Studs had been one of the last names on Parish's list. I knew now why there had been so little work just lately. He'd started with the major crime bosses. Big Louis, Enrico the Axe, Knuckles DeFreitas, Mad Mike Murphy… How Parish got face to face with these guys I don't know – though I could vouch for his skills of persuasion – but one by one, after he'd made his visit, they got religion. Big Louis took to wearing flowing robes and spreading Hindu teachings. Enrico joined the Sufi sect known as the Whirling Dervishes. Knuckles took up with the Rosicrucians and Murphy the Baha'is. So it went.

Clearly there should have been henchmen waiting in the wings to take the lead when the guys at the top of the pecking order demonstrated the first sign of weakness. But it didn't work out that way. Instead there was a kind of chain reaction right down to street level. And across the board too, reaching out to the gangland associates. Corrupt city officials, politicians, mouthpieces, even crooked dicks — they all began to preach the word. Peace and good will to all men and women.

It was hard to believe. That's why Parish had told me to go check it out myself. First Studs and then the rest. The word was spreading anyway. Seems that all too soon there was money available for welfare, education and housing programmes; drug abuse was in sharp decline, small businesses thriving. Once as sick as just about every other place on earth, the city had found a cure.

It was revelation to revolution and all down to just one guy, Garfield Parish, private detective. Who *was* he working for? He'd said he'd tell me once I'd seen what I needed to see.

"He's ready for you now." Gina put down the phone. Even she had traded her nail file for a rosary. I picked up my car keys and headed for the street.

∞

Lola was nowhere to be seen. I let myself in through the open door of Parish's office. He was not there either, but the cup of liquorice tea on his desk was still warm. I looked in the drawer where I'd figured he kept his gun. It was gone. I pulled out mine, a Glock 23, and began – with extreme caution – to look around.

The rooms were empty. No one jumped me and I did not discover any corpses. Out in the stairwell, I noticed sunlight from above. The roof door was open. Treading soft and slow I made my way up there, Glock at the ready.

Hugging the doorway I paused to let my eyes adjust to the bright sunlight outside. Adrenaline was kicking in, my senses attuning themselves to danger. I was the eye shadow. I was the guy who rooted out the crooked dicks and my occupation left no room for any false sense of security.

"Mr Mallett." Parish seemed to step out of a shimmering heat haze to stand beside the top of a lift shaft, smiling. "So glad you could make it. I figured you'd find me up here. This is a good place for us to talk, my friend."

"Six of one." I said, waving the Glock slightly for emphasis. "Now spill, Parish! You've been busy. Who's picking up the tab?"

"Do you not have any appreciation for what I've achieved?"

"Appreciation ain't in the job description."

"Then let me show you something. Something that will... enhance your understanding. Over there, by the edge."

"You first. And keep your hands raised. No sudden moves or I'll plug you."

We reached the edge and looked out across the city. From this hillside location it was quite a view. Civic buildings, mansions and green leisure parks to tenements, docklands and sprawling industrial development.

At first I could not be sure what it was that Parish wanted me to see. I glanced at him questioningly, but he merely gestured back with his eyes to the view.

It was then I began to notice something. The sun was high and strong and there were pockets of the heat haze that, a few minutes earlier, Parish himself had seemed to step out of. But the haze was spreading, the isolated parts of it were joining up. The view of the city was becoming distorted, less substantial, even as the haze itself began to take on form.

At first I couldn't figure out what it was. It was like looking into one of those pictures where the image itself is camouflaged in the speckle of seemingly random 'noise'. Your eyes take time to adjust, to pick out the shape — which then, quite suddenly, becomes both substantial and three dimensional.

That shape was loosely human in its form, yet far more than human. Its dimensions were greater than three, for it seemed to include time itself, and in time every shape and form of every living thing that has dwelt or will ever dwell on this earth. Somehow it was both perpetually still and yet bustling with vitality and myriad, shifting detail. I still struggle to find words that could picture what I saw. What I felt. It was essence. It was all. It was nothing. It surged with potential. It reeked of finality.

My hand seemed distant and numb. The Glock fell to the floor at my feet. "Oh my god," I said. "Oh. My. God."

"That's right," said Parish. "My employer."

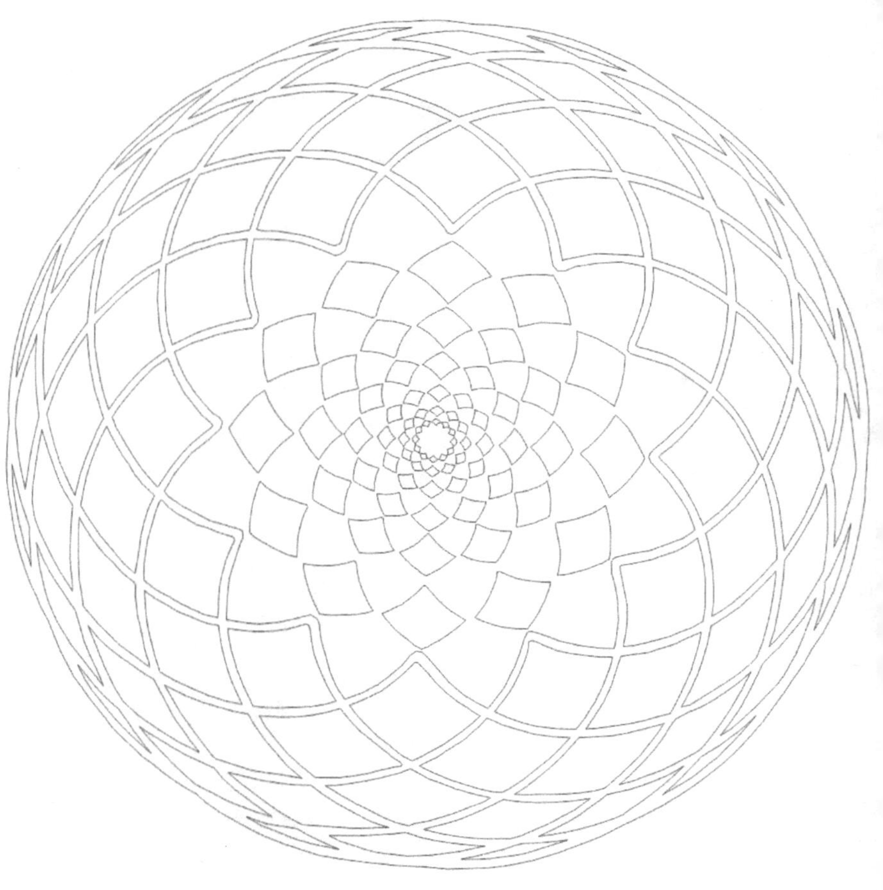

Coyote Ltd

January 15th

Coyote Ltd have included this device in their lavish information pack. They advise me to make recordings here as a sort of journal for the entire period in which I have engaged their services. A playback at a later date, they say, will enable me to "appreciate and reflect" upon the work they are undertaking on my behalf. Since I have paid them a considerable sum of money I suppose I had better make the effort, though frankly I am of the opinion that the keeping of journals, diaries and the like is for introspective navel gazers. Let others make a record of my achievements. And they have. There are books about how I made my way up from the gutter and revolutionised the world of Sanitary Disposal. Books!

I'm supposed to make a start with how I heard about Coyote. Dinner party I attended late last year. Dicky Bronson, the airline fellow. Damn good do, as I recall. Anyway, he told the story over the brandy. Keeps his image quite 'hip' does Dicky, so he gave it all a bit of that New Age gloss and everyone lapped it up.

He'd signed up with Coyote, he told us, to have an 'Intricacy'. The idea was for an elaborate hoax to be played upon oneself and quite literally at one's own expense. Bonkers, I thought. But the idea, Bronson explained, was that one gained "valuable insights" through the very experience of being tricked.

In his own case he'd been in a lift in one of his office blocks when there was apparently a power failure. Alone in the lift he'd called for assistance, but had then been overcome by an overwhelming drowsiness. When he came to, he was still in the lift but the lights were on and it was moving again. When it stopped he got out. Bit of a shock. He wasn't in his block any more but somewhere looking more like a luxury hotel in Dubai. And a sincerely perturbed receptionist was approaching him with a briefcase, which she said he'd inadvertently left in the foyer. It contained a stack of paper currency and his room keys.

Well obviously he twigged that this was the hoax he'd paid for. But then came the twist.

Fifteen minutes later he was surrounded by armed policemen and arrested. He had no passport, no papers, and, they told him, no legitimate reason for being in their country. It was no use telling them who he was. What proof did he have? On went the cuffs, over his head the hood, and when that came off he was strapped to a chair in a windowless basement. What was his real business there? He knew he couldn't answer to their satisfaction. The hoax appeared to have gone badly wrong and Dicky Bronson was shitting himself. They were just setting him up for a spot of water boarding, when a man from Coyote Ltd stepped out of the shadows. Gotcha.

Bronson made out that this had been a profound experience, motivating large donations to Amnesty International and the like on behalf of those unfortunate folk for whom what he'd just tasted was no hoax.

Of course, I thought, the story did his public profile no harm at all. A bit of openness, vulnerability, compassion... people like to see those things in their millionaires. Not that my rep is founded on having a 'caring' side, but it wouldn't do any harm if I could get people thinking that beneath that tough exterior there was a heart of gold. Or at least a bit of mush. Whatever.

Assuming of course Coyote Ltd were up to pulling the wool over *my* eyes.

February 8th

More than three weeks later and I'm still waiting. All right, I've been over in Taiwan, pulling a lame duck subsidiary up to scratch, and they're not going to follow me round the world. But I've paid good money for this bloody hoax, this oh-so-humbling experience that I will then make as much PR capital out of as I can.

Not that, as I said, they're going to have an easy time making a fool out of me. I've been looking at their brochure testimonials again. I mean just how easy is it to convince some people that black is white and vice versa? Take this gent they got this tight-fitting rubber insect costume onto while he was asleep. He wakes up and he's on his back and it's very difficult to move, and there's all these little legs in front of him waving up and down. Well, it's a clever outfit, and they've got his family in on the act – all treating him like there's been some sort of horrible transformation. But did he really, at any point, believe that he had genuinely metamorphosed? I don't think so. Unless they'd drugged him or something.

Whatever. Thing is, he gets himself a load of interviews after the event. Talks up the insight it's given him into what it feels like to be viewed with disgust and loathing; and how he's planning to divert some of his wealth into providing employment for people who suffer with disfigurements and what-have-you. Nice story.

Or there's this geezer who one day finds himself being 'sectioned' and forcibly removed to what they've set up as a fake mental hospital. And there, apparently, they manage to convince him that the very idea that he is a powerful business magnate is entirely a delusion. He is – in fact – an intruder found trespassing in the mansion that he'd thought was home. Well, I can see how you could do that to some people – but this guy's got the knowledge that he has paid to be 'intricated', as they call it. All he's got to do is play along with it and figure out how he's going to profitably present himself as a beneficiary to mental illness sufferers when the experience is over.

Come on, Coyote. Get on with this bloody hoax on me, will you? I need some material to work with.

March 15th

I've had some hard words with Joel Piltner, my A.D., today. When I first considered contracting Coyote to hoax me I still had a lot of doubts, and it was after discussing it with Joel that I made my decision. He assured me he'd investigated them thoroughly. Their operation was absolutely legit and above-board. Safe bet, he said.

Well, I'm beginning to have my doubts again. I've told Joel I want to know exactly what Coyote Ltd are up to, what they have planned for me and when they intend to carry it out.

They're dragging this thing out, and it's turning into a bit of a farrago, frankly. I've had my legal team look over the contract again and there's a withdrawal clause. If I don't get satisfaction out of them soon, I'm using it.

April 1st

It's nearly midnight.   You'd think if Coyote had something planned, they might have pulled it off today.

Mind you, when they profiled me I told them I'd never had much time for fooling around, April the First or any day of the year for that matter. Newspapers doing stories about spaghetti growing on trees. I ask you – haven't they got anything better to do?

I told them straight. I was only going into this because of what it did for Dicky Bronson. Him and another one I heard about – old Leon Katz. Now I've done a few deals with Leon in my time, and I know he prides himself on being astute. So how they managed to convince him to invest capital into a company marketing squirrel-meat burgers, I don't know. But it did make me smile. They'd done it full on, with the packaging, the design themes, logistics – the lot.

Or maybe that was another one where he saw it coming. At any rate, he turned it round. He had received, he said, "a lesson in humility" which would inform his future business practice. Then he had the whole of his marketing team make a study of the Coyote package to see what they could learn.

Lesson in humility? My arse.

PR. That's the real name of the game.

Piltner contacted Coyote as per my request and came back to me with some airy-fairy story about how they had something "under way." I told him. I said: "That was not what I asked you to find out." He said that they were not prepared under any circumstances to reveal their plans prior to the event and that – just as everyone else had – I would find out in due course what they had in mind for me.

That wasn't good enough, I told Piltner. Gave him his marching orders there and then. No monkeying.

April 20th
They've had the bloody cheek to ask me for more money!

They sent this glamorous bit of totty—heels, short skirt and legs right up to her arse. I wouldn't have given her the time of day, but being as she was from Coyote I thought I'd have a few words.

I told her straight. If your lot can't get on with it, I said, or they can't put me in the picture, then I shall be withdrawing from the contract. It doesn't matter whether it's a publicity-generating hoax or a consignment of widgets from Shanghai, if you can't deliver the goods you don't get the business.

She started to give me some flannel about how I was a "special case" and that what they had in mind for me was probably going to be one of the most spectacular pieces of work in their entire portfolio. I wasn't having any of it. I sent her out with a flea in her ear. She could tell her bosses that if they couldn't deliver in the next two weeks I would be requiring a full refund.

May 6th
Nothing. And they're not answering my calls.

May 10th
The bloody number's 'unobtainable' now. I got the legal boys onto it pronto when the deadline was up, but it turns out the address that Coyote Ltd were apparently working from is on the thirteenth floor of a twelve-storey building. The mail was being diverted, but where it went no one can tell.

I got onto Dicky Bronson to see if he still had any kind of a fix on them. He was a bit distracted getting himself kitted up for one of those bungee jumps he does. Couldn't remember who they were and when I reminded him he dismissed them. Very much a 'last year's thing'. Does a lot of that, does Dicky.

As for Leon, he's not spoken to me since I undercut him on the Number Two contract for Indonesia so it's no use trying him. I've been onto the police, of course, but they don't call them 'plods' for nothing. They wanted to speak to Joel Piltner since he was last to have visited Coyote. In their thirteenth-floor office. Turns out he's another one that can't be traced.

Coyote Ltd have vanished into thin air with my money. And that's untraceable too. Just got channelled through a series of holding accounts into some sort of financial void.

So there's not much point in recording any more of these. I shall not be doing any "appreciating and reflecting" because the "work" they've done "on my behalf" amounts to nothing more than elaborately defrauding me.

Is this their idea of a hoax?

Frankly speaking, I fail to see the joke.

Quack!

Picture this. Two people walking around a corner simultaneously from opposite directions bump straight into one another. Or someone really does slip on a banana skin. Or there's a bunch of ducks on a lake, all cackling raucously like they're sharing a powerhouse joke. Cartoon moments.

That's how it gets started.

They call it 'Sepia', the condition. Teresa wasn't too sure how she came to be suffering from it but slowly, surely, it seemed to be taking a hold. Cartoon moments occurred with increasing frequency and startling intensity.

Only the other day she'd been walking home from work when a human body had come flying out of a window as if shot from a cannon. She could see the speed lines trailing after the blurred figure until it hit the opposite wall and concertina'd against it. It slipped to the ground, a flat disc, twitched a little and then, with a sharp 'pop', re-inflated to three dimensions. It was a man in a business suit. He dusted his hands together, whistled once and walked off. He didn't look like a cartoon any more. She stood staring at his retreating figure.

She glanced back at the window from whence he came. It was closed. Shaken, doubting her own sanity, she continued to walk home, eyes peeled. Fortunately, further events that defied the laws of physics and biology did not ensue that afternoon.

The first time when it stopped being 'could be a cartoon' and became a definite 'was', a postman was knocking at her front door. Approaching it she stopped, terrified. With each deafening knock the door was bending back towards her as if made out of living rubber. Small puffs of white smoke were bursting from curved gaps between the bulging door and frame, then disappearing as quickly as they emerged.

The knocking stopped. The door looked solid once more. She opened it and stared amazed at the postman. Apparently unaware of anything out of the ordinary, he handed her a parcel. And that was an end to it. Reality as she'd known it re-established itself. She put it down to her imagination, but she couldn't put it out of her thoughts.

Not long after that people began to develop hard black outlines. The play of light and shadow and the crease lines of their faces and clothing would begin to look stippled, as if drawn painstakingly with a mapping pen. And their most characteristic features – a prominent nose, say, or pronounced cheekbone – would become acutely exaggerated. This would last for a few minutes. Then the effects would fade. She made an appointment with Ian Cuthbert Clearly, her optician.

The eye test began normally enough. We've all been there. However, with lights restored following a test involving an illuminated screen in darkness, she was disconcerted to see that the optician himself had developed a very substantial black outline. He gave her a smile and his teeth appeared, shining with glowing gleam-lines that radiated around his mouth.

"Is anything the matter, Ms Tybhal?"

"Uh, no, everything's fine."

"Are you sure?" He leaned towards her and as his face expanded everything else foreshortened, creating a bizarrely disconcerting fisheye lens effect.

She tried desperately to disguise her reaction. "Yes, of course I'm sure. I was just a bit... dazzled when you put the lights back on."

The optician turned to adjust another piece of equipment, and as he did so, the outline faded. Normality was restored and presently he revealed there was no detectable deterioration in her eyesight.

So it had to be her mind.

After the window incident in particular, she was ready to accept that. Seeking psychological assistance, she found her way in time to the premises of one Marina Mallard, specialist in Sepia Therapy.

Nervous, dry mouthed, Teresa took her seat in the waiting room. She'd read of the condition in a magazine in another waiting room, but what she'd been waiting for then she couldn't recollect. Nor could she recall the prognosis for sepia sufferers, the probable cause, or even its treatment.

On a coffee table in front of her she noticed a jug of water and a couple of glasses. She was about to reach forward and pour one for herself when the jug began to move. It rose slowly to reveal a pair of sturdy, undetailed legs extending from its underside. As Teresa's eyes steadily widened, it took a few stiff steps over to one of the glasses and then tilted itself forward enough for its contents to pour. Thus filled, the glass itself walked to the edge of the table nearest Teresa. She reached for it impulsively and took a few sips, then held it up high enough to examine its legs. But there were no longer any such appendages to be seen.

Teresa began with this incident when asked by Ms Mallard to explain why she'd sought therapy. She backtracked then to the various earlier events. The specialist listened attentively, occasionally jotting in a notepad. In her fifties, dressed neatly and neutrally, her greying hair was tied in a tight bun that left just a few strands hanging by her cheeks. She had an easy, relaxing air about her, enabling Teresa to unburden without fear of incredulity.

"So when things turn into cartoons it all seems as real to me as... as you and I are sitting here. And then it goes. And it's as if it never was. I can't understand what's happening to me. I mean, I know about sepia, but why have I started to suffer from it? I've always been, well, what I think of as normal..."

"That's 'normal' as in 'conventional', would you say, Teresa?"

"Yes. I've never been a person who likes to stand out in a crowd."

"And you're not in a relationship at the moment. You live alone. And there is no one you've felt able to confide in about these episodes?"

"No. They'd just think I was, well... nuts. That's why I came to you. So am I right? Is it really sepia?"

"I think we need to do a little work, Teresa, before we can properly answer that question. For a start, insofar as most people know of sepia, there are many misconceptions. If it is a dysphoria – that's to say if it is causing you distress – we need to look at why that may be, what it is in you that triggers the discomfort. Then I would hope we could clear up the misconceptions. All this over, say, five or six weekly sessions. How does that sound?"

It sounded good. The relief in confiding what she'd not dared to tell her closest friends was a helpful start. For the remainder of the hour there was no more talk of Sepia. At her therapist's request she carefully described the emotional landscape of her childhood, her adolescence, etc.

Leaving via the waiting room, she could not help but glance at the coffee table. The water jug and glasses were nowhere to be seen. Had someone come in and moved them to a kitchen somewhere? Or had they taken themselves?

Despite her relief that day she found no change in her intermittent experiences of cartoon realities. Often, for example, people would morph into hybrids of human and animal. Or any form of impact would involve previously solid objects quivering and twitching. Ms Mallard was still gathering information, she consoled herself. Then the cure would come.

Her life story continued over the next three sessions. By the end of the fourth there seemed little more to describe. The therapist asked her to stop and look back over all of which she'd spoken. "Do you notice anything extraordinary about it?"

Teresa considered. "I suppose I have been very lucky. A loving family, financial security, good friendships and... Okay, I'm not in a relationship right now, but I'm young and I've no reason to believe that the right person won't come along. I've had an incredibly happy life."

"Incredibly. Yes. Suppose, Teresa, that someone made a movie of it. Can you imagine what the style of that movie would be?"

"What a strange question! I don't know. It wouldn't be one of those nasty films, obviously. Um..." Teresa laughed, uncomfortably. "Walt Disney?"

"Well, that's all for today. I'll see you next week."

On her way home, lost in thought, Teresa was unable to take evasive action when – seemingly out of nowhere – three wolves on a steamroller came zooming towards her. She had a moment or two in which to observe them. Each wolf was wearing ragged but colourful clothes. Two wore bowler hats, the third a crooked stovepipe. They were smoking fat cigars and cackling. Then she was under the roller.

The sensation of being crushed was deeply unpleasant but surprisingly painless. Consciousness remained even as the bulldozer clattered away. There was a feeling of absolute discomfort, but one that could be overcome by the tensing and releasing of her crushed muscles. She could hear the now familiar 'pop' sound as she stretched, quite abruptly, back into three-dimensional form.

Examining herself for signs of damage, she noticed immediately the black outlines which now surrounded her, and the way her clothing had adopted clear primary colours. She scampered towards a nearby shop window to observe her reflection.

Her first thought on sighting herself was that she could have done worse – she resembled some shapely starlet or an image on a cocktail bar napkin, stereotypical but unexaggeratedly so. However, then the shop window took on a life of its own and began to bend, first concave, then convex, to distort her. Fat. Skinny. Fat. Skinny. It was obvious she should walk away, but she felt compelled to distort her own strangely pliant features as best she could in a vain attempt to compensate. This must be what it felt like to be a character in a cartoon. An endlessly flexible clown.

It continued for some time. Sequences that followed included walking tightrope on telegraph wires after being unable to make headway on a ludicrously crowded street, and clinging on for dear life inside a bus that performed a dance routine. Somehow she reached home, stippled now, but sliding back to a reality without outlines.

In the week that followed, her cartoon-self manifested more frequently and for still-longer sequences. Champion, victim, buffoon and sage – she could be any of these or more. Only when the speed lines and smoke puffs faded away did she find herself, bewildered, in flesh and blood. She thought frequently of phoning Ms Mallard, but any attempt to do so brought on another transformation and she would lose herself in obsessive attempts to outwit some funny animal or other.

Nothing was predictable any more. That she made it to the appointment at all was a surprise. That her therapist was now a bright-eyed duck in human costume was not. "So, tell me," she squawked through a vivid orange beak, "what sort of a week have you had, Teresa?"

"It's… It's just all become so much more intense. Sometimes I feel more like a cartoon character than an actual human being."

"Is that so?" The beak curled to a warm grin, one clear white tooth revealed at the corner, sparkling. "Then I think we are making excellent progress."

"Progress? I don't understand. How can you call this progress?"

"Teresa, why don't we…? Oh, I don't know… Let's walk up the walls and sit ourselves down on the ceiling for a chat, eh? It can be surprisingly comfortable up there.

"You've had some quite overwhelming misconceptions about the condition known as sepia, but you're recovering very well now and I think it's time we got them cleared up."

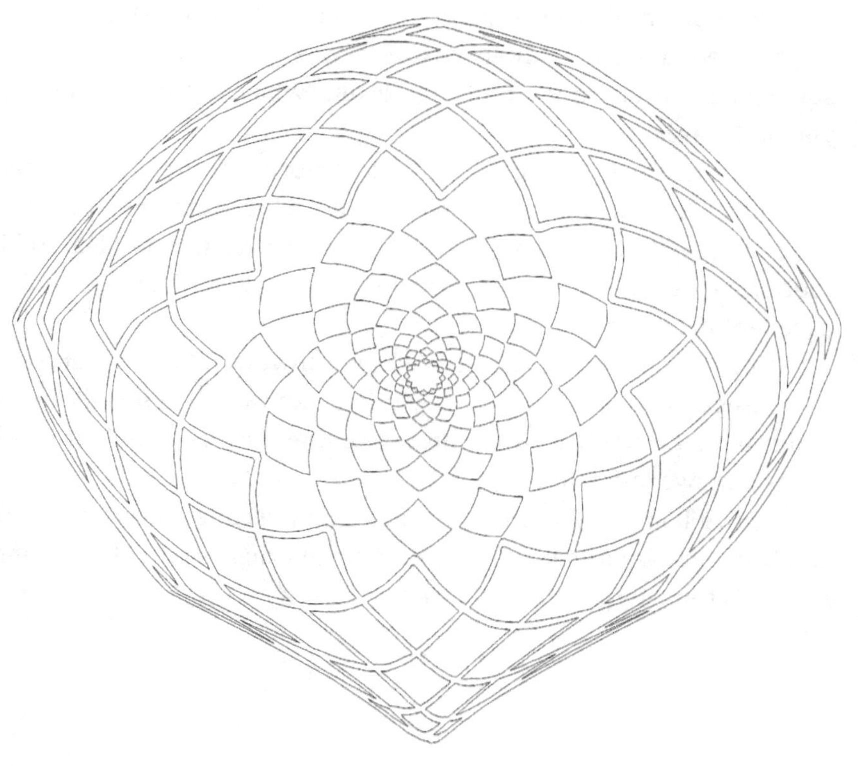

River Man

'River miles' are a measure of distance from the mouth of the river or the confluence of a tributary to a destination. If one man walked more of those miles than any other I have known, it was Dane Carthy, who has recently – and regrettably for the rest of us – reached his final destination.

His name will be associated for years to come with the Art of Streamline, a method of riverine divination not practised since the early Middle Ages. Many years of deep documentary research in the British Museum, the Bodleian and elsewhere, combined with programmatic experimentation and observation of natural waterways across the world, engendered Carthy's revival of this practice. He described his first published book on the subject, 'The Fluvial Art', as "a spring from whence we can be carried to an ocean of information." And when he said things like that he had footnotes to authenticate them.

I well remember my first encounter with Dane Carthy at that venerable circle the Rollright Stones. Crouched for a closer observation of one of the 'King's Men', I glanced up to see approaching me a dapper and striking ginger-haired man, wearing a flowing purple cloak, matching fedora and a lovingly waxed moustache. It was the early 1970s, so we were still used to seeing folk who looked like they'd stepped off the cover of 'Their Satanic Majesties Request' – particularly in the vicinity of ancient monuments. No fop though – there was an energy and vitality to Dane Carthy that was immediately apparent, more than matching the flamboyance.

The fact I had been studying the megalith was quite sufficient to convince him that, although he had never seen me before in his life, he could immediately address me as if I were an old friend. He affected a kind of self-mocking upper-class accent in those days, greeting me with a jovial: "What-ho, my good man!" and began immediately to discuss with me the stones and their surroundings. For the sharing of knowledge, my enthusiasm rose to meet his. It was not long before he was asking what I knew of local streams and rivers. I was immediately impressed by the wider sense of topography that he brought to our topic. His perspective was holistic. Though not quite always.

As he proceeded in his life to unearth and finesse the Art of Streamline, another aspect of him became apparent. His meticulousness. He always maintained that, no matter how otherworldly the subject matter, one should be vague about nothing. The Art required numerous forms of observation, amongst them precise measurement, not only of the passing water but of the entire riparian environment and its underlying geology. It was not uncommon to see him at riverbanks intently working a battered theodolite.

The core measurement, as he would always remind us, was a stream or a river's 'Sinuosity Index'. This was expressed as a ratio: the actual path length of the river over the shortest possible path length (i.e.: a straight line descending seawards). The higher the resulting figure, the more curved the waterway. "That's the key that unlocks it all," he'd say. "It's the first of a set of numbers that lead us to words. This is how our planet sends us letters to read." From here he would take us on to gematria and geomantic technique, through which numbers become words, words reveal layers of meaning and randomness generates concept.

Born and raised in Somerset, Carthy described his parents as 'free thinkers'. He excelled academically but avoided the more lucrative career paths he might have taken, cultivating the eccentricity I witnessed that day at the Rollrights. Later in life he toned it down, shaving the 'tache and confining his delight in brightness to rainbow braces and hand-painted ties worn with light, 'English gentlemanly', tailored suits. Even in more relaxed attire he was never less than elegant.

He married Margaret Portman in 1976 and they had one son, Zachary. Unfortunately the marriage failed after some eleven years, which came as a surprise to those of us who knew Dane and Margaret. They had seemed a well-matched couple.

Having maintained our friendship, we had often talked of engaging together in a writing project. This occurred at last in the late 1980s. Carthy had expanded his writings on the Streamline with two more volumes, both sharing critical acclaim, but was looking to apply his ever-enquiring mind to connected topics. "Expand the old repertoire somewhat," as he put it.

We embarked on a work that was to become 'The Links – Contextualising Earth Mysteries', and during this time I got to know him a lot better. To connect to the man you had to penetrate the broad front of his conversational prowess. He could talk with fluency, erudition and wit on a seemingly unending series of topics: politics (he once considered candidacy for parliament as a 'Radical Eccentric'); artworks (I remember a long discourse concerning the artwork on picture card gifts offered with a well-known brand of tea); people (you had to hear him on sailing the Nile with two Rolling Stones and a Beatle, or on the self-appointed master of Pungsu–jiri-seol with whom he studied the 'patterns of wind and water' in South Korea). I could go on.

But at the core of him were aspects very rarely revealed. He would tell of his personal experiences with timeslips, relocations and other visionary phenomena. In writings and lectures he would refer to these with clinical detachment. In the heat of *conversation* he conveyed the sheer wonder and exhilaration of instantaneously finding yourself fifty yards from the spot where you last were, or seemingly slipping for strange moments into the Neolithic or Dark Ages.

Another mystery was centred round a reach of the River Wathwell, within a few miles of the Midland village where he settled in later life. I had asked him if there were stretches of stream or river that he still found himself unable to 'read' and he had replied by taking me to one.

He had, he told me, a very full set of measurements, right up to its confluence with the Roachleigh. How many gallons of water flowed past any given point during the passage of a minute. The composition of the river's substrate, and of its 'benthos' of plant and animal life. Such things he knew for its every mile. From these he had derived the locations of what Pungsu-jiri practitioners refer to as 'hyeol', sensory openings in the landscape where earth's chi and heaven's chi can mingle. Correlating them with the all-important sinuosity index, he had made accurate predictions concerning the progress of much human activity in the vicinity. This was all part and parcel of the Art of Streamline.

"But from here for as far as the eye can see," he said, after a short trek from the car, "my dear fellow, I come completely unstuck."

I was aghast. Such an admission from Dane Carthy was unexpected to say the least. This glide of unturbulent water, lined with ash trees, tall reeds and occasional clumps of bramble, seemed quite unexceptional in its quiet surround of rolling green fields and woodland copses. Its curves here were gentle, giving a low sinuosity index, which should have fitted comfortably with all his other readings and observations. "But instead they clash, you see? What do they say, these days? 'Number crunching', isn't it? Well I've crunched these into a fine powder and still got no sense. And there ought to be at least one opening on this reach. Blowed if I can find it!"

"Well, there we are," he added, after a thoughtful pause. "I've worked the Grand Canyon to the Ganges and never stopped short. But this... this stubbornly remains... an enigma."

I muttered sympathetically, unsure how to respond or what to suggest. The subject was not raised again for many years.

'The Links' was accepted as a major work in its field, and for Carthy this led to further commissions – the broadening of his reputation. Such was the subsequent demand on him, not only for his writing and lectures but also increasingly for media appearances, that I saw little of him for too many years.

During this time I was distressed to learn of Zachary Carthy's imprisonment on drugs charges. Carthy's relationship with his son had, I knew, been a difficult one. He was to tell me eventually that his tendency to become utterly absorbed in his work for long periods of time, rather to the exclusion of most other matters, had contributed to the breakdown of his marriage. How much this had also led to the circumstances in which Zachary developed a heroin habit is difficult to gauge.

These matters are now public knowledge amongst those who have an interest in the life of Dane Carthy. After consultation with both Zach and Margaret and with their approval, I would like – before concluding this commemoration of his life – to add an account of one more visit to that enigmatic reach of the River Wathwell.

It was in the autumn of 2006. I received an unexpected phone call requesting I visit him as a matter of some urgency. This I somehow managed, and within one or two hours of my arrival, I found myself standing beside him once again at that quiet stretch of the river. The trees had mostly shed their leaves and it was a brisk but sunny day. Carthy had charmed me as always but had seemed uncharacteristically quiet. We walked for a while along a muddy public footpath that paralleled the riverbank. At a certain point he guided me to a section that was free of vegetation, where we could stand at the edge and look down.

"So," I said, "is this a breakthrough? Or still an enigma?"

"Perhaps both. You're aware, my good friend, that I have the fullest possible knowledge of this waterway – its morphology and its content. I thought I had seen all there was to be seen, and that it was my interpretation that had failed. Well, tell me... Look into the water on this fine day. What do you see?"

"Not much. It's rather murky."

"Yes, yes... high turbidity... but what else? What else?"

"Uh... ripples, leaves floating by..." I laughed. "The reflections. Two men in later middle-age, gazing down at the water!"

"Yes!" He smiled ruefully. "And that's what I missed. In... what? Forty-five years? I never once considered the meaning of my own reflection on the surface of the stream."

Carthy was drawn to this location, even made his home as close to it as he could. He thought the lure was its mystery, his inability to decode the message from its Streamline. But there was one possibility he'd never considered. The message was for him. The Streamline on this reach of the Wathwell could only be read with the understanding that it told of nothing other than *Dane Carthy*.

Perhaps we all have such a point, on some natural waterway somewhere, where our story is written. We could walk past it daily and never know. Or perhaps get a glimpse of our reflections, and receive some momentary hint.

Dane Carthy however, with absolute calm, predicted to within an hour the point of his death. He knew, long before any diagnosis, what would be its cause. He foresaw himself, in the last years of his life, setting aside all his work and doing what he could to salvage his relationship with his son.

A tough call, that. No end to the humble pie.

But the Wathwell had told him. And it all came about as the river outlined.

Now, what more need I say? We were with him, of course, Margaret, Zachary and I, at the moment of his death. We saw him pass to the depths of the ocean. We saw him pass to the source of the spring.

A Statistical Improbability

If it hadn't been for Jacob Rice it is conceivable that East Poddlebury would not be the craggy crater it is today.

He was wayward. At school he refused to become a prefect on account of its being unpaid policing supportive of an archaic hierarchical structure. In his youth he became an anarchist but found the movement hidebound by conventional ideas. East Poddlebury simply could not contain his like. He moved on to the city to merge amidst diversity.

Then some family related matter brought him back. His visit happened to coincide with the East Poddlebury Annual Field Day.

For those who may not be familiar with the concept of a 'Field Day', a brief digression is called for. Like that of every other village in the area, East Poddlebury's was a compulsory event, in which every able-bodied person was required to stand for the day in a designated field from dawn until dusk.

Beadles would patrol the area for the duration. Woe betide anyone they found who should have been in the field and was not. They also presided over the site itself, enforcing various Field Day Bye-laws. For example, someone had once suggested that some sort of entertainment could be provided for the day. A brass band, perhaps, or a skiffle group. No, said the Beadles, Bye-law BB81B stated clearly that the provision of any form of entertainment was banned. A subsection of BB81B also pertained to personal entertainment devices, reading material, games, puzzles etc.

In short, all the residents were actually allowed to do was to go and stand in the designated field. They could talk quietly amongst themselves, move around or take a rest as required. That was about it.

Jake Rice had not been to a Field Day since his adolescence. Although most villagers tended to greet the event with weary resignation, it was something of a spree for the young folk. A section of the field would soon become theirs exclusively and there certain ribald courting-related ceremonies would take place. Wisely, these were permitted by the Beadles, though carefully monitored to ensure that nothing got out of hand.

Now in his twenties, Jake's memories of Field Days were vague but not unpleasant. Thus he was somewhat surprised to hear his sister complaining: "Oh god! Tomorrow we all have to go and stand around in that field all bloody day." He had forgotten that attendance was mandatory. Immediately something within him began to baulk.

He tried to remember the reason for Field Days. Essentially, the belief was that if each village did not have one, and if all who were able did not attend, then sooner or later some terrible disaster would occur and everyone would suffer. An often-quoted example of a place where the practice had lapsed and catastrophe had followed was the Lynton and Lynmouth Flood Disaster of 1952. "If they'd only gone on having Field Days that river would never have changed its course," they'd say.

Dawn broke with heavy rain – the worst case scenario for a Field Day. Bye-law BB22aB prohibited the building of any form of shelter in the field. People just had to trudge through the day in waterproofs and wellingtons. Even the village youth seemed reluctant to get started.

"Why are we doing this?" said Jake despairingly to his sister after half an hour.

"Because that's what we do," she said, "unless you want to try hiding under a bed or in the attic all day hoping the Beadles don't sniff you out."

"But it's ridiculous. What is the point of it?"

"Oh, don't start! Don't start! If you want to argue about it go and talk to one of the council men or something."

He did.

Several village dignitaries were standing in a cluster, having appropriated for themselves the partial shelter of a large oak tree. As he approached, one or two of the younger ones – recognising and remembering him – quietly slipped away to get a place in the Portaloo queue. A sub-section of Bye-law BB22aB limited the provision of conveniences to an absolute minimum, thus ensuring that both men and women had to queue. This, in fact, constituted one of the few ways people found to help pass the time on this long, long day.

"Why are we doing this?" said Jake to the remaining dignitaries. "There's absolutely no reason why the entire village should spend the whole day standing here."

"That may be what you think," said a portly, red-cheeked dignitary, in a sou'wester and waxed jacket with dripping shoulder flaps. "But it isn't what the majority think. And, around here, what the majority thinks is what goes."

"And you can't deny what 'appened in Lynton and Lynmouth," added another.

"Lynton and Lynmouth was just one place," said Jake.

"Well, it were two actually. Lynton... and Lynmouth."

Ignoring this Jake continued. "If, back in 1952, every other village in the area had stopped having Field Days, would they all have flooded?"

"That's nonsense, boy," said the first dignitary. "They're not all situated in the vicinity of rivers. But some other calamity would have occurred, you mark my words."

"No," Jake said. "Not everywhere! Statistically speaking, that's just not possible."

"Ah," said the second dignitary, "but there's 'lies, damned lies and statistics', ain't there?"

"There is also common sense. Or is that inapplicable here? I mean all these ludicrous 'Bye-laws'. No shelters, minimal toilets... It's demented!"

"Not from Farmer Brown's point of view, it isn't." said the first dignitary. "He's got to make use of this field for the rest of the year. You start knocking up structures all over it, how's he going to manage?"

"They can be dismantled. Same as at festivals."

At this point a third dignitary chimed in, realising that the debate might help to pass a fair chunk of the day. Pretty soon more joined them. The arguments flew back and forth until, as arguments do, they became repetitive. Tiring of it, the dignitaries referred Jake – following an enquiry he'd made concerning origins – to the village historian.

After he had departed they shook their heads at the folly of youth, then fell to debating how best to eat their packed lunches without them becoming soggy in the rain. But as the day progressed, more than one was heard to say that some of the points that Jake had made might just be worthy of consideration.

The formidable Ms Pettigrew, village historian, stood some yards away sheltering under an overhang of the hedge. As Jake trudged through the damp meadow-grass towards her, she recognised him. She had taught him at school.

"Rice, isn't it?" she jollied, "and what has the city made of you, young man?"

"Bit of a long story, Ms Pettigrew."

"I'm a historian. I like long stories."

"With respect..." said Jake, and it was very hard, even for a rebel, not to respect Ms Pettigrew. She combined a bulky but eminently healthy physique with an acute mind. "I've come to ask you something. These Field Days... they just don't make any sense to me. How did they get started?"

"You attended history lessons, did you not, Rice?"

He shrugged. "Sometimes."

"Ah. Then let me remind you."

Ms Pettigrew briefly sketched a ninth century, when Viking marauders swept Britain bringing chaos and terror. Fearing the worst, the inhabitants of nearby Upper Dipton sought advice from one Odfrey, a local mystic, as to how best to protect themselves. The first 'Field Day', its date determined by astrological means, was the suggestion they went with. As did the populace of Nether Dipton. But not, however, that of Lower Dipton.

It was Lower Dipton alone that the savage Danes chanced to find, sack and loot. The others survived. Word spread, and soon Field Days were the practice of every village in the area, East Poddlebury included.

"So," said Jake. "Let me get this straight. The whole thing is based on some sort of mystical divination. Without which, chances are the

Vikings might still have missed those places. As I recall, they're not exactly on the beaten track. Anyway – who was this Odfrey? What was he about?"

"I'm sorry, Rice, but the occult… it's hardly safe ground for an historian. If you want to know more about Odfrey, you'd best talk to Reg Turvey, the village warlock."

"The village warlock? Poddlebury has a village warlock?"

"Why yes, of course. I think I saw him over there a few minutes ago."

Upon Jake's departure, Ms Pettigrew began to reconsider the historical perspective. There was, she had to admit, a certain logic to young Rice's attitude. Should primitive superstition remain a guiding factor in these modern times? It was… debatable.

With his long grey hair, copious beard and black leather coat, Reg Turvey was not hard to spot. He was dowsing in a quiet corner of the field.

"Found out there were no Bye-laws concerning dowsing," he explained, once Jake had made himself known. "Passes the time."

"Not short of water today though, are we?"

"Heh! Point made! What can I do for you, Jake Rice?"

Jake explained that he had so far failed to find any valid purpose for holding Field Days, and that he wondered if the mystic, Odfrey, really did have any coherent reason for introducing them.

Reg Turvey sucked breath through pursed lips. "Odfrey? No. Far as I can tell, the guy was a complete loony. But there we are. In my business, a little bit of madness can take you a long, long way."

Jake could barely contain his exasperation. "So Field Days were conceived by a lunatic who was mistaken for a mystic. They've gone on for centuries without a shred of logic, and become enshrined with draconian laws, enforced by uniformed bruisers. Everybody loathes them but there's no alternative."

"Well, that's certainly one way to see it."

Jake shrugged and sighed. Was no one else prepared to challenge this dogma? But he'd had enough. He was cold, tired and hungry. Soon it would be dusk. Best to wait it out, get away, and never, ever in his life return here on a Field Day. Or indeed to anywhere that shared the custom.

And he never did.

But in East Poddlebury the seeds of doubt had been sown. The village dignitaries began to discuss the issue, questioning its continuing validity in modern times. Several attended a debate at the Historical Society, instigated by Ms Pettigrew, questioning the actual efficacy of Field Days. Meanwhile, Reg Turvey began to advise all with mystical leanings that there was more than one way to look at Field Days. Perhaps, for too many centuries, people had been choosing the wrong one.

To what extent the day's unending rain contributed towards this nascent revisionism cannot be assessed, but many in the village were open and receptive to it. The following year a significant number of them instigated an organised boycott.

The Beadles, truncheons at the ready, were preparing to put a stop to this when orders came from the council that the boycott should be permitted. That was the beginning of the end. A halt to Field Days was formally declared. The Beadles were instructed to ensure that no one so much as entered Farmer Brown's field on that day of the year.

The odds against one house getting hit by a meteor have been calculated at 182,138,880,000,000 to one. The odds regarding a small village and a somewhat larger meteor have not been estimated. Nevertheless, whatever those odds, in this incomprehensibly vast universe of ours such an event can conceivably occur.

In this case it did.

There were no survivors.   Other villages, where Field Days continued, had watched with interest to see whether a calamity would occur in order to validate their caution.   They got their money's worth.

Jacob Rice remains to this day a man of radical views and a questioning nature.   But on the subject of Field Days he is uncharacteristically tight-lipped.

Friendly Smiles and Calm Voices

There are bright, exquisitely designed banners hanging over the entrances that catch your eye with their sunrise colours as you take the short, pleasant walk from the plane to the terminal building. 'Welcome,' they say. 'Welcome to Analgesia'. And somehow – wherever you come from, whatever your tongue – the signs read in your own language.

Beyond the terminal are green shrouded hills, dotted with scintillatingly picturesque buildings designed in harmony with their surroundings. You breathe air scented with honeysuckle and a hint of some exotic spice. You feel the warmth of the sun on your skin, the absence of excess humidity, and – whatever the rigours of the journey you've taken to get here – you begin already to relax.

Inside the terminal, staff with friendly smiles and calm voices whisk you efficiently through minimal arrival procedures. At each stage you are offered refreshments and comforts.

Then, it seems all too soon, you are in your sleek, fuel-efficient courtesy car and driving along elegant, smoothly surfaced boulevards, your destination clearly signposted. You arrive at your accommodation with a feeling of absolute confidence. Justifiably so. It is perfectly suited to your individual needs and desires.

By the end of your first evening in Analgesia you have discovered the unique excellence of the local cuisine, the easy-going yet respectful friendliness of those whose task it is to serve you. You've taken a rest on the padded lounger and watched a rich and splendid sunset from your balcony. You've listened in the bar to talented musicians playing the lively yet gentle music of this region. You've considered at least some of the many and varied landmarks, sights and vistas you might check out during your stay here. Now you're ready to sink into the soft comfort of a large and inviting bed.

∞

You wake from a deep and restful sleep, shower, dress lightly and go in search of breakfast. Soon you're comfortably settled at a table in an open air space that functions as both eatery and exotic garden, with a selection of fresh fruits, local breads and cereals in front of you, as you take your first delectable sip of fresh brewed coffee. And yet, for all this medium of perfectly judged luxury in which you have exulted since your arrival in Analgesia, you realise you have woken with a sense of unease.

At first you can't place it. A bad dream whose feeling lingers though its content is forgotten? Or a premonition of the mundane and stressful life to which you will inevitably return when you've had all that you've paid for here?

Hey! Lighten up. It's the first day of your holiday. Enjoy!

$$\infty$$

You can't resist the sandy beach, the inviting crescent of the palm-lined bay. There are plenty of shades and tables for your convenience and from time to time tempting light refreshments are discretely served with easy grace. You gaze across the lazy waves at a clear, bright horizon and you realise that still, you do not feel entirely at ease.

What's wrong? Your mind returns to the problem and a possible indicator presents itself. You are, it occurs to you, in a kind of heartland where the sun shines to order and all is as it should be, ever was and ever will be. But how can this be so? We are human. Our nature is flawed. How can anything of human creation be as perfectly pleasant as this?

Like an Arabian rug, this place requires an imperfection. Find that and you can relax. A bit of plumbing that doesn't work perfectly. An irritable official who will only cooperate when bribed. An idiot on a motorbike driving too fast across the beach. Just one example will do. Then the disturbing feeling will abate.

$$\infty$$

You make a few enquiries amongst the staff and discover that minibus trips are available, and amongst them there is one to a nearby fishing village and a small town. Its purpose is to give the curious visitor a sense of life as it is lived in the communities here, outside of the tourist-oriented aspects of the Analgesian economy. It all sounds educative and worthwhile, though you don't doubt that it will be a little stage-managed at least.

That would be flaw enough. A bit of obvious play-acting.

So a driver whisks you and a few other more thoughtful tourists off in a luxurious vehicle (with cocktail bar and videogame consoles) to the dainty little port of Aspiri and the charming market town of Ibupro. There you discover that the fishing folk are all happily synched into a smoothly running workers' cooperative which distributes wealth equitably throughout the community. In the town you hear of similar enterprises and their success. From praise for the government's provision of exemplary medical and educational services to enthusiasm for a range of colourful cultural activities, you speak to no one who does not appear to be genuinely happy and contented with their lot. If this is a performance, you can only say 'bravo' to the performers.

∞

On your second night you do not sleep so well. You are content enough with your first day's activity. It has been good to get a sense of life here outside the holidaymakers' bubble. You've nothing but respect for Analgesia's loving and resourceful people. But this 'just right' quality to everything you encounter is beginning to feel oppressive. There's something in you that wants to stir it up, to disturb the placid surface of these waters and see what lurks below.

It seems curious, in the most comfortable bed you've ever had the opportunity to occupy, that you toss and turn through much of the night. But the time of your wakefulness is not spent idly. You conceive of a number of experiments to be conducted the following day.

∞

The experiments, however, fail to provide the result you seek. You cruelly and vindictively insult a waiter, only to find that he responds with such winning wit and unaffected good humour that you end up apologising and offering to buy him a drink.

That lunchtime you drink heavily and rapidly until you are incapably drunk. This will surely cause some stress, you think, as thought itself becomes incoherent. Just then your friend the waiter approaches you and offers you a drug, which he says is legal in Analgesia and acts with alcohol in a way that restores calm and capacity but enhances the euphoria to the point of ecstasy. It sounds irresistible, and once you've taken it, proves so delightfully effective that you completely forget the remaining experiments you planned.

∞

It does occur to you the next day that if you simply relaxed, chilled out, accepted the place for what it apparently is, you could have the finest holiday of your life. The experience would rub off on you and you would return home happier and contented. Perhaps the world has a great deal to learn from the exemplary inhabitants of Analgesia.

No! You baulk at this blissed out thinking, no doubt engendered by yesterday's drug ingestion. It just can't be true and you'd be a complete fool to let yourself buy the lie. Something needs to be done to expose it, something drastic. And soon – so you can get it over with and then relax.

But what? The answer comes to you swiftly. All it requires is a bit of research on the Internet and a series of purchases at some of the shops you observed in Ibupro on the minibus trip. You are not by nature a criminal or violent person, so it must be done with care.

∞

Some hours later you return to your accommodation with the requisite chemical fertiliser, a small can of diesel and the other equipment you need. You feel a little nervous, unsurprisingly. You've never made a bomb before.

But the instructions make it sound quite simple and the target you've identified is a public memorial, well away from any habitation. It will be an act of vandalism, no more, but the slogans you intend to spray paint in the vicinity should stir up ill feeling, enough to disrupt the façade.

Obviously from what you've observed, the response will – in the main – be calm and rational. But there should be a degree of outrage. And people seldom retain their better nature when outraged. All you need is a little glimpse of the crazy edge of the Analgesian psyche.

You are just re-reading the print-out notes on fertiliser bombs when you hear a firm and urgent knock at your door.

∞

Through the reinforced glass window you can see the airport and the green shrouded hills beyond. The sun still shines brightly, but you have been gently yet firmly advised to remain in this room until the arrival of the flight that will take you home.

Everything, from your discrete arrest at the resort to the serving of the deportation papers, has been done with the utmost civility. Officials with friendly smiles and calm voices have whisked you through the minimal legal procedures. At every stage you have been offered refreshments and comforts.

It has been quietly and clearly explained how your good friend the waiter had reported your increasingly erratic behaviour to the authorities and you have been under observation for the last 24 hours. They are quite used to this sort of thing in Analgesia. They recognise that a certain proportion of their valued visitors will react in the way that you have. Not only do they recognise this, but they show a fine understanding and even a degree of sympathy for your motivations.

Nevertheless, they obviously cannot permit you to go through with your plan. You or anyone like you. Since there is no crime whatsoever in Analgesia, they are able to devote their security forces exclusively to this kind of problem and invariably, as they like to put it, 'nip it in the bud' before any unpleasantness occurs.

Shortly before your plane arrives, you dine for one last time on the exquisite local cuisine – a superbly spiced fish dish – and browse through a number of brochures that they have thoughtfully provided, detailing possible holiday destinations that might be a little more suited to your psyche.

And they're right, of course. They always are. You begin to seriously consider a couple of weeks in the lively state of Neuralgia. Or possibly the quieter island resort of Lumbago...

Long John Nights

"So how was the meeting, then?"

Julie had come to bed wearing one of her cutest babydolls, a frippery of frills and dangling ribbons. Keith guessed that she would not be requiring a particularly lengthy answer to her question. "Oh, you know, like all the other ones, really. Some of it's just ordinary and boring. Some of it's, well... a little bit peculiar."

She giggled. "Peculiar? Mm. Tell me about *those* bits, sweetheart. I want to know all about them. There weren't any women involved were there?"

"Certainly not. I told you, Ju, women are a no-no at the Long Johns. It's strictly men only. Businessmen, tradesmen, councillors – it's like a little network that sort of runs the town, you know?"

"Yes, but what about these 'peculiar' bits?" A sly smile creased his young wife's dainty face. She was slight, small boned, delicate.

Though no great size himself, Keith often felt like a big lug in her proximity.

He was enjoying the salacious tone of her questions, even if it did feel somewhat inappropriate. "Well, they like to call us new blokes the 'acolytes', and we have to go through these 'rituals of acceptance', yeah?"

"Rituals?" she repeated, in a slightly singsong voice. Keith could feel her hand lightly stroking his thigh. As was sometimes the case, he wasn't quite sure what was going on. Above the duvet, she was apparently all intent on hearing about the meeting. Below it, her intentions seemed to be directed elsewhere.

Best to keep talking, he judged, until she lost interest in the above-the-duvet part. "Well, there's a lot of bowing, for a start. And how much you bow is according to the rank of the gentlemen who are there to judge your worthiness. So, like, for an Upper-John, you bow from the waist, right down. For a Mid-John it's more of a sort of halfway bend. And for an Under-John, you just nod your head."

"How can you tell which is which?"

"Well they arrange themselves according to rank, see? For the ritual, this is. The Acolytes have to bow to each and every one of them, to show respect, like, until they are accepted as Under-Johns. So in this ritual you go further down as you move up, so to speak. And the Upper-Johns, Ju – you should see who's in amongst that lot. Bank managers. Factory owners. Police inspectors. I tell you, love, once you find yourself playing golf with one or two of them, you've made it. But you have to get the bow just right. They judge you on the strength of it. It's like... performing in a dog show or something."

"Oh, baby... I'd go to Crufts to watch you perform."

"Really?" he said, attempting an erotic tone as he sensed that below-the-duvet was about to take precedence.

∞

"I did the Pre-Initiate Ritual tonight. All being well, this time next week I'll be an Under-John."

Julie cuddled close. She was in her scanties again, and Keith wondered whether to embroider the telling, add a few details to turn her on even more. Best not, he decided. He couldn't always be that sure just what it *was* that turned her on, and besides, it was the truth that seemed to do the trick when he described the Long John rituals. And trick it was. He'd always enjoyed making love with Julie but these post-meeting sessions had... He couldn't quite put it into words. Just something *extra* about them.

"Ooh. My Keith, an Under-John, I can hardly wait... You'll get to wear one of those special lanyards, won't you?"

"I will. The Order of the Laundered Lodge. And a medallion bearing the image of the eternal Trouser Press."

"And what did they make you do in the Ritual this time, my darling?"

"I had to... I had to put on this very special set of green underwear – green symbolising regrowth and renewal, I think it was. Then I had to cross a threshold and answer lots of questions that the Upper-Johns read out from the Great Book of the Inner Leg." At this point, Keith became aware of gentle, probing fingers on his own inner leg. He pressed on, the pitch of his voice rising slightly. "Only, the thing was I couldn't answer them very easily, 'cause they'd told me I had to keep a pebble in my mouth at all times. *Zo I cud only chalk like thizh.*"

Julie began to giggle. This he took as a cue to respond to her advances, reaching to stroke her, progressing through each of the places he could remember where she liked to feel his touch. She wriggled provocatively. "Mmm... Oh Keith! Answering the Ritual questions in your green underwear. But why did you have to have a pebble in your mouth?"

"Something to do with 'overcoming adversity'. I knew all the answers, see? Like: 'I seek to ascend from the dark shadows to the illuminating lights.' Learnt 'em by heart. But the challenge was to say them clearly enough with this pebble in me mouth for my 'interlocutors' to recognise."

"I bet you did it really well."

"I wasn't bad. I wasn't bad." He rolled himself closer to her and began, copiously, to kiss both skin and satin.

∞

It felt anticlimactic to get into bed alone, after such a momentous event, but that was what Julie's text had instructed him to do. She'd been visiting a friend that evening, one of her Wednesday 'coffee morning' pals. There was a problem. She'd be with him very soon. He was to make himself comfy. And he was not to wear his pyjamas.

Presently, there were hurried footsteps on the staircase. Julie appeared in the bedroom doorway flushed and breathless. Poor love, she'd not even taken off her overcoat. "I'm so sorry, Keithy. Your special day..."

"Yes. I am now an Under-John, an honourable member of the Laundered Order of Long Johns."

She advanced slowly into the room, unbuttoning her coat with clear and pre-calculated finesse. Keith's eyes widened. Was she wearing nothing under that coat? It looked that way until a tiny, white, diaphanous garment was revealed covering some of the curves he so loved to caress. It had a low cut, scoop neckline and hung from her shoulders in what would have been a loose way if not for two gold braids tied around her waist. These pulled it tight enough to emphasise her pert breasts and the swell of her hips most desirably.

"Let me get close to an honourable member," she said, the coat dropping to the floor around her. She let him feast his eyes for a few sweet seconds, then swiftly eased herself into the bed beside him. His honourable member stiffened.

He touched the delicate fibre of her garment. "This is new," he said, approving.

"It's especially for you, my darling, to celebrate your John-hood."

"Looks like something out of an old painting. Greeks and that."

"Whatever, my sweet, whatever... Now tell me about what you had to do at the Lodge," she said, voluptuously, "to become... a Long John."

Eager for under-the-duvet time, he glossed the description of the Initiation Ritual – in which he'd ceremonially role-played a traveller who is beset by blackguards. They demand that he renounce his loyalty to the Long Johns. He refuses to do so and is symbolically 'asphyxiated' with a small pillow, then brought 'back to life' as an initiate. By the time he'd got to this point in the telling, he and Julie were already in a passionate embrace and he was finding it as difficult to speak with clarity as when he'd had that pebble in his mouth.

Their lovemaking was wild and wonderful. Julie seemed possessed with desire for him. He was inspired, testosterone-charged by the status he felt he'd gained that night. They rocked. They rolled. The bed could hardly contain them.

When at last they were done, and lying, sweaty, in one another's arms, something dawned on him. "You... You weren't really delayed at your friend's at all were you? You just wanted to make an entrance."

She laughed. "Yeah. Good, wasn't it?"

∞

Returning home after his first meeting as an Under-John, there was for Keith a rather perplexing turn of events. Julie was asleep already and – he noticed as he got into bed beside her – wearing the long cotton tee shirt she used on nights when she had no intention of lovemaking.

She groaned lightly, momentarily returning to consciousness. "I'm tired tonight, sweetheart," she said as he reached to stroke her.

"Don't you want to hear about...?" He paused, attempting to make it sound provocative. "The meeting?" But even as he spoke, he was aware of how absurd he sounded.

"Tell me about it in the morning, love."

Perhaps it was that time of the month he concluded, before falling asleep beside her.

∞

He was wrong. In the weeks that followed, it became clear that Julie's interest in the affairs of the Long Johns had taken on a more businesslike tone, even – Keith sometimes felt – proprietary. Their lovemaking reverted to its old patterns of ebb and flow, none the worse or better for his Long John status. He was tempted, of course, to question her about what had happened, but some sixth sense suggested to him strongly that this might not be a good idea. Best to keep it under the lid. Except for the question that impulsively escaped his lips one evening.

"That little white thing you wore the night I was initiated. You know, that shifty thing. You looked so good in that! How come I've never seen it since?" He braced, ready for a cool response, thinking immediately that he'd broken a taboo.

To his surprise, however, she smiled. "Yes, my love. Sweet little thing, wasn't it? And rather special." Her demeanour and voice had become hazily suggestive. "Just something for very special occasions."

"Oh." He tried to match her tone. "Can I ask what sort of occasions?"

"Ahh. Perhaps you should apply yourself to becoming a Mid-John. Yes. Yes. Perhaps that might be special enough."

She paused, her eyes meeting his directly. Keith wasn't sure, but he thought there was a sort of glow shining from within them. The future, he realised, was beckoning with arms wide open.

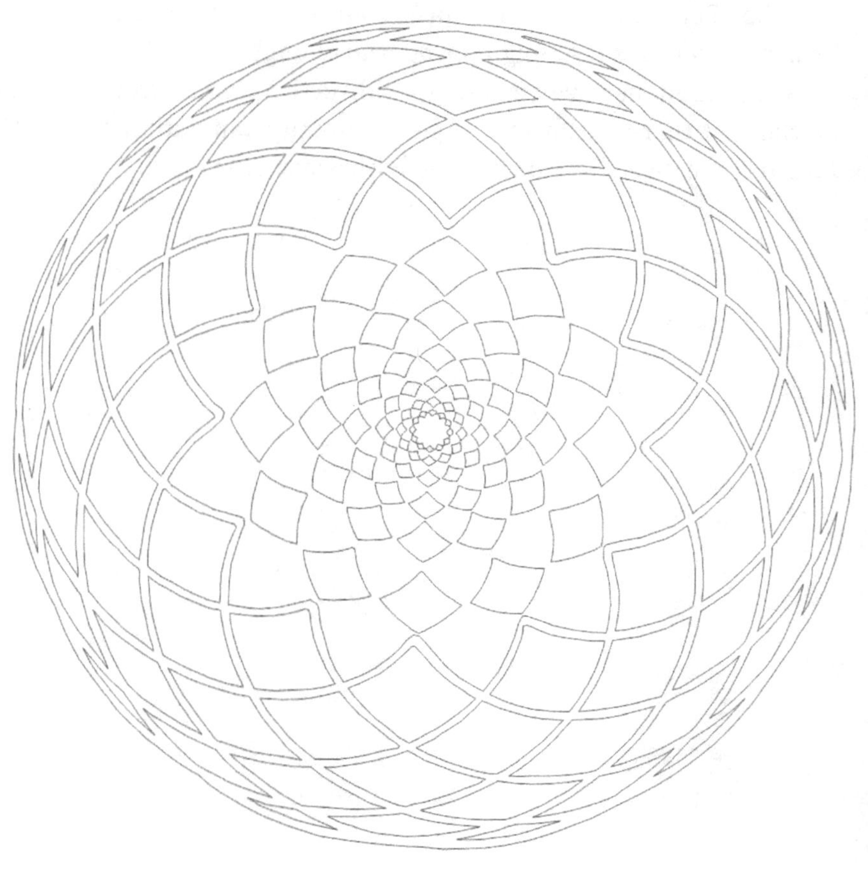

A Pair of Loose Ends

Well, as I'm sure you can understand, Derek and I, we were very distressed. I mean, in modern day Britain you don't expect that sort of thing from the *Council*. It beggars belief! And as we realised just what it was these local authorities were getting away with, we felt we ought to jolly well try to do something about it.

Of course, now, we are rather suffering the consequences.

We first became aware of it not long after Derek got his pension. Life had become more leisurely. We'd decided to devote more time to our little hobby of visiting old churches. We'd often heard St. Andrews in the Marsh at Norton Hensbury was well worth a visit. Some fine Norman arches and a superb rose window overlooking the nave. Oh, and he does love a good rose window, does my Derek.

We set off on a Tuesday in May. The weather's been so good in May these last few years, we always set aside some time for our little 'pilgrimages', as we like to call them. And with Norton Hensbury only a few miles north of Toncaster, it's surprising we'd not got round to going there before.

Oh that GPS is a blessing though. Derek always insists on doing all the driving and I never was much good with maps, but with GPS you're there without a worry in the world. And there we were at our destination, just on the edge of that charming little village.

But there wasn't a church.

I mean, there was a boundary wall, even a little bit of grass and some gravestones left around the edges – so we knew it was the right place. But in the centre of the plot there was just bare soil and some holes in the ground where the foundations had been. It was extraordinary, as if the building and its immediate surroundings had just been ripped off the face of the earth. Well, as I say, it was rather distressing.

A lady came by, walking her dog. We asked her what had happened. "It was one of them Council Dislocations," she told us. "Happened a couple of weeks ago."

"Council Dislocations?" We both repeated the words simultaneously. The effect might have been quite comical were we not so perturbed. "And what might they be?" added Derek.

"You'd have to ask the Council," said the woman with a shrug of her shoulders, and then off she went with her dog.

∞

We got hold of the phone number of the Parish Council Clerk, but he wasn't a lot of help, really. He and the Parish Council appreciated that it might be a source of distress to both locals and visitors, but that the Dislocation decision had been made at a higher level, the right and proper protocols had duly been observed and the necessary paperwork completed. "But why?" Derek was almost shouting down the phone. I do worry about his blood pressure at times like that. The clerk said he regretted that he was unable to comment any further on the Dislocation of St. Andrews in the Marsh. The matter was now closed to discussion. Fortunately, Derek had the presence of mind to ask, with what civility he could muster, who he might contact in order to discuss the matter at a higher level.

And that's how we found ourselves in the office of Councillor Kimberley Crouch of Toncaster District Council. We were confident that we would get to the bottom of the matter with Mr Kimberley Crouch, especially as I was on reasonably good terms with Mrs Kimberley Crouch with whom I'd become rather cordially acquainted at the Women's Institute. At first we listened as, quietly and not without charm, he explained about the protocols and the paperwork and how we were not to worry, the Deconsecration Department of the Dislocation Division would have carried out the necessary procedures so the land could be put to other use. Red faced by then, Derek could no longer contain himself. "That's not the point! St. Andrew's was a historic British Church. It had a rose window! You can't go just knocking down buildings like that and taking the stonework away!"

To which Councillor Kimberley Crouch said: "Mr Cox, may I enquire as to how often you and your wife attend a church for the purpose of worship these days?" And with that enquiry he launched into a series of statistics detailing the decline in church attendance. The case put simply was that resources were no longer available to maintain such buildings. Whilst there were, he admitted, other uses to which they could be put, the Council had found that in this case Dislocation was the most economic, efficient and sustainable procedure.

Later, in the car, neither of us the wiser than before we'd entered the Toncaster District Council offices, Derek looked at me sadly. "I think we're being stonewalled, Rita," he said.

∞

And what a stonewall it was! You'd think we could have found someone to help us but we proceeded to draw blank after blank. The Citizen's Advice Bureau explained that, since we were not residents of Norton Hensbury and therefore not directly affected, there was nothing they could do for us. It was the same story or similar with legal advice agencies and even the rather hopeful sounding Community Land Advice Service. We wrote about the matter to local newspapers, even contacted the media. No one got back to us. We looked in Record Offices and through all of the source material we could find, hoping to come across at least *some* reference to the legal and legislative background. There was none to be found.

We did, however, gradually begin to discover precedents. Friends of ours, for example, told us of sites of interest that they had tried to visit that had somehow 'just disappeared'. On a visit from London, our son Martin told us of a friend of his who used to visit an Arts Centre that had, one day, 'just gone'.

This young man had then made enquiries of his own and learned of other places similarly 'dislocated'. A 'lido' swimming pool; a museum; a housing block in South London that had been occupied by a well-organised group of squatters... Not that we approve of that sort of thing, but nevertheless it was quite a list. We asked our Martin if we could meet this chap but Martin explained that he had lost contact with him somehow, and that not even mutual acquaintances seemed to know where he could be located any more.

Now Derek and I, we're not political by nature. We've voted Conservative all our lives, of course, and though we're not too sure about some of the cockier youngsters in the Party these days, we still think the country is safest in their hands. But as Derek said, someone had to be accountable. After all, it couldn't be that entire Dislocation procedure had just been made up by some anonymous official, and everyone had just quietly agreed to get on and do it because it was easier that way. Not in a democratic country! So Derek decided that he would go to the top. He would write to the Prime Minister.

It took a few weeks for the reply to get back. It said that Her Majesty's Government regretted any distress that Dislocational procedures might cause, but that in all cases the right and proper protocols were duly observed, the necessary paperwork completed and all Dislocations had been carried out within the Law of the Land.

∞

I said to him. I said: "I think that might be far enough, Derek. If we go any further, I've got a feeling there's going to be trouble."

But he wasn't having any of that. Not my Derek. Once he gets something into his head he has to see it through. So the next thing was that he was going to organise a public meeting, start a movement of his own to expose and challenge the practice of Dislocation. He was all fired up. Well, it's my belief that a wife should support her hubbie at all times, so I threw myself into helping with the organisational side of things.

Truth to tell, it was a welcome distraction from some rather troubling developments at the WI. Mrs Kimberley Crouch had stopped talking to me for some reason, as had her friends. Then one day, Mavis, our secretary, had called me in to say there were 'irregularities' in my membership details, and that I would have to be suspended whilst they were looked into. "I'm ever so sorry, Reet," she said – and it seemed to me that she'd been pushed. Derek told me he'd had similar experiences at the Buffs.

But we were having trouble finding a venue for our meeting. Halls where for months on end nothing seems to happen were completely booked, or 'closing for refurbishment'. Finally we heard of a place on the outskirts of town and we drove out to meet a rather unpleasant man who demanded an exorbitant amount of money for the use of his premises.

Dejected, we set off for home. "Never mind," I said, "I've got some lovely fresh salmon in the fridge. I can get it ready in a jiffy. Let's open a bottle of wine and forget our troubles for a bit, eh?"

∞

Unfortunately, however, we found that we had no home to return to. Another Council Dislocation had occurred. Everything was gone. The house and all its contents, from the fresh salmon in the fridge to Derek's marvellous collection of War Memorial photos. Gone. Even the garden – my azaleas, Derek's greenhouse where he grew his prize winning tomatoes... Gone. Gone. All gone. Just bare earth and ditches.

I was too distraught to speak, but Derek found out that none of the neighbours had *seen* the act of Dislocation take place. They'd all been out somewhere or... I don't know. Asleep?

All we had left was the car, our clothes and the bits we'd taken with us. But there was worse to come. I'll spare you the blow by blow account of how we went to the police, only to be told that it was a civil and not a criminal matter. And how we discovered, in our subsequent attempts to find accommodation, that none of our credit cards had remained valid. Within a few short hours, Derek and I had become homeless and destitute.

But I must say we have jolly well tried to make the best of our life now, in our little room in the hostel for homeless people. You'll find me down in the kitchen helping out on a daily basis, and I put a great deal of time into organising outings for some of the more sedentary gentlemen here. As for Derek, well, perhaps he hasn't tried so hard as I. But he needs to rest. His blood pressure, you see... He did keep on leaving messages for Martin until the credit ran out on his mobile but we had no reply. And of course, to this day, he'll talk about how something ought to be *done* about these confounded Dislocations. But as to *what* that might be, he does seem to be at rather a loss.

Besides, he's started to worry a lot about Martin. And even about us. He keeps remembering how Martin's friend, the one who'd accumulated all those examples, had apparently 'just disappeared'.

Whoever it is that co-ordinates these events, they clearly don't like to leave any loose ends.

Humping and Buckling

Betsy has probably lost track of a marble or two in the past few years but no one is prepared to take what they'd get if they suggested this to her face. Yet remembering how things used to be, she can handle that just fine. And that's why the boy with the recording machine keeps coming back for more.

"Now where exactly do you put the tape in that little doohickey, boy?" Betsy wants to know.

"No tape, Betsy. It all goes onto a hard drive."

"Hard drive?" When Betsy giggles it's phlegmy. "I've had some hard drives. But if you want me tell you about those, boy, you have to loosen ol' Betsy's tongue."

"I like what you have been telling me just fine, Bets. And the trouble is, if you get loose I can't understand a word you're saying."

"That's because you oughta get loose too. Now what you want to know about today, boy?"

He wonders how much he's going to be able to decipher of today's talk. It's noisy. There's a domestic in full swing in one of the shacks down the way, and wired sound everywhere – thudding hip-hop competing with the wild exhortations of airwave fundamentalists.

"You started telling me about the dancehalls, last time. Where you kinda made a living when you were a young woman." She's told him quite a lot, in fact. But he likes to get her going over things more than once, because she tends to pull out different details each time and he can edit it all into one when he transcribes.

"Well that's because the only work you could get them days was trash work, you understand? Weren't nothing to be had that wasn't drudgery, an' somehow you always ended up *owin'* the people that was supposed to be *payin'* you. Now I'm talkin' about the ladies here. If you was plain, well then trash work was about all you had. But if you was a pretty girl, well there was better ways to make a living. An' if you was good at dancin'..."

"Yeah, you told me, didn't you — how you used to practice when you were a little girl?"

"Damn right! I was one hell of a dancer, boy. I could dance the Patio like you would not believe."

"The Patio?"

"Ain't you never heard of the Patio? Tchah! Where you come from, boy?"

"Uh, place where nobody's heard of the Patio, I guess." They trade a grin. Humour is a good bridge for the age gap. "So what was it? How did you dance the Patio?"

"Two things. Two things. First thing was the footwork. You'd point with your feet to the beat. This way. That way. Whole set of directions. An' the guy you was dancin' with, he was the mirror. His set would fit with yours. Second thing was all the *rest* of you. We used to call it the 'hump' and the 'buckle'. You'd hump and you'd buckle, and all the while keepin' to the footwork. That was the Patio That was a dance." She belts out the last word, like there's not a lot of room for contenders.

He looks at her for a moment and no further question springs to his lips. He's trying to imagine this frail but feisty old woman sitting at a table outside the shanty where she's lived more than half her life as a nubile beauty in a twinkly ballgown, gloss lips glistening, kohl-rimmed eyes like sparks in the dark.

Then he's noticing her eyes right here and now. She's looking at him shrewdly. Fair bet she knows just what he's thinking.

"But, uh, dances come and go. There must have been others."

"Oh sure. There was the Hullaballoo, and, uh... the Flutter, that was kinda fun. But the Patio... Ahh! That was a dance."

Betsy slips into reverie. His nostrils pick up the scent of wood-smoke from somewhere nearby, and a rich, herby stew that is probably simmering over the selfsame fire. Time is passing. He needs to cut to the quick.

"Okay... Making a living, you said. You were a professional dancer?"

"Huh? You mean like a ballet dancer? What you talkin' 'bout? There weren't no 'professional' dancin' in the dance halls. But there were the guys, the guys that wanted to dance with pretty girls. Now I'm not talkin' about fine lookin' boys like you, sweetheart, I'm talkin' about guys the blessed lord did not see fit to grace with good looks and charm. You followin' me?"

"You mean these guys paid you to dance with them because that was the only chance they'd get to dance with a pretty girl?"

"What I'm sayin'."

"So this was kind of a 'hostess' thing. Maybe went a little further than just dancing, yeah?"

"Depended. Me, I was respectable. I made good money just by dancin'. An' you know what? Didn't matter whether a guy had a pot belly, bald head and an ugly face, so long as he got the moves that was all right with me. Hell, that was good work. Feet be killin' you by the end of the night, but that was good work."

"Wow. The music? Bands? Singers?"

"They played *music*, them days. Real music, fine musicians. My Georgie, he was in a band. The Attaboys, they called themselves. 'Patio, baby, you look like a queen... Patio, baby, you dance like a dream...' That was one of theirs. Then there was the Conundrums, the Wakusi Five... Oh, I don't remember the names so good. You can go look 'em up. They got books..."

"Georgie? He was the guy you married, right? You met him in one of the dancehalls?"

"See, the years were rollin' by an' I was gettin' kinda mature. Seemed like it was the younger girls that was gettin' the action. Now I'd been friendly with Georgie a good few years. We'd take a drink together end of the night an' he'd always tell me how it made him feel good when he saw me dancin' to his music. I liked that, but I didn't pay it any great mind 'cause I figured he'd have the same line for some other girl in every dancehall he played. An' maybe he did.

"But there was one night when I didn't get no dances at all. An' the Attaboys were on stage, an' Georgie, he was lookin' out for me. But of course he couldn't see me nowhere, 'cause I was sittin' an' waitin'. Maybe some real old guy would walk in an' I'd get my dance... But I wasn't gonna be makin' money anymore, an' there were vacancies at the canning factory, an maybe it was time to think about that. Now Georgie, he played the tenor saxophone, an' I'm sittin' there listenin' to the Attaboys an' it don't sound quite right. Where's the tenor?

"An' then there's a hand on my shoulder an' I'm lookin' up, an' it's Georgie. 'I got no coin to pay you,' he says, 'but I sure would like to see you dance. Shall we?' Next thing we're down the front, an we're humpin' an' we're bucklin', and the footwork is just perfect between us. Just perfect. An' we're barely aware of it but there's a gap openin' around us an' people are just stoppin' to watch because we are... we are immaculate.

"An' the band keep playin', whippin' it up, an' the other folk get to dancin' again. An' it's like I feel the years slippin' away an' I'm the little girl that practised dance moves to the old gramophone an' Georgie... why he's the boy I always loved an' I just never did know it.

"An' then when the Attaboys finally wind up the tune, he's holdin' me in his arms an' he's tellin' me how he loves me an' he wants me to be his bride."

There are tears in the corners of Betsy's eyes. For a few seconds she lets the emotion wash over her, then – remembering she is being observed – she hawks noisily and spits into the dirt at her feet. "Too bad he turned out to be a lazy, good-for-nothing drunkard. Which I found out after I married him. Hard times, boy, hard times. That's most of what livin' is.

"But I never stopped lovin' him 'til the day he died."

"And that was—"

"Boy... You turn that little doohickey off now. I'm tired. I don't wanna talk no more. You come back another time, hear?"

It's been a short session but a good one. He knows there's no point trying to persuade her to carry on. Betsy won't be moved, and he knows from folk hereabouts that she's got a fierce temper and she can bear a grudge for years. Diplomacy and patience are part of his job, and the Foundation pays him well. He clicks off the recorder, thanks her warmly and tells her she's doing great.

"Doin' great!" she quotes him contemptuously, and spits once more. But she's smiling. "I'll see you again, boy. I'll see you again."

Exiting Betsy's yard, he has to sidestep hastily to avoid two squabbling hens, and it takes him a moment or two to regain the rhythm of his walk. He thinks maybe he can hear a viscid gurgle of laughter from behind him, but he holds himself with dignity and does not turn to look.

'*Boy*'! Jeez! He's in his thirties, married, one kid, divorced... And to Betsy he's like someone just out of the starting gate. Still, it makes him smile to think of it. He'll take '*boy*' as a compliment.

Kids from out the schoolhouse walk past him sucking at bags of ice. His nostrils wrinkle. A sharp reek from the impromptu gutter at the centre of the lane. He's sweating already, even at the start of his walk. And wary – the 'doohickey' in his pocket cost plenty bucks and this is not the safest of locations. In cut-off Levis, torn sleeve surfer t-shirt and beach sandals, he's dressed down so as not to stand out. But it doesn't pay to be complacent.

So this is where Georgie brought her when she became his bride. This was once the man's home turf. Kind of hard to imagine the romance lasted long.

Of course he knows more about Georgie than he's letting on. The Foundation are big on the whole Bill Russell jazz archive thing. He's seen sepia photos of Georgie in a wide-lapel, pinstripe suit and fedora, hanging out with the dudes in one of the big bands he went on to after the Attaboys. Cross-country tours, dancehalls, no doubt with Georgie eyeing up a lady dancer in every one of them, while Betsy waited home alone.

And today he'd been particularly disingenuous concerning the Patio. It was well known and recorded as the dance of its day. Back then, if you couldn't do the Patio, you couldn't do shit. But if he'd not played dumb, he wouldn't have got that great description out of Betsy.

Those glorious terms with all their onomatopoeia and innuendo. '*Humping*' and '*buckling*'. He rolls them through his mind as he walks. Humping and buckling. Humping and buckling.

So Betsy humped and buckled her way into a dead-end marriage and continuing poverty. But she went on loving Georgie even as he drank himself to death, for the sake of that one night when they danced immaculate and for a few minutes the whole floor stopped to watch.

Now he sits in the hotel bar nursing a tequila and he wonders. Was it worth it? Can a whole life's value be pinned on one magnificent moment, when all the crap and the detritus drops away and we are bathed in glory? Or does that moment deceive us 'til we find ourselves later drenched in its slops?

It's a tough call.

One of these days he might have to make it himself.

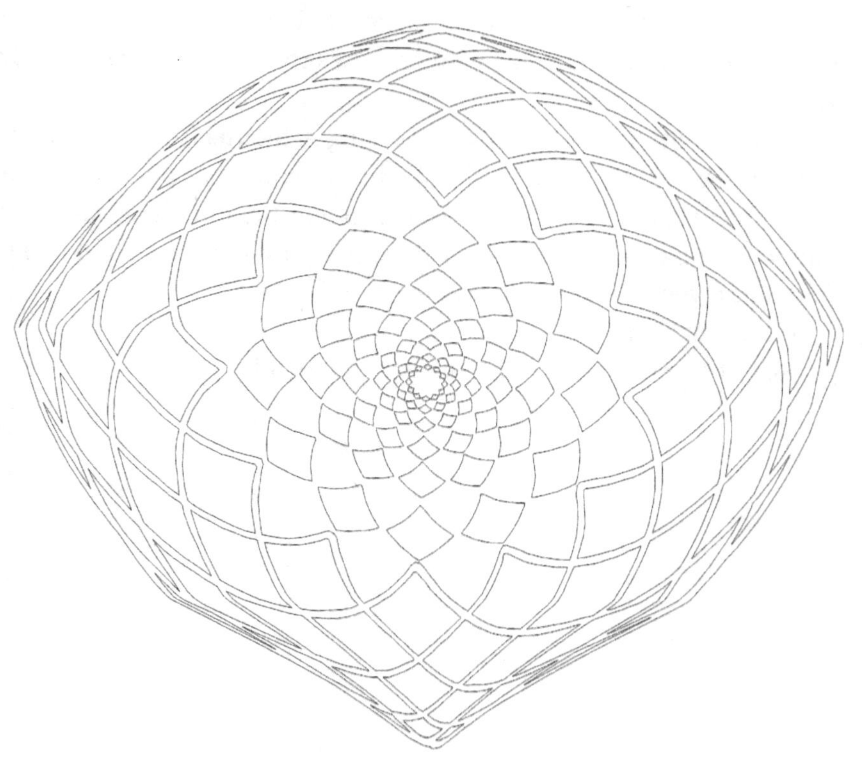

Short

Every two or three years our dad used to say: "I think I'll go and stretch my legs." He'd usually be gone for a good few days. When he returned, he'd be a bit frail and shaky for the next week or so. Walking was obviously difficult. He'd also be somewhere between one and two inches taller than he was when he left the house.

I've looked at old black and white photos in the family albums and it's clear that he started out short, maybe five foot tall. Shorter than Mum, in fact. Not that it appeared to have bothered them. Dad in his demob suit and flat cap, Mum in her flared frock, lipsticked lips beaming a characteristic, slightly lopsided grin. Ooh, they were lovely together. Bless.

We didn't really notice it when we were little. Grown-ups are big, that's all you know. Some of them are taller than others, but you don't keep a track of their size because they're supposed to have stopped growing. Except for our dad, that is.

It was my brother, Al, that first cottoned on. He's always been the observant type, our Al. "'Ere, Rosie, 'ave you noticed 'ow Dad's different when he comes home from 'stretching his legs'?"

"'Ow do you mean?" I said, thinking back. It wasn't long since one of his interludes away, and he'd seemed like the same old dad to me, sitting me on his knee and telling me I was his 'cosy Rosie' or some such nonsense.

"Watch 'im when he goes through the coal shed door, Rose. 'E 'as to duck. 'E never used to. 'E's got taller."

And it was true. He even got a nasty bump on his head one time when he must have forgotten he was those couple of inches up on himself. So one day I asked our mum about it. She laughed. "Don't be such a daft ha'porth, Rosie, 'course 'e ain't got taller!"

"Well then 'ow—"

She cut me off. "It's just the rest of the world. It's shrunk." Then she started laughing, and in such a funny way that I had the feeling it was best not to ask about it anymore.

And that's how it was ever after. If me or Al ever brought it up, they'd make some sort of offhand comment. "Don't worry. You'll catch up one day!" "'E's just learned 'ow to stop slouching, that's all." And they'd laugh, and you'd feel a bit daft for asking and like it wasn't really a good idea to mention it in the first place. So we stopped.

And besides, we forgot all about it for a while, because the next day after that little chat our dad came home with his first ever car. Vauxhall Viva, it was, in a very nice shade of blue. Soon we were going on 'outings to the countryside'. Almost every weekend, it seemed like.

The seasons all rolled by a few more times and then, one day, we were all having our breakfast and Dad announced: "I'll be off again today... stretching me legs..." And then he gave me and Al a look as if to tell us: 'Don't you dare go asking your mum any awkward questions. Either of you.' We got the message.

I wasn't sure our Al was that interested by then, anyway. He was in his teens and you know what boys get like at that stage... So I was a bit surprised when later that morning he said to me quietly: "It's 'appening again, Rosie. Let's keep an eye on Mum tonight. See what she gets up to."

As it happened, Mum had the sewing machine out. That wasn't unusual in itself, she still took a lot of pleasure and pride in making clothes in those days, even with Dad telling her that hard times were over and she needn't really bother. She'd sit there for hours, whirring along, taking the occasional sip from a brandy and ginger ale, Home Service on the radio, happy as a lark. But this time Al ushered me into the kitchen and showed me the brandy bottle. You could see she hadn't left much room in her glass for the ginger ale. And she was making alterations to a pile of our dad's trousers. Lengthening them.

It was all a bit obvious really. When we came into the workroom she looked at us sheepishly at first, then you could see tears beginning to well up in her eyes. "'E's doin' it for us," she said in a cracked voice. "Doin' it so we can have a better life."

"But 'ow big's 'e gonna get?" I burst out. "Is 'e gonna be a giant?"

"Ooh no," she said, making her best effort to sound reassuring. "'E says 'e'll probably only have to do it once or twice more. There's only so much you can stretch a man's legs." At this point she could no longer hold back the tears. "Or he'd just topple over."

Same as the joking and laughing had done before, that nipped us right in the bud. I just rushed to hold Mum as best I could with my little arms while she cried. After a bit, Al got the brandy bottle from the kitchen. You could see she needed it. I ended up doing a load of those trouser legs myself. She'd taught me well.

When Dad returned, treading very unsteadily, supporting himself with a pair of walking sticks, he knew straightaway that he wasn't the only one who had changed. Me and Al, we'd both grown up a little too.

∞

The last time he got it done it was different. For a start he'd told Mum not to bother with any alterations. When he got back, he'd be buying himself new trousers. From a tailor.

A lot of other things were different too. We'd moved from the old terraced house where me and Al were born to a posh secluded place right on the edge of town. It was so big that our mum took on a lady to come in and do for her. Our dad, he'd bought himself a Mercedes and he looked proper swanky, sat behind his chauffeur in these handmade suits he'd taken to wearing. And holidays, well... Weymouth Sands on a dry day was once our idea of paradise, now we were jet-setters, globetrotters, whisking off twice a year to the most exotic and exclusive resorts you could imagine.

It wasn't all sweetness and light though. Mum seemed to get more and more stressed out as the years went by, and if it wasn't for Valium I don't know how she'd have managed. What was it? Me and Al used to talk about it sometimes. Same thing that had brought her to tears that night we'd gone in to see her at the sewing machine, we reckoned. But it was obvious she didn't want to talk about it.

That last time it took nearly a couple of months before he could walk again. He had physiotherapists coming in daily and everything. He was just short of six foot six inches tall. The first time he stood up, he looked magnificent... for the minute or so before he had to sit back down in his wheelchair. But I'll say this for him. He was determined. He was going to get himself walking again and nothing was going to stop him.

198

And so it was that, one day a few weeks later, he came into the living room where I was sitting on my own reading Vogue. "Rosie," he said... I was in my late teens then, I wasn't his 'Cosy Rosie' any more, I was 'quite the little lady.' "Rosie, why don't you and me go out for a nice walk, eh?" Well, I thought he was up for something therapeutic, like, a stroll in the country, but no...

The chauffeur took us to the business district of town. The parking space where we pulled up was exclusively reserved for our dad, but we didn't go into the office block where he worked, not straight away. We just ambled around. Even though he still needed a walking stick (he'd got himself this beautifully carved cane with pearl inlays), he had this overwhelming dignity and grace about him, which everyone we passed or met seemed to recognise. A lot of them knew him. They'd greet him warmly and it was always either 'Sir' or 'Mr Jephcott'.

As we approached the shopping centre, there was this little tobacconists we went into. The proprietor greeted dad like he was an old friend, a fellow connoisseur of the finer things in life – in this case cigars in fragrant wooden boxes. When Dad had made his selections the manager insisted they were 'complimentary' and wouldn't charge him.

Outside, he handed me a wad of notes, gave me a wink and gestured towards an extremely fashionable shoe shop just down the street. "See you back here in an hour, eh?"

I was getting the point.

Once we'd met up again, we did a quick tour of his place of work – where, guess what, everyone seemed to think he was the bee's knees. After that, it came as no surprise to me that we ended up in a lavish restaurant, eating stuff you usually only see on those TV-chef programmes.

"Did it 'urt, dad?" I said. "When they did what they did to your legs?"

He shrugged. "Not so as you'd notice if you weren't paying attention."

"But this last time, you might have lost the use of 'em."

"Oh no... You've got to stay on your feet, girl. That's what your legs are for...." He paused thoughtfully, looking around him with the clear intention of reminding me where we were and what we'd done that afternoon. "That's what your legs are for."

∞

He died on the operating table. They were trying to do something to relieve this terrible, agonising sciatica he'd developed. And this wasn't the first time. Well, he'd had enough. His heart gave out.

I expected there to be a lot more people than there were at the funeral.

Afterwards, it was just Mum, me and Al again – all three of us on the brandy and ginger ale. And finally, late in the night, when we'd all been telling some of our secrets for a while, we asked her. What was it, just as our dad was going up in the world, that had brought her so far down?

"Well, my darlings, truth is..." And there was that lopsided grin again, only with a rueful edge to it. "Truth is simple, I s'pose. I just liked 'im a whole lot better back in the days when 'e was... short."

Marinating Jeff

Attics, basements, crawlspaces, cavities... In the dust, detritus and cobwebs – amongst the spiders, the centipedes, the earwigs and the silverfish – there they congregate.

But don't mistake them for mice or rats or any earthly vermin. There's no poison you can put down to tempt them, no trap into which they will stray. For they are not made of the stuff of which living things are made. They don't play by the rules that bind earthly creatures to life and death. They are Inklings, escapees from the apertures between realities.

Acquiring a house, for example, especially when drawn to older buildings for their 'character', it is as well to ensure – if at all possible – that no one has practised ritual magic beneath those rafters. It makes no difference whether the practitioner has acted for good, evil or simply out of pure curiosity. If an entity has been summoned, then a portal has been created. And through that newly opened gap the Inklings are ever-eager to emerge. They creep through, rarely noticed amidst demonic spectacles of unearthly lights, tentacles, slaver-dripping fangs and bloody claws.

And once through, the Inklings don't ever go back to the slime encrusted crevices from whence they came.

Why?

Because the food here is wholly and enticingly succulent.

∞

Like most of humanity, Jeff Edmundson had no idea that Inklings come to dwell so frequently in our world. And besides, the house he'd bought, downsizing after a bitter divorce, was not particularly old – a 1940s semi in a suburban city street.

He wasn't to know that between 1953 and 1964 the place had been occupied by one Aloysius Batt. Batt was a would-be alchemist who had, more by luck than good judgement, attained the mysterious practitioners' goal of Nigredo and thus had the extreme good fortune to release the Golden Lion. This was shortly before his mysterious disappearance from our earthly plane. It is said, by those in the know, that had the unfortunate Aloysius Batt but ensured better ventilation in the basement he would now be both fabulously wealthy and practically immortal.

Nevertheless, like effluent into a mountain stream, Inklings made their entrance. Ventilation was a matter of minimal importance to them.

Jeff, blissfully unaware of these events, had found the house a bargain. The previous owners had seemed anxious to move on and had accepted his skimpy first offer without quibble. He moved his few retrieved possessions in and proceeded to explore the potential delights of a restored-to-bachelorhood lifestyle. Within a few weeks the place took on a smell of old socks blending – towards the kitchen – with that of rotting food on unwashed plates.

The Inklings were at rest, paying some careful attention to this latest human manifestation but for the moment biding their time. They had fed well, if not completely, on the former occupants. They were replete.

Before long, however, their appetites returned. It was then that they began to prepare their own special marinade for Jeff Edmundson.

∞

Shaving one morning in the bathroom, Jeff noticed a movement behind him reflected in the mirror. All he could make out was something dark, of indeterminate shape. It appeared to drift past. He turned to see what it might have been, but there was no sign of it. There was no sign of anything. With a shrug of his shoulders, Jeff returned to his own reflection.

This proved a shock.

The image in the glass was no longer the familiar figure and features of a mildly overweight man with a receding hairline. The skin on his face appeared to have shrunk, tightening intensely around bone and sinew, giving him a stark, utterly gaunt appearance. It was as if he had been mummified, taking on a grey pallor, like some ancient body long preserved in a peat bog. There was an unremitting look of revulsion locked into his eyes. Held in thrall by this ghastly reflection, an idea then occurred to him, an idea so profoundly disturbing that it seemed to make perfect sense of the dehydrated vision at which he gazed.

He shuddered. That involuntary movement alone was enough to restore the reflected sight of his normal, chubby, half-shaven face.

Simultaneously, that vile idea – whatever it was – flitted from his short-term memory and was gone.

All that remained was a feeling of overwhelming thirst. He reached for a mug on the bathroom shelf, filled it with water and drank rapidly until it was drained. Not enough. He filled it and drank again. And again. And again.

∞

Blearily Jeff surveyed the few remaining men, on the turn with middle age and unacknowledged health issues, who – along with himself – had once been a legendary crew of comrades. 'The Berserker Boys'. Legendary, that is, amongst themselves. And perhaps a few select acquaintances. On this evening they sprawled in his dimly lit living room around the flat screen watching sports on Sky.

"Anybody need another beer?" Grunts of approval ensued. Jeff exited to the kitchen.

He switched on the light and was, for a few instants, curiously conscious that not all the darkness had been dispelled. It was as if blobs of it remained – some sweeping across the floor, some hovering in the woozy air. In an attempt to clear his eyes, Jeff blinked rapidly. By the time his gaze was steady, they were gone. "Too much bloody TV, that is," he muttered on the way to the fridge.

When he returned to the living room he almost dropped the beers.

The guys had changed. Beyond recognition.

Three of them were hollow cheeked, ancient, bodily wasted, nodding and drooling in their chairs. They stared at Jeff with an air of advanced dementia and no apparent sign of recognition. Deteriorated beyond even this stage, the remaining pair were rotting corpses, rife with writhing maggots and clusters of flies.

Then, in the time it took an announcer to say: "and if the scores stay like this they are relegated," he was seeing them as themselves again.

"Fuck's up, Jeff?" said one. "You look like you just trod in dog shit."

∞

"So, uh, yeah, that was like the second time it happened. Shocked me rigid, the guys all looking like that.

"Then it was the noises in the night. Like I had mice in the attic, not just a few, but hundreds of the fuckers up there, all skittering around. 'Course, I get up the ladder with a flashlight and there's nothing to be seen. Except I'm hearing hundreds more of them, all running around in the sodding *basement*. Ain't had a decent night's sleep in months.

"So then, this one time, I've been nodding out on the sofa and I wake up with this weird feeling. Look around. And the house... it's like a ruin. You know, windows all gone but for a bit of crumbling old wood. Grass and nettles growing through the floor. And it's so cold and icy. I get the feeling that every other house in the neighbourhood is the same, or worse, and there's no one... no people left. Not anywhere.

"And then another time, I'm coming out of the khazi and it's like I've stepped into a fireball, there's just nothing left, it's all melting and burning up..."

Tracey, Jeff's recently acquired girlfriend, gave him a long, frightened look. "You know, I don't think you and me are really that suited to each other," she said as she reached for her coat.

He never saw her again.

∞

Jeff was one to savour, they agreed, one from whom to draw every last drop. When, inevitably, he lost his job, they networked in order to keep him alive. Soon, unrequested Disability Living Allowance payments were arriving regularly in his bank account. He hardly noticed the change. He'd always ordered his supplies online, hadn't he?

The delivery drivers had a name for him. They called him 'the ghost'.

His old mates, the former Berserker Boys, had stopped coming round. Jeff was definitely losing the plot. He never left the house any more, which was out of order given their undying loyalty to the Swallows Inn. Not a one of them felt they could have a proper conversation with him these days – the guy seemed perpetually distracted by events that only he was aware of. Used to be a bit of a laugh, he did. Not anymore.

There was a little discussion regarding whether he might be in need of some kind of help, psychiatric or whatever. But the consensus was that he'd probably snap out of it, just as the rest of them did when their marriages fell apart. Shame he didn't hit it off with Tracey, though. She'd have got him sorted.

∞

It was cold. Absolute zero cold. Infinitely, ultimately cold.

Had the stars all burned out? Or, with the expansion of the universe over inconceivable lengths of time, had they moved away so far that you just couldn't see them anymore? All that remained was darkness. He could not observe any part of himself, or even conceive of what, if anything, his feet stood upon. It was not certain that he had a body at all, or eyes with which to see. He was merely some fragment of consciousness, lost in some emptiness where everything had ended, where the only hope was that the unimaginably immense cycle of existence might begin again. But not so much of a hint as to when or how.

Then he was back in his bed, shivering.

In their hidey-holes throughout the house, the Inklings capered and skittered. So close to the final feast, they were. And the food... The food was rarely this well prepared.

∞

It seemed to Jeff, the following morning, quite incredible that dawn had come at all. There was a universe around him, its lightless depths extending in every direction, an infinity beyond comprehension.

He, in all his Jeff-ness, was so much less than a minuscule speck in this doomed and desolate expanse. Any perturbation on a cosmic scale could wipe his entire world out of existence.

It was no more than dust. Dry dust.

Any last shred of willpower gone, he lay on his back on the bed staring up at a ceiling where cobwebs waved their dusty strands in a faint draft from the doorway.

There was a vague memory of what one does on waking of a morning. Urination, defecation, cleansing, eating, drinking... That sort of thing. But what would be the point?

What would be the point?

And besides, the room was darkening. Perhaps the day had passed and night was already encroaching. Except that the darkness seemed to consist of strangely pulsating blobs. More and more of them, cramming their way into his bedroom, jostling one another in their eagerness to get close to him. Opening their openings, drooling their drool, the Inklings were pressing their way into him, seeking to savour the sucked-up marrow of his blighted being, to drain every last drop of the juice in which he'd steeped.

And oh, tasty he was.

Oh, he tasted good.

∞

When the police eventually forced entry to the house and found it in the bedroom, Jeff's corpse was incomprehensibly drained of all body fluid, as if somehow mummified. His eyes were wide open, locked in a stare of horrified revulsion. The room was foetid. Strange, oily deposits glistened on the floor. Nausea overwhelmed them and they were forced to retreat.

They called in forensics in their coverall whites and facemasks.

"You know, it's almost as if this guy was..." said one of the team, looking up suddenly from his work, eyes wide with dawning realisation.

One of the others looked at him expectantly.

He shook his head. "No, forget it... Just a passing thought."

The Long Haul

I watch them in the night from the unearthly shores where I stand
– even as I also lie in bed a-sleeping. Their great mainsails billowing
in the brutal, gusting wind, they are the dreamboats, whose
mariners know nothing of sleep or rest; and thus nothing of their
cargo, the ornate caskets in the holds that contain the fragrant stuff
of dreams. These craft, the dreamboats, they sail both sky and sea,
seeking harbour wherever the dream traders do their intricate deals.
They moor in ports where dreams are brokered. The caskets are
hauled onshore to lie in waiting, subsequently to be distributed and
at last assigned to the sleepers.

And I find that I yearn to be aboard such a boat. I am not content
merely to be one more unknowing beneficiary of this ethereal trade.
I wish to return with the dreamboats, when the last of their cargo is

unloaded, to the place from whence they first set sail. And there to seek out the craftspeople, the shapers of phantasm.

What manner of beings are they to intricately tool this dream stuff, to build towering edifices from little more than soap bubbles and dust? I have no idea. But I hold them in awe, whoever they are. For their creations keep me a-hold of life in this dark time when I am robbed of waking hours.

∞

I have been press-ganged. Rounded up by blackguards and forcibly removed from the coastlands where it had been my custom to take those solitary walks. Head in a black sack, cruel treatment, humiliation, all these came to me, and passed. Yet I am satisfied. It was worth it. I am now a crewman, stationed perpetually on the afterdeck, hauling the yard, in the company of seemingly somnolent men whose stories of detainment most likely echo my own. We none of us now know anything of sleep or rest, for this vessel, which goes by the name of the 'Wendigo', is apparently one of the dreamboats.

Our captain is a will-of-the-wisp. His name is usually Johnny Handel, and when not at his duties he seems at times to be more of a mist than a man. Though vapour in clothing, he is possessed of a sharp tongue. Even seasoned crewmen regard him with respect.

No one cares to tell me of our current destination. Until we make land and are called upon to move the caskets, I have no way of knowing the extent to which our lastage remains loaded. Communication with anyone aboard the Wendigo, it appears, is more a matter of gesture than of verbiage. Spoken queries are answered with nonsense; ask a man where we are bound and he will tell you of tiny insects that creep in his clothing.

Day follows night, night follows day, but not with any regularity, for when we sail between the stars there is nothing but night.

∞

"The dreamboats, my darling, remember the dreamboats. They don't just sail the seas, you know. Oh no. Dreams are of anywhere, and anywhere dreams can take you, so go the dreamboats.

"That's why they'll bring you back to me. They will. I know they will."

∞

We have unloaded the last of the caskets in a tiny port that harbours little more than the local fishing fleet and carried them to a cavern whose owner is a dwarfish man, given to wearing a variety of animal furs and copious adornments of rough jewellery. We stand a-waiting, whilst the buyer and Captain Johnny Handel appear to argue furiously, the latter summoning all the weight and solidity he can muster. Eventually they appear to reach some kind of settlement, with a far from friendly handshake and the passing over of gold to conclude the proceedings.

It is only some hours after we have left the harbour that our good captain at last relaxes his grip on solidity. So much so, alas, that a sudden gust sweeps him out of his clothing which falls lifeless to the decking. He, himself, is dissipated. We are never to see him again. Although sometimes, when winter is bitter and the wind is sharp, we may feel his presence still.

It does not appear to make any great difference to us that we are without a captain. Each of us is familiar with the tasks lying ahead. We know neither rest nor sleep and we are navigated by providence. We have supplies to pick up, which will be paid for with a small proportion of the gold we now carry. These goods that we will acquire are highly valued by those whom I seek at last to meet.

∞

Somewhere between the populous region of 'here' and the lonely wastelands of 'there', we are caught in a terrible storm. The Wendigo is shattered. Those of us who survive the wreck are soon assaulted by a mighty and malignant leviathan. I alone survive.

Washed onto a beach, I know not where, I am rescued and adopted by a gentle tribe of cyclopean natives. Soon, I find that, with the advantages afforded me by the possession of two eyes, I am considered some sort of saviour. So I am honoured. Luxuries are pressed upon me. I am offered the hand in marriage of the King's beautiful daughter, with whom, fortunately, I have already formed a close friendship.

∞

"I'm with you, my love. If you find you've lost your way, listen for my voice. Let me guide you back to the shoreline and, sooner or later, you will see them again.

"And you'll remember... remember those great white sails, how they billow in the wind."

∞

From time to time I am called upon to complete tasks which my advanced spatial awareness enables me to accomplish with far greater ease than any of the tribe. I am able to assist with the building of the elaborate and decorative structures in which they live, the hunting of various forest dwelling creatures and so on.

From time to time, however, I am troubled in mind and spirit. There is a sense of something that I was trying to do, some place I needed to get to for some reason that I appear to have forgotten.

But this feeling is quick to pass and my existence seems contented and idyllic — until, one day, the natives find another man washed up upon the shore. They carry him to the village and revive him. This man has three eyes. It transpires that, with his third eye, he is able to see into the realm in which the tribal ancestors live and thus communicate with the dead. It is possible that he takes advantage of the position of influence that his ability grants him amongst the tribe. At any rate, the respect and privilege to which I had become accustomed soon dwindles away and I become a pariah within the village, the recipient of mild scorn and general indifference.

Only my good wife remains loyal to me. Even when, self-exiled, I leave the village and build a lowly dwelling close to the ocean. There by night, unable to rest or sleep, it becomes my custom to take long walks on the shoreline. Now and again in times of twilight, I notice magnificent sailing ships passing by out at sea. They intrigue me. I long to know who sails them and where they are bound. I ask my wife if she has any knowledge of these vessels, and she tells me of the tribal belief that they are the 'dreamboats'. Their holds, she tells me, are laden with ornate caskets containing the stuff of dreams; and the dream stuff is the work of immensely gifted craftspeople in the distant lands from whence these boats set sail.

And I find that I yearn to be aboard such a boat, and most especially when its time is come for returning to those distant lands. For I remember that I am in a bed a-sleeping. What life I have is attributable to the dream-makers alone. I have to meet them. I have to learn from whence all this comes.

∞

"No change then?"

"Nothing we can detect. I'm sorry. Your husband remains alive but profoundly unconscious."

"But he's in there somewhere, isn't he? He isn't lost?"

"We can only be sure of that if he comes round."

"I have to keep talking to him. Hoping."

"Of course, of course. Though it must be hard to find things to say."

"I tell him stories. Over and over. Like the one about the dreamboats that bring our dreams. He always loved that idea. I tell him maybe, if he could just get aboard one of those mysterious ships, he might just sail his way back to me..."

∞

They've seen me. The man on the crow's nest has spotted my drifting raft. I built it with the assistance of the wife who awaits my return at the shoreline. He has called out to the crew. Now they are lowering a rope.

A long haul awaits me. In treacherous waters such as these, it may never end.

A Curious Dream

Cecilia was beginning to get very tired of sitting, drowsily, by her sister on the riverbank with nothing to do. Suddenly, a strange man ran close by her. A policeman pursued him, blowing a whistle.

The book her sister was reading must have been a very good book indeed, because she did not so much as look up from its pages. Cecilia watched as the man hid behind a bush. The policeman ran past him, as did two more who came following. 'I should tell them where that man has taken refuge,' thought Cecilia. 'But how do I know that he is guilty?'

She told her sister that she was going for a little walk. Her sister nodded without looking up (which is hardly polite, but can be forgiven if the book you are reading is very good indeed). Then Cecilia walked over to the bush, and although she could make out only a little of his stripy shirt through the leaves, she asked the man: 'Please sir, *are* you a criminal, or do those policemen just *think* you are?'

'Why miss,' said the man. 'That is a very well put question. I am most grateful to you for not revealing me to those policemen before you could ascertain my criminality for yourself – though criminal I certainly am.'

'Oh dear!' said Cecilia. 'Then I should have revealed you.'

'Not necessarily,' replied the criminal. 'For at the point when you *could* have revealed me, you did *not* know. And besides, you had no knowledge of what an *interesting* criminal I am.'

'Then please sir,' said Cecilia politely, 'I would very much like to hear what makes you so interesting.'

At this, and seeing that the three policemen had not returned, the criminal stepped out from the bush. Cecilia could see that he wore a black beret, and an eye mask. He had a neatly trimmed moustache and a rather pointed chin. He gave Cecilia a friendly smile. 'And so you may,' he said. 'For I am no ordinary criminal, I am a *toddy*!'

'That is most interesting, I'm sure,' said Cecilia, although in truth she was not quite certain she could remember what a toddy *was*. 'Please tell me more.'

'I was just about to,' he replied, a little testily. 'For – as *most* people know – we will only commit crimes that are bewildering and puzzling. So, it is not sufficient for a toddy to burgle a house and steal a lady's jewellery, he must burgle a similar house nearby and exchange the jewellery from each to the other.'

'But what is the point of *that*?' exclaimed Cecilia.

'The point?' said the criminal, even more testily, 'I shall come to the point, shortly. But the illustration comes first, which is an elementary rule of composition, as you should know.'

'I'm very sorry,' said Cecilia. 'Do please continue.'

'We also rob art galleries and exchange their displays with the posters and notices we've stolen from the walls of a post office or laundrette. However, these exchanges are but one thing. If a toddy steals a car, it's to return it later with a unique and multi-coloured paint job. If a group of toddies surrounds you in an alleyway, we'll perform a dance routine, sing you a song and conclude by offering you lottery tickets. If we rob a bank and take hostages, we'll teach them advanced origami using whatever documents we can find.'

Cecilia could not help her lips curling up into a smile as she imagined all this. 'Well,' she said, 'that *does* sound bewildering and puzzling. I'm sure it must leave people quite perplexed.'

'Oh definitely,' said the criminal. 'And that *is* the point of all we do. When our work is over we meet up in toddy-bars and describe to one another the looks of bewilderment, puzzlement and – yes – even perplexity that we have brought to the faces of our victims. It's quite the most pleasant way to pass our lifetimes.'

'I wonder,' said Cecilia, 'how a person could possibly *learn* the way to commit all these rather complicated crimes and not get caught.'

'Patiently,' said the criminal. 'You spend many years as a 'toddler', before you become a toddy.'

As he spoke, Cecilia was distracted by the sight of the three policemen, who had quietly returned. They were approaching the criminal from behind – one directly, one to his right and one to his left. She thought to warn him, but so intent was he on his speech, that she simply could not get a word in edgeways.

'Oh yes, you see we have our own terminology, we toddies. If one of us works alone, he is 'on his tod'. If he finds himself identified and pursued by the police, as I was, he is a 'hot toddy'.'

By then the three policemen had closed in, surrounding the criminal. The one behind him said: 'And if the aforementioned 'hot toddy' is eventually detained by officers of the law, then he will shortly be doing 'tod-time', won't he?'

'Ah,' sighed the criminal, looking around. 'I have let down my guard.'

'That you have,' said the policeman who first spoke and who appeared to be in charge of the other two. 'And now I must inform you that you are under arrest and that anything you say may be taken down in evidence and used against you.'

'*Anything* I say?' asked the criminal.

The chief policeman looked to the constable at his right. 'Notebook, Johnson.' At this, Johnson removed a notebook and pen from his breast pocket. 'Now write down: "The accused questioned my statement. This is a clear indication of his guilt." Then he added, addressing the criminal. 'Well, I think the evidence is mounting up, don't you?'

Wisely, in Cecilia's opinion, the criminal said nothing.

'Now, let's get you down to the courthouse. And you too, young lady, since you are a material witness to the crime.'

'But I didn't see the crime!' exclaimed Cecilia. 'All I saw was this gentleman running away from you.'

The chief policeman looked at her, sternly. 'Well,' he said, 'an awkward customer. Any more lip from you, and I will begin to suspect that you are an accomplice.'

Wisely, Cecilia said nothing, and followed on as the three policeman led the criminal towards the park's exit. She glanced across at the riverbank where her sister was still completely engrossed in her book, and hoped that she would not be detained too long at the courthouse.

Cecilia had never been in a court of justice before, but she had seen how justice is dispensed on television shows, and she was quite pleased to find that she knew the name of nearly everything there. 'Those three gentlemen and the lady,' she said to herself, 'are the judges. And they will hold up placards with numbers that add up to the 'sentence'.'

'And that box on a plinth is the witness stand. And that one over there is the dock where the accused must stand.' Sure enough, there stood the criminal. He gave Cecilia a little wave as her eyes met his. Then up spoke the chief officer of the court, whose nose seemed to have a permanent upward tilt. 'Waving is not permitted in the courtroom,' he said. 'Please refrain.' So the criminal just smiled instead.

'Let the trial commence,' said the chief officer. The judges, who had been looking rather bored and fidgeting until now, suddenly looked pleased. 'Yes, let it,' said one. 'On with the show,' said another.

'Ladies and gentlemen of the court; let it be known that this man stands accused of a heinous crime, that he did force three innocent people, at gunpoint, to strip off their outer clothing, then dress in fish costumes. And furthermore insisted that they would not be released until they had each managed to toss at least one pancake.' The chief officer then turned to the criminal. 'And how do you plead? Guilty or not guilty?'

'Neither one nor the other,' said the criminal. 'It was the act of a toddy.'

'I think you'll find that we'll be the judges of that,' said the first judge, suavely; and then everyone had to wait as approximately twenty voices in turn shouted: 'Call the first witness.' This seemed rather unnecessary as the first witness had been sitting next to Cecilia the whole time. He was wearing a blanket over his underwear. Looking a little nervous, he went to the witness box. The usher removed a fish suit from a bag marked 'Exhibit A' and handed it to the chief officer.

'Is this costume the one you were forced to wear at gunpoint by the accused?'

'It is. And a very poor fit it was.'

There were gasps from the courtroom. The judges were all writing busily in their notebooks. Cecilia noticed that many of those present were frowning rather severely at the criminal. Even more so when 'Exhibit B', the gun, was produced – although it appeared to be more like a child's toy gun.

The other victims, various witnesses and the chief policeman were all briefly questioned, adding little of any substance to the story. Then it was Cecilia's turn to go to the witness box.

'What do you know about this business?' said the chief officer.

'Nothing,' said Cecilia. 'All I saw was this man running from the police.'

'*There!*' said the chief officer, conclusively. 'Running from the police! Clear evidence of guilt!'

'I think you'll find that we'll be the judges of that,' said the first judge again. 'Now all this has gone on far too long, and we are ready to give our judgement.'

'As you please, M'lud.'

'I will begin. And, I must say, I am quite unimpressed. Fish suits? Pancakes? Yawn. When excellent peacock costumes and three-course meals are freely available at many retail outlets? No, this just won't do.'

'I must disagree with my colleague,' said the second judge. 'Whoever heard of tossing a three-course meal?' (A ripple of laughter passed through the courtroom, with the chief officer frantically signalling everyone to be quiet.) 'It is my feeling that this combination displayed both *je ne sais quoi* and *sangfroid...*' (Cries of 'eeyew' and 'oo-er'.) 'And that the accused has committed an act of toddyism *par excellence.*' (Applause.)

'But,' said the lady judge, 'we must remember the stakes are high. We're looking for a winner today, not a loser. And I'm afraid I see a loser.'

The fourth judge was just about to speak when the first judge cut in with: 'And *I'm* afraid that's all we have time for... It's time to vote!' And each of them, with a little build-up, held up their chosen placards to gasps, 'oohs' and applause from the courtroom. The second judge gave a score of nine, the others were all below five.

'And that,' said the chief officer, 'adds up to a total of seventeen. That's seventeen years tod-time to y—' He had turned to the dock with a grand flourish, only to realise that the criminal was nowhere to be seen, having escaped the courtroom whilst everyone's attention had been on the judges.

There was uproar. Everyone was out of his or her seat. They were craning their necks, trying to spot the accused. People shouted: 'Find him!' and 'He can't have got far!' The policemen ran around blowing their whistles.

Cecilia, who had remained in the witness box, was quite bewildered and not a little puzzled. The proceedings in the courtroom had made no more sense to her than the crimes of the toddies. And despite the commotion all around her, she was feeling rather drowsy and the little witness box seemed safe and protective. So she lay herself down on the floor and was very soon asleep.

'Wake up, Cecilia!' said her sister, who had completely finished reading her book.

'Oh,' said Cecilia, finding herself lying on the riverbank once more. 'I've had such a curious dream!'

Apparition

It being my practice as a meridian, I have sought out herbs, roots and berries from each of the five points of direction. The last point is the most difficult, for without recourse to magnetic guidance the nature of Centre must itself be divined. Having done so, I chanced upon mandragora and shuddered, contemplating its intimations and implications.

Nevertheless, returning to my hub, I processed my gatherings with spirits to make a tincture. This I ingested by my fireside with all accompanying ceremony on the next Questioning Night of our ancient calendar. To soothe my passage I smoked two tender buds of leonitis, settling my body in comfort and warmth to stare at flames until they sunk into the glowing embers. And therein, with only my spirit-pouch for baggage, I commenced my transit.

Around me the walls of the chamber appeared to alternately expand and contract. Expanded, I marvelled at the map-like detail of their surfaces. Contracted, I felt as though crushed from all directions and struggled to maintain enough perspective to combat paroxysms of fear. So it always is. Mine is never an easy passage.

I was not too precisely aware of the moment at which, retaining my pouch, I left my physical body and began to find my way through. It might have been as the walls became filled with the faces of clowns and jesters, their jaws wide and mechanical. Or as a scratchy, wiry form of music filled my ears. At this time the soothing leonitis became my friend, for the first sensations of transit can be overwhelming. Like an amputee sensing a lost limb, I can still have an illusory sensation of body. Nausea and worse often follow as I begin my weightless drift.

In the drift I sought to make a dance, responding to what little melody and rhythm I could detect in that harsh music. In time, as I developed my movements, it grew less abrasive. Or perhaps its nature did not change – I had simply found a way to recognise its hidden harmonies.

By then my memory itself was melting. I had no more idea why I was undergoing this sequence of experiences than a snake knows why it crawls. I was immersed in fluttering, enveloped by a multiplicity of wings, slipping through layers of downy cloud to some objective that I had already forgotten.

Then I became as though bodied once more and my lowest limbs rested upon solid ground. I looked around. I was amongst great blocks of stone-built towers that may have been dwellings. At my destination, but disorientated and lacking memory of purpose, I was vulnerable.

On the ground, between the towers there was a streaming of souls. Their corporeal forms wrapped in a bewildering variety of clothing, they scurried about, sometimes stopping to gaze at the wide, lower floor glass frontages, or darting in and out through doorways.

In this profusion, instinct told me, there might easily have been demons. I needed to orient myself and to rediscover purpose. I have trained long and hard for such moments. The necessary meditation is virtually a reflex.

But alas, before I could complete it, there was a demon already confronting me.

I was, at that point, unseen by any except this one creature. "You!" it snarled. "Meridian! You are not welcome here!" Darkly coated, it was long faced and craggy of feature. It carried a placard on which there were incomprehensible symbols. "Here!" It raised its free hand, which crackled and flashed with azure energy. "I shall cleanse you from this place."

Around it the other beings glided by, either oblivious to this apparently one-sided confrontation or not wishing to pay any attention to the demon's rant.

"Cleanse you!" Jagged bolts of that energy flew towards me with stinging, spitting ferocity.

Resurgent memory informed my reaction. I flung myself backward and upward, rolling limbs over head into the air, and on up to the downy layer through which I had descended. This the blue energy could not penetrate. I rolled like tumbleweed through its lower reaches to remove myself to some quieter location and evade the demon.

I then recalled why I'd taken passage to this destination. A family hubbed within three spits of me had asked for help. Their youngest daughter was stricken and in need of deepest healing. I had divined that the oppression was sourced from parts beyond, and also from which parts I would obtain the required healing substances. That was my purpose here.

I needed a liquid from one who was close to death and another from one close to birth.

I rolled back to earth, having sensed a quiet place quite unlike the towers yet still within the great span of stone architecture that spread so far and so wide. This location was an open surround to a structure that stood alone, with its own small tower at one end and windows of leaded, coloured glass. Amidst trees, shrubs and grasses were shaped pieces of stone, engraved with symbols. Some were elaborate, carved and decorated; others simple and plain. This, I knew, was a ceremonial place. A good place to begin my search, even in the encroaching twilight.

I heard the sound of singing. It was a faltering, hesitant sound, lacking in melody – the voice hoarse and threadbare. "Jee-zus wunts... me... for... a sunbeam..." I sensed acidic irony in that frail, frayed voice as it rasped out the innocent sounding words.

I followed the sound to a deep, arched doorway on one side of the construction.

He was sprawled on the ground in its shelter, back propped up against a wall. A greybeard, huddled in a rank and filthy garment, clutching a bottle of darkened glass. I perceived a spirit within him that was mired in confusion and deep, dark anger.

He sensed me and looked up sharply. "Hoozat fuckin' standin' there? Show yerself, I can't see yer."

For his benefit, I became opaque. This brought forth laughter. "Ohh! Heh heh! Ain't you a big one?! Fine fuckin' figure of a meridian you are. Oh yes, I know, youse lot turn up here regular. Yeah. Yeah. Like birds on a fuckin' wire." He lifted the bottle to his lips and gulped noisily. This, I realised, was the first liquid I needed, the man being closer to death than most of his kind. But he caught the intensity with which I'd gazed at the bottle, and grasped that this might afford him some leverage. "Wunna drink, d'yer? Well, me, I like to make a trade. Know wot I'm tellin' yer?"

I did. But what had I to offer? He had his bottle. He was wrapped against the cold. What else might he need? Then I noticed a change in his expression. He winced, whimpered, shut his eyes as his face twisted into distortion. I waited to see if he would recover. He did, regaining his focus on me. I made a gesture of squeezing, and then let my limb go limp.

He nodded, comprehending.

"All of it? All the fuckin' pain?"

I nodded in turn and he handed me the bottle. Taking a small container bulb from the pouch I poured in a few drops, then handed it back. He was laughing again, "Heh heh, savin' it for later, huh? Savin' it for fuckin' later."

I turned away to make a quiet entreaty on his behalf. Without resistance, he simply ceased to breathe.

Outside the arch, I remained in vigil until the morning light. Beyond the low wall that surrounded this place, I could see some way down an approach to where a small group of living souls were gathering. One of them held aloft a banner.

I crept low, round to the other side of the structure. Then I ran. Long, long I ran, passing beyond where so many beings dwelt, until I came to softer places where most of what could be seen was in growth from the ground. But even here there were numerous dwellings.

By one, I saw two beings out and enjoying the warmth of sunshine in clear sky. A female, relaxed but watchful. Her offspring played with small objects on a rug on the ground.

The charm of this sight slowed me from running and, as I passed, the little one looked toward me and called out, in a sing-song voice: "Oh Mr Merry Dene, Mr Merry Merry Dene. Oh Mr Merry Dene, where have you been?"

I stopped, looked behind me – no sign of pursuit – then back at she who had called to me.

Girl child. A few years from birth. She had been playing with small replicas of eating and drinking vessels. But they did not appear to contain any liquid.

I made a smile, which she returned. "Would you like a drink?" I nodded. She proceeded to 'pour' with a display of concentration, from a 'jug' into a 'cup', stepped up to the low fence and offered it to me.

I was about to continue the charade by taking it and pretending to drink, when I realised that I did have what I needed – perhaps more powerful for being imagined, not actual. I reached into my pouch for another container and repeated the mime of pouring, this time from my 'cup' into the bulb. Then I gestured my thanks and turned to go.

She resumed her singing. "I've seen Mr Merry Dene. He pops a drink into a pot, he pops a drink into a pot and saves it for his dinner." Her mother was looking at her fondly, enjoying the seeming babble, unaware of what had taken place.

Checking again that there was no sign of pursuit, I risked a back-flip up into the downy underside once more. I had recalled and achieved my purpose here. Now, I recollected also that I needed to get back to the location at which I first arrived in order to make the Passage of Return.

It occurred to me that this was not without risk. Having failed to catch up with me as I gathered the liquids, the demon would almost certainly know that I was compelled to reappear there.

Remembering the crowds of beings present at my arrival, it seemed to me that my best strategy would be to come to ground a short distance away. Then I might reach my point of exit moving in concealment amongst those teeming souls.

As I did so, I could not but feel the weights and the slipstream drags of their emotions. Blending with these I would remain hidden. But it was turbulent. Joy buffeted against anguish, lust against grace.

It was all I could do to remember my wariness regarding the creature I feared – or others like it.

With absolute accuracy, however, my persecutor had positioned itself at the exact spot I sought to reach. There it waited, scanning the passing crowd.

This required a new strategy. I became opaque, guessing this would startle those around me.

Indeed, it did! There were cries, gasps, screams. As I'd hoped, a stampede followed. The demon with the banner was swept along by the fleeing crowd, unable to hold its ground.

Reaching that precious spot, I leapt up into what seemed to the onlookers to be sky.

On the ground, the demon must have somehow anchored itself. I could hear the crackle of its bolts reaching up below me. All of me was protected, but for three of my lower limbs. That pain was excruciating, that damage beyond restoration. In all my time since then, I have remained lame in my walking.

Back in my hub, agony-racked and exhausted, I still had nevertheless to conquer the pain and limp as best I could to that stricken child who lay waiting for my bulbs of liquid.

As I have said, such is the toll I must pay.

For mine is never an easy Passage.

The Hanging Post and the Banging Post

It began with the hallucination.

So far as I can tell, it is the only one I've ever had in my entire life. Vivid though. We were out for a Sunday afternoon walk, myself, Pete and the kids. Alan was 7, Lana was 8. It was on the footpath edging one of Bob Roberts' pastures. The three of them were engaged in a running game and well ahead of me. I'd been thinking about Bob – a slow spoken, thoughtful man and a long time friend of Pete's family – when there it was, manifest, in front of me.

An old field-gate, the wood aged to grey and with traces of rot, though still standing sturdy enough. On each of its knobbly, weather-scored supporting posts I could make out a roughly carved zigzag in a small, square panel. Some craftsman's trademark perhaps. Tall grasses grew around them but the posts were attached to nothing else – no fence or boundary that I could perceive. The gate just stood there across the path. I was startled. How had I not seen it on previous walks here? I drew closer. It looked solid and real enough to lean on, pull open or climb over.

The others were out of sight. I called them. I must have looked away from the gate for a moment and, when my eyes returned to its location, there was no longer a gate to be seen. Only the clumps of tall grass remained.

My call had gone unheard, yet Pete and the children were now in clear sight. I caught them up but decided not to mention it until Pete and I got to bed that night. "Wow," he said. "A gate! What a thoroughly rural sort of a vision!"

"Well, maybe there was one there once."

"Not that I know of, Liz, and I've lived here since I was ten."

I remember thinking as I fell asleep, 'There *ought* to be gate there.' That stayed with me. Whenever we walked the path thereafter, I'd feel that there was a need for that gate to be constructed. It seemed an absurd train of thought. I had a part-time job in the village shop, devoting the rest of my days to the family. I didn't build gates.

Then we learned about *surrogates*. On holiday in the South West we came across one, standing on its own in a field just as I conceived of mine. Locals identified it as 'one o' them surrer-guts'. It had simply been built there some years before, for no apparent reason. By whom, no one knew. Or at least no one admitted to know. Such structures, it turned out, were dotted across the country. Nowadays there's actually a website where enthusiasts have them mapped.

"Well, my love, there's plenty in the village who'd be able to knock you up a gate," said my ever-amenable partner when I told him of my plan.

"Which of them is good at keeping secrets?" I said.

I put it to Bob Roberts myself. "I want to pay for it, Bob, and do it as anonymously as I possibly can."

"Ah," he said, deliberately thickening his accent. "Eliz'beth Golding. So you're the one to build the gate, are you?"

I laughed nervously. "What do you mean, Bob?"

"But it's got to be done," he said. "So you say Wally'll be putting it up. Good choice, girl, good choice."

Conversations with Bob were rather like that. They came to sudden ends.

But Wally was great. To this day, as far as I know, has not told a soul. Knocked it up, discretely somehow, and showed me when I paid him. "This one," he said, proudly pointing to the sturdy post on which the gate was hinged, "this one's the hanging post. And that one, where it shuts, that one's the banging post."

So there it was in Bob Roberts' pasture, the gate. My surrogate. Lana, when she first saw it, thought it had been built by fairy folk but Alan reckoned it was far too robust and solid-looking for fairies. He proclaimed with authority that it had to be the work of dwarves.

I admit we had fun, Pete and I, years later, when we told them the truth. "You, Mum? A hallucination! Wow! You?"

So walking there, as we still chose to through the years, did always feel just a little bit strange. Because I knew, as of course did Pete and two of the older gentlemen of the village, that it was the gate that I had brought into being. No one else did.

Sometimes we'd be there on a weekend with many another walking the same path and overhear adult speculations as to its origin. Some would identify it as a surrogate, soundly enough. Others thought that old Bob had intended to put up a fence and divide the field there for some reason but hadn't got round to finishing the job. Or that he'd sometimes set one of his horses to jump it. A distinct lack of hoof marks in the vicinity rang a death-knell to that one!

Once there were two girls, barely teenagers. It was a sunny day and I'd lain down in a hollow nearby to sunbathe. Well, all right, the choice was intentional. I'd come to enjoy overhearing such talk. My two were both at university by then and I had more time for such dalliances.

"You stand on that side," said one of the girls authoritatively, "and you get him to stand on the other side and kiss you over the gate. And that's it. He's yours."

"But what if he doesn't kiss me?"

"Then you're better off without him, stupid. It's this old gate, see? It's where the true hearts meet."

I hadn't thought of the gate as being 'old', but to them it had been there for as long as they could remember.

A year or two later the coloured ribbons started to appear. I don't know why, but the practice seemed to be to tie them to the diagonal braces, though a few would stray onto the cross rails. They would have pairs of initials felt-tipped onto them, with the occasional heart motif – so again the 'custom' would appear to have developed amongst village youngsters. I never saw anyone come and tie one on. They just appeared – presumably put there later in the evenings or at night. My occasional liking for eavesdropping did not extend to making a lengthy 'stakeout' in order to observe this phenomenon. The relative anonymity of the act seemed in keeping somehow, a little cloak of mystery around hopes and desires. Nevertheless I sometimes wondered how well those sentimental tokens worked, whether the unions they marked were enduring.

I asked a friend's daughter about it. "Oh yes, I know a few who've done that."

"But does it work?"

"Well they have to do it right. They say it has to be done by the light of a full moon. Some think they can just do it at any old time and I'm not sure that always works. Sometimes it does, though."

She smiled dreamily. I had the feeling she'd tied one there herself, properly, one moonlit night.

After a few wet summers, moss and lichens began their slow spread across the wood. The ribbons rotted and gradually fell away. More would appear at times but another practice also became established. You'd see small 'offerings' in the grass around the posts: posies and trinkets, bits and bobs. And there'd be little notes with them on tightly folded scraps of paper. Tempting as it was to the eavesdropper in me, I could not bring myself to open them. That would have been a desecration, I think. But the gist of them, I found out later, were written wishes – some personal, some for the good of the world.

This sweet practice did not endure for long. Respect for the gate proved less than universal. The notes were getting read and mocked by others. Probably just as well. They were becoming a clutter.

After a solo walk one winter, Pete returned to tell me that someone had carved a 'sort of' zigzag pattern on each of the posts. "When you had that remarkable hallucination, Liz, didn't you see something like that?" I felt as though a very cold gust of wind had just blown right down my spine.

I checked for myself. It did not resemble the neatly carved 'trademark' that I remembered from my vision. More of a rough gouge, it looked like a stylised lightning bolt. Later, I mentioned it to Wally when he came into the shop and there was no one else there. I wondered how he'd react. "That'll be vandals," he bristled. "No respect for craftsmanship."

The impact of what I had done was becoming clear. I have a good friend in the village, Carolyn, who is inclined at times to be fey. She sweetens it with humour, but she was unusually serious the day she began to tell me all about the gate. She was knowledgeable regarding surrogates, more so than I. Though tempted, I'd never told her of my part in its creation. I felt this instinct had probably been correct as she spoke. "These friends of mine, they took one look at it and they said: 'That's a portal, that is.' They reckon they'll be up here next Beltane for contact with the fairie folk."

"Really?" I said. "And do *you* think it's a portal?"

"Best to keep an open mind."

Up by the gate another day, I chanced upon Bob Roberts. His son Ben had largely taken over the farm as Bob himself was becoming frail with age. So I suppose he had a bit more time for standing there looking at it. As he was.

"Well if it isn't Eliz'beth Golding!"

"Bob... This gate. You were *expecting* someone to build it, weren't you?"

"That's the way of it, girl. Told you then, didn't I? Had to be done."

"Why?"

"There's a pretty question. Well, you've got most of the pieces, Eliz'beth. You'll put 'em together."

Again, I got no more out of him. Characteristically, nor did he see fit to mention that he had been recently diagnosed with the emphysema that was to end his life a few years later.

Prior to Bob's funeral, in accordance with his persistently expressed wishes, mourners made a detour with his coffin, taking it into the meadow and passing it respectfully through the surrogate before going on to the church.

At the wake, up at the farmhouse, I asked Ben about this. He smiled, "Do you know, he said you'd ask? Said if you did I should take you over to the old barn and show you something."

"Really?"

"Oh yes. Come and have a look."

It had that mildewed hay and damp stone smell, the barn. Its original function transferred to more modern structures, the ancient building now contained rusty disused equipment, nesting birds and shrouds of cobweb. Ben pointed to one corner where two objects lay on the ground. "He'd had these lying here for as long as I can remember. Didn't ever want them touched."

Their lower parts rotted away, all that was left of them was what had stood above ground. For all the years that had passed between my hallucination and this moment, I recognised them that instant. The hanging post and the banging post – with their knobs of many knots, their grey and deep-scored, lichened surfaces – now close to crumbling with decay. The hanging post and the banging post of the gate I saw in my vision: lying before me, as real as ageing, on the dirt floor. And, on each, a few last traces of the old zigzag carving.

Bob's words came back to me. He was never a man to hurry.

I have the pieces now. I am beginning to put them together.

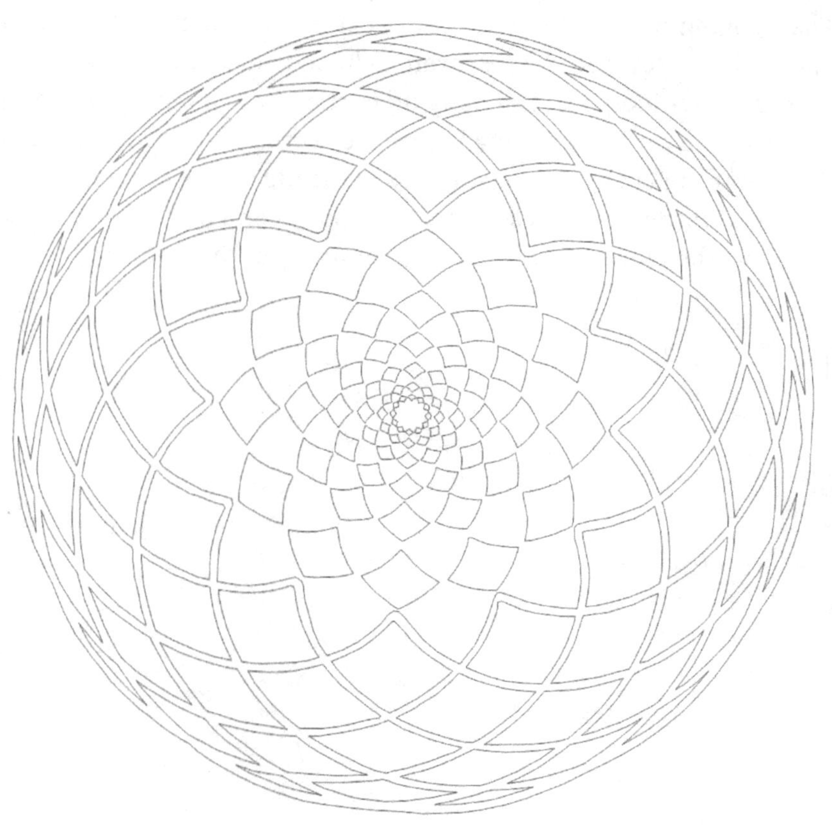

Peacock Feathers

The venue was a disused warehouse just out of town. A glim. All-nighter. No booze. No drugs. 'The music gets you high' was the spin.

Kris Jameson didn't buy it. Too many boozers and druggies he knew went glimming. But he'd pocketed a flask of his namesake, just in case. Couldn't work without some fire in his belly. Cal was driving, so Kris hit the flask.

Cal would be taking pictures. Brief was to get a handle on the glim scene and its supposedly synaesthesia-inducing soundtrack. If he came across anyone who looked like they could string more than two words together, he'd flash cash for spilt beans. Decent spread in it, at least. Pay dirt. Even if he didn't connect with any substances, he'd work something around the old 'repetitive beats' riff – dodgy legality, why wasn't the Criminal Justice Bill being applied here? Whatever. Something to scare the readers. That's what they paid for.

"What are they calling it again?" shouted Cal. Cal always shouted. It was useful anywhere noisy and crowded, annoying in a car.

"'Sub-Gliminal'"

"Right. Puns, innit? What was that other one now? Yeah, 'Glim-Pses'... I liked that one."

"You did, hmm? I'm so glad you're not a writer, Cal."

"Fuck off."

Background. Started with an old hand from the nineties, who had this thing about 'unfinished business'. The rave scene had been going somewhere, but it just hadn't got there yet. Vet's name was Zeeb Ruesome (allegedly) and he'd been working on this project he called 'Sonic Alchemy' ever since. Mad scientist stuff. Attuning sound to alpha, beta and theta brainwaves in sequences supposed to generate spontaneous experiences of synaesthesia and ecstasy.

All packaged with a lot of New Age bullshit: Ruesome coining the header 'glim' – slang for 'light' or 'the eye'. He got the marketing just right, the punters zeroed in and within a year or two it was worldwide, viral etc.

Time for gentlemen of the press to bring the public up to speed.

∞

She was wearing an outfit that appeared to be made entirely of peacock feathers, the colours somehow permuting into ever-shifting patterns. Dancing, she sparkled and radiated, a multicoloured furnace burning exhilaration and energy. Kris was glad that Cal was taking plenty shots of her. Front cover stuff, maybe.

Hers was the wildest yet, amongst a hell of a lot of elaborate and vividly colourful costumes. Carnival vibe. Plentiful pockets of tripped-out delirium. Wild screams. Whoops of delight. A friendly, chaotic bacchanalia. Not a hint of aggression or paranoia.

Kris still anticipated both before the night was out.

The music was borderline enjoyable – rave or Goa trance revived with some progressive elements thrown in, he reckoned. Hadn't induced any synaesthetic experiences. Certainly no ecstasy. Ruesome's spiel was looking thin. Kris was prepared to bet that the more manic dancers at least were off their faces on some chemical or other, including Ms Peacock Feathers.

There was a lot of incense burning somewhere, hard to locate in the dry-ice haze. Neat trick, whoever was manipulating it, to keep the smell changing in synch with tempo shifts to the music.

She'd stopped dancing. Kris realised that her stare was directed at him. Still shimmering intensely, she took two steps towards him. "Hey, man with the intense stare," she said. A voice that penetrated. "Dance."

He was on the point of laughing her off, but it dawned on him that her face was the most perfectly symmetrical and unutterably beautiful face he'd ever seen.

Dance? He'd not come here to dance. He wasn't succumbing to any of that Pied Piper crap. But he weighed it up. Maybe a dip into the experience would give him an angle. Especially now, given that the music was actually flowing around him in some sort of liquid form.

Hadn't noticed it before, but yes, there were eddies and currents of it just swirling and sloshing through this labyrinth of dancers. It was a flood, an immersion, so to dance was clearly a preferable option. He could swim in the liquid music, writhe to its rhythms in muscular harmonies.

The peacock feather woman smiled, watched his body as it began to sway and gyrate. Her smile played on his ears like bar after bar of some celestial tune. And he was in love, immersed in the scent of it.

And later, somewhere in a quiet light, he told her he'd like to see her again.

∞

"Get any effects?"

"You mean from the music?" yelled Cal. They were back in the car.

Kris nodded.

"No chance, mate. Ear plugs. Don't wanna loose what's left of my hearing. How about you? You looked like you were getting well fazed when you were dancing with that piece in the peacock feathers."

"Fazed? Kris Jameson? Excusé moi! Got her mobile number."

"Smooth..."

"Not like that, dickhead. For an interview."

"Oh. Bit of a shame that, then."

"How come?"

"I 'ad a quick shufti back at the shots I took, while I was sittin' 'ere waiting for you. Some weird reason, none of her pictures came out, like. All the pixels just went crazy. Rearranged themselves into random noise."

∞

They met in a world-food place, downtown; her choice. At least they did decent coffee. Fifteen minutes late and he didn't recognise her when she sat down at the table. Was this a wind up? The girl in the peacock feathers was beauty incarnate; this was some sort of plain Jane, with lank, mousy hair, bad skin and watery eyes. She wore a dull-green combat jacket over black jeans and a sweatshirt. No hint of a feather.

"Hi Kris." The voice, however, was unmistakable. A kind of luminescent quality to it that he'd felt even on the phone. It was her.

"Hi yourself, Nadine." Hard to believe though that he'd felt such an overwhelming attraction. Perhaps some of the euphoria had rubbed off on him that night at the glim, after all. More likely those shots from the flask before going in.

No call for romance then. Might pay to keep her thinking something was on the cards, at least 'til he had an interview in the bag.

Her hand lay on the table. For a moment, he thought he could see right through it to the grain of the pinewood below. Transparency. The moment passed. He saw flesh again.

∞

"...and Zeeb, he's listening to the vibe of the cosmos, and he's looking for the chinks in the human armour, for the light to get in and do its work. So that's why it's glim, Kris. It's like, I don't know... like the eyes in a potato, where the new life sprouts, get me? It flies out and flowers. And the sensory mix-up kicks in and you're realising that the high is kind of more substantial than anything you ever had with drugs, or whatever..."

She'd been talking like this for an hour. Pure psychobabble. Yet the intensity with which she spoke was distinctly intoxicating. That *voice*... He had only to look away or momentarily close his eyes and she was in feathers again.

Much of what she said he found ludicrous. ("Like the *eyes* in a *potato*..." Get a *grip*!)

Some of it brought back a time when he'd once, too briefly, dreamed that life could be better.

∞

There was a sound system in the room. It was playing the scent of fresh rose petals. Time back, brought him here, she had. She had shadows, shadows that slowly slid like some sort of slithering, shining—

No, wait. He remembered something. Sound systems don't play scents. They play... What *do* they play? Oh yes, coruscating cascades of colour. Colour you could roll about in, get wrapped up in, colour you could *drink*.

Hang on. Wait a minute. That didn't seem right, either. And why was he waiting for the minute? How does it feel to touch sixty speeding seconds, each wrapping their packages of uncountable nanoseconds, femtoseconds...? Answer: like featherings, tiny featherings brushing the skin.

Featherings? Yes. The fronds of the peacock feather, the feathers of finery furling around her. Nadine. Her cross-sensory sound system. Her. In this room of comfort and delight, where she could control the intensity with carefully defined arm movements, each leading a trail of increasingly hazy afterimages in the air.

The essence of moon goddesses, her substance the ether. She was thrilling through him, now, waving him into her. She was drawing the deepest, deepest feelings up within him, until he could not but express his love, in all the ways and with all the devotional, confessional words he could muster.

Being naked helped. It was possible that Nadine was too, but it was hard to be sure because of the feathers, which could have been clothing. Possible too that she was some sort of hybrid, both bird and woman. Indeed, there was more than a chirrup in her voice at times. This seemed funny to him. He began to laugh.

Catching, she too began to laugh. When the laughter died down, she said: "But you know what the joke is, don't you?" and then paused.

"Go on then," he said. "I like a good joke."

"'Reality'. That's the joke. When *this*... this is as close as it gets to the *real*... We are one step from timelessness. You can't get much closer without ceasing to exist."

"Oh. Sort of a metaphysical joke, then?"

∞

With its clutter of mugs, digital devices and printouts, there was little to be seen of the original surface on Cal's kitchen table. Kris sat shivering in the intense, quivering glare of the fluorescent light, and took a sip of the whiskey the photographer had poured for him. Jameson's, no less.

"I don't know how I got here, can't even clearly work out where I came from."

"I had that once," boomed Cal. "Not sure... but I think I'd just been born."

"Well, fuck you, Cal. At least I got out of it wearing an overcoat."

"If nothing else. Hey, why are you staring at those? They're fucked up, Kris. I printed some out to check, but it's just digital dirt, man. Peacock feather lady – no pics."

Kris' voice was barely a murmur. "You're so wrong, Cal. These are pictures of Nadine. Look, she's dancing. And—" He slid out another from the small pile of prints. "This one. She's speaking. Her lips are moving. Fuck! I can hear her. I can hear what she's saying..."

Cal looked quizzically at the journalist. "Yeah? So what's she saying?"

"She's speaking in maroon, and... and streaks of dark purple. No, more of an indigo. And she's saying... she's saying that I'm still with her. I'm still in the room with the rose-petal sound system. Always was. Always will be. The idea that I'm here in your kitchen, Cal. That's the unreal part."

"Stay put right there, pal. I've got some tranqs somewhere."

∞

Those close to the source, Cal amongst them, chose to keep the real story quiet. Between themselves, though, they'd sometimes speak of it.

His identity had been in the hip flask. Without that vessel for company, Kris Jameson had not only lost his edge, but had gradually uprooted himself from any reality they shared. It was after the first glim, of course. He just kept on going back and back again whenever they ran one. He was cutting adrift. Each time he'd return less substantial, less of a presence in their lives.

The last time his old colleague ever encountered him, Kris was near subliminal. You could almost see through the guy. Sometimes there would be a sense of brightness or illumination, swelling around him in patterns of iridescent light. You'd catch it for a moment, and then lose it. A momentary impression of peacock feathers.

Patience

I think I shall go back – though I don't know when – to that place I so freely and frequently visited so many, many years ago. It has lived on inside me to this day, but my return was not permitted. Adulthood intervened.

You might ask: 'What was it like, this place?'

It was a place of absolute, intense colour. Neither living thing nor inanimate object was without its lustre. It was as if made of the stuff of rainbows, but rainbows whose spectra greatly exceeded the hues with which most people are familiar.

It was populated by an endless variety of curvilinear creatures. Some possessed limbs and bodies in shapes that might be recognised as approximately human or animal in form. Some were of a more abstract nature – shapes resembling spinning tops, architrave, balloons, lathed wooden doorknobs and tool handles. But these creatures also had a flexibility of form. They could break apart to reveal organic shapes, resembling those you might find in the artwork of Tibetan tankas: sinuous and symmetrical, coiling and interlacing, rich with lotus blossoms and always, always a great multiplicity of eyes.

The visual splendour of this place was matched by its scents and sounds. These have not lived on within me in quite the same intensity; yet I have only to sniff ananya, jasmine or neroli... I have only to hear a few bars of Duke Ellington, Hoagy Carmichael, or the Boswell Sisters... and its presence begins to load itself, to unwind and reveal its nature within my mind.

Did I miss it when access was denied? Of course. Ah but my eyes were open – and opening further – to the world in which I lived; for I would not want you to think that I did not appreciate the splendour that I share with you. Oh no. There was no end to my good fortune.

∞

"Hilda! Whatever are you doing, Hilda?" asks the nurse.

"It's under the bed! I always keep the best ones under the bed."

"Ah yes, your pictures! Hilda, this is not your home. You cannot keep them under the bed here. The health and safety men, they would scream and cry!"

She makes me laugh, this nurse. I remember her. She always has me laughing. Her name is... Her name is... Oh, if only I had the right glasses on and I could read her name badge!

"Those that fitted, they were put into this drawer here. The biggest drawer that you have in this room, that is where your pictures are."

"Oh yes, I'm so sorry, nurse, I quite forgot."

"You do not need to call me 'nurse'. I have told you my name. I am Patience. I am Patience."

"Ah! And so you are!"

Deftly, she helps me to my feet. She even hands me the proper glasses. I can see her face clearly now. Her brilliant face; those wide nostrils with their perfect, splayed curves, the rich ochre of her skin, the width of the pores on her cheeks. Only for a moment; until she moves, slips out of focus.

Patience, Patience… I must devise a mnemonic so that I will not forget her name.

"Now may I help you take your pictures from the drawer?"

"That would be most helpful. Thank you, Patience. But I will only need one. It should be the one on top."

"This one?"

"Um… Ah… Oh yes, yes, that's the one."

"You made this? You painted this?"

"Oh yes. Yes. Forty… forty-six years ago."

"Hilda! This is… Hilda, this is very beautiful."

∞

How *can* there be colours that most cannot see but some can? It was long, long before I could even clearly conceive that question. I knew, even as a child, that other children could not see what I saw. I don't mean seeing the place I spoke of earlier. In that respect I was not alone, for many children have their secret worlds. It was what I saw in *this* world and in its colours.

I will give you a simple example. Leaves. You will remark how leaves change colour in autumn, from green to glorious golds and reds. This is not such a dramatic change for me, as I see those colours blended within the green, from the very moment a leaf reaches maturity. The effect is, to my eyes, to make the leaf glow, almost as if luminescent. And another. Flowers I see as birds see them; the sunflower petal is for me a gradation from yellow through a series of exquisite tints to purple.

So of course when I reached adulthood I became a painter! Oh, but I was the dark sheep of the family! 'Our daughter, an artist! How absolutely scandalous!'

Ah, the thrill of it! The life I lived, disowned as I was. The prodigal daughter! I never returned. I made my own way. And whenever I was able, I painted. If I could not afford to buy paints, I made pictures with whatever I could lay my hands on – pencils, crayons, pastels, charcoals, chalks... If I could not afford canvas or cartridge paper, I worked on scraps, cardboard, objects, even walls.

I depicted the place I remembered so vividly from my childhood. My pictures were populated with the creatures I saw, whose every detail I was able to remember and reproduce. And when I had colour to use, I made my images shine with the known hues and – by dint of lengthy periods of experimentation – also with the unknown ones.

Which brings me back to the question: what was it that enabled me to see those colours? I found out, eventually, from an optician. I am tetrachromatic. I have four types of colour receptor in the retinas of my eyes, rather than the three types the majority, the trichromatics, have. It is, however, not enough simply to possess them. The brain must learn to recognise the information they pass on. In this respect I was fortunate, the visionary experience of my childhood served to familiarise me with the gift of these colours, priming me to see them in this world.

I was an elderly woman, my eyesight already starting to fail, by the time I learnt all this. Nevertheless, through my work, I had met a few others – always women – who saw what I saw. It is a human urge to name things, and we shared the frustration that our colours had no names. So we named them. Our primary fell close to orange in the spectrum. We called it 'overt'. To the hues that were created as overt blended with the other primaries, we gave a variety of fanciful names. Lumin, passionette, granade... Oh, we were poets in the service of tint.

Those women... dearest friends. Dead, gone, lost to me now.

I stare at my painting, as close to the window as I can be to see it in natural light. A large creature – with a little of the rhino, a little of the warthog, its body a spectral wash of intensely bright fur – strides through a clearing in a forest of twisted trees whose bountiful fruits hang like jewels. These on occasion catch the sunlight, casting light beams across the visual field. Above the tree canopy, the sun is close to setting. The sky... That sky still takes my breath away. Even now, with my failing eyes. Still.

That's why it is on top of the pile I keep under the bed. Or wherever it is I'm told they've put it now.

∞

"I have your medication, Hilda. Do you have some water?"

She is back. Her name is... I had a mnemonic for it. That's gone now, too. But she doesn't like to be called 'nurse'. I'll have to bluff.

"Oh yes, dear." I point to the jug on the bed-table. "Or is that my vodka, perhaps?"

When she laughs, it is full-bodied, huge. "Ah, you would be as high as a kite if you were drinking so much vodka, Hilda!"

"Really? And I was thinking that it was these pills you keep giving me."

"No, no, these are good for you. Here..."

"My glasses, please?"

I put them on, steal a quick glimpse at the name badge. "Thank you, Patience."

I swallow the pills. A doctor told me what they were for. I'm sure Patience is right. I'm sure they're good for me.

I hand back the little plastic cup. Casually, she puts it down, and then reaches to touch my arm. She is tactile. Warm. "May I ask you something?" she says, and there is a seriousness in her voice. She is ditching her professional jollity. "I have been thinking all morning about your picture, Hilda. It is very, very special. May I see it again?"

"Of course." I point to the bed. "It's under there."

She makes a clicking sound with her lips and tongue as she bends to reach for the picture. There should be a pile of them down there. I don't know where the others are.

We sit on the bed, each holding one side, and look at it together. She points to the purest section of the sky. "I have never seen this colour in any picture. Tell me, you, the lady who has made this— some people will say this is orange, but no. It is another colour. What is the name of it?"

"It is 'overt', my dear. The name of this colour is 'overt'."

∞

This is the last place in which I will dwell on this earth. I may be gone tomorrow, I may be here for some years, but it is clear that I am too frail to support myself in the way I managed for most of my long life. It's not a bad place. There is love here.

You might think that I achieved fame as an artist. This was not the case. I tried to make my mark in the first decades of my career. Critics deemed me an outsider, childlike – childish even – or 'primitive'. It was suggested more than once that I might have done better as an illustrator of children's books.

I carried on regardless. There was no other work for me than making my paintings and pictures.

In the 1960s and early '70s I was re-assessed, sold paintings sporadically, even had a few commissions. Good times. By the 90s I was largely forgotten. A footnote.

Now, I sit at the window – lights out in my room – so that I can see into the twilight. The colours of the day have faded, to be replaced with a new range. Inevitably, they are not as vivid to me as they once were, but they are still there. Pinks, greens and lilacs where trichromatics would only see shades of grey. They may even be the product of my mind now, rather than the decaying cones of my retinas. But I drink of them and take refreshment nonetheless.

Presently, I will press my buzzer and request help to get down to the day room, where I will sit and watch a little television with some of the other residents. That's what you do here.

Sometimes an image from the place of my childhood comes back to me, and there is a catch in my mind that releases, filling me with the urge to find brushes, crayons, canvas, napkins... anything with which to picture it. But my hands tremble now, my concentration wavers, my eyes tire quickly. The painting days are over.

Ah, do not feel sorry for me. Today, one of my carers has become a friend. Whenever we can, we will talk of things known only to us. She will look at my pictures and speak of what she sees. She will tell me of her own experiences as a child, seeing those effulgent and unique colours herself.

We have no reason merely to sit and wait. Our journeys of discovery are never done.

The Panel Which Cannot be Beaten

Cecil Oakley, panel beater, dressed habitually in shades of brown. Constantly serene, he was often mistaken for a Mormon. People were disappointed when he failed to offer them a leaflet.

He was a man of careful thought, of measured speech, slow enough to make others question their own quicksilver conclusions. Of his expertise there could be no doubt. Show him a dented panel and his dark brown eyes would go to work, gauging the force of restorative blows, assessing the angles from which to apply them. His sensitive fingers would probe for stress, eyes closed, caressing the contours of buckle and bend. He'd work with the grace of a sculptor and the gravity of a judge. Within an hour or two, that panel would be perfect.

"Tricky one here, Sess," said Derek the Manager.

The panel appeared to have undergone torture by a meticulous and maniacal metalphobe armed with a claw hammer. It was a mass of ridges and hollows, close to corrosion.

"Hmm. Well, there's a challenge," said Cecil quietly. "How did it—?"

"The usual. An accident. But it's priority. There's a VIP needs it done ASAP. The Lady Staines-Wrangler, no less."

∞

In the workshop, Cecil contemplated the panel. Once coated in paint of jade green with rims of sleek and graceful contour, it was – even in its currently crumpled state – redolent of wealth, luxury and power. To restore it; to return it pristine to the good Lady, that was a challenge indeed.

He selected a series of hammers and mallets, then set to work. A firm blow here; a series of sharp taps there; a long look followed by a lengthy probe; the mallet again; a deft swipe of the hammer... So, without ceasing, he worked for an hour and then for another.

In the third hour, though showing no outward sign, he became perturbed. He had long been a secret admirer of the Lady Staines-Wrangler. From all he'd read and seen of her in the media she seemed to him, with her wispy figure, her porcelain features and haute couture apparel, to embody the elegance of the nation's aristocracy. The work in hand was therefore an honour.

But it defied him, this panel. Though somewhat straightened now, it remained pocked and crimped. It manifested strange resistances, equal and opposite reactions at unexpected points. To adjust one section seemed always to worsen another. Trickier than anything he'd yet encountered; but – jewel amongst panels – it demanded restoration.

Knocking-off time came and went. "Keys through the letterbox when you're done," said Derek the Manager as he departed – appearing unsurprised that Cecil hadn't finished.

Cecil continued — tapping, hammering, probing, staring. Still the panel defied him. It seemed to have a will of its own.

Then it occurred to him. This panel... this panel could only be 'The Panel Which Cannot Be Beaten'. It was not merely a test. It was the greatest test of his art. Almost legendary, spoken of in hushed terms by panel beaters from Bournemouth to Bratislava; a test that – it seemed only apposite – had been assigned to him and him alone by the Lady Staines-Wrangler.

With renewed vigour he began to experiment: applying heat, clamps and weights. Calculations crawled like giant turtles through his mind. It was, he concluded, a matter of sequencing. The knock-on effects of one action required immediate compensation with the actions that followed. The series must run smoothly from beginning to end, like an unspoiled break on the snooker table.

He was ready.

∞

Cecil looked upon his work and was satisfied. There was no more he could do; other than go to the storeroom, select an appropriate shade and finish the job with a re-spray. Then he looked upon it some more. Even watching the paint dry was somehow exhilarating.

It occurred to him that this was no longer a matter in which Derek the Manager had any part. He'd get it wrapped and ready here and now.

In the morning he would put on his best brown suit and take the panel to the Lady Staines-Wrangler himself.

∞

"I'm sorry," said the doorman, "the Lady Staines-Wrangler has no wish to peruse any form of religious literature."

"No! I have the panel. The jade panel."

"Ah. Come in."

∞

The Lady Staines-Wrangler, dressed in an exquisite morning gown, appeared at the reception room doorway. Cecil rose to his feet. "It's here, Ma'am." He pointed to the parcel he'd leaned against a velvet chaise longue.

"Open it, please."

He deftly untucked the folds and tabs of the packaging until the panel was revealed.

Only then did she step from the doorway. "Quite incredible," she said in hushed tones, "the panel has never been so marvellously beaten. This is your work?"

"Yes, Ma'am."

But, as he looked at it, in bright morning sunlight pouring through the window, Cecil noticed that there were still imperfections. Slight ridges, faint depressions that he'd failed to notice before the wrapping. He'd been too hasty, too foolish.

He had apparently achieved the greatest mastery of his craft, and yet it galled him that he could have done better.

There was talk of reward, honours, remuneration. Cecil refused it all. He would return to his workshop and continue in the employment of Derek the Manager, just as he'd always done. A small bonus, perhaps. That would do.

When he'd gone, the Lady called for her butler. "The panel," she said.

He knew what to do.

In an outhouse, he spent the rest of the day attacking it, meticulously and maniacally, with a claw hammer. He had a deep hatred for metal. And panels, he hated them most of all.

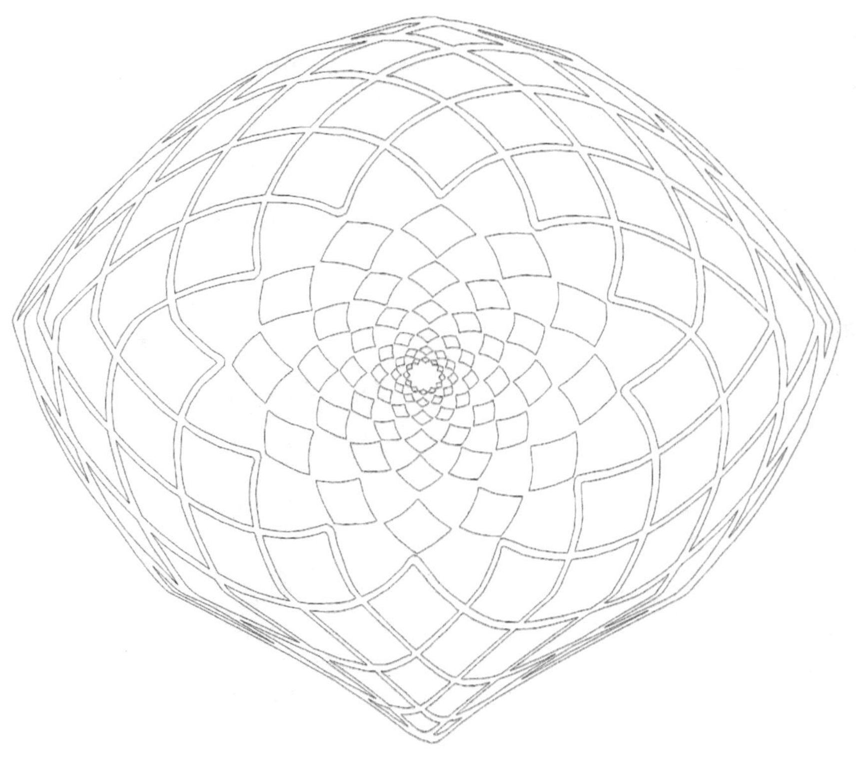

The End

"'The End'? What kind of a title is that?" Eric made a noise that a convenient gap in his front teeth had no doubt enabled him to customise over a number of years. A sort of 'ppphh' sound that conveyed contemptuous dismissal. "Title like that, I'd bloody well jump to the next story, I would."

"Ah," I said, incapable of concealing my overweening smugness, "but you won't be able to. It's the last one in the book."

"Ppphh," he repeated. "Smart arse!"

Some of the spittle reached me that time, splatter drops on the skin of my face. I was almost regretting my choice to read at this particular workshop.

When I was young, insofar as I can remember anything about it whatsoever, the word 'workshop' referred to a room or building where handmade objects were crafted into existence. Somehow, in the leap to my now advanced years, I had entered a world of 'level playing fields', 'solutions', 'blue sky thinking'. I had, as it happens, entered it 'big time'. In this peculiar milieu, you only had to mention a potential enterprise and those around you were seemingly compelled to 'workshop' it. Nevertheless, I had succumbed to the lure of 'writing workshops'. And, it had to be said, this one was at least a nicely democratic affair.

"For Christ's sake," Eric interrupted. "Get on with it. We don't want to know your opinion about workshops, you supercilious prat. You told us all your bloody stories are supposed to be only up to two thousand words long. Well you've used up two hundred and fifty-nine already and the damn thing hasn't started yet."

I looked at him wearily. He was balding, skinny, unkempt and unshaven. He wore a faintly grease-stained waistcoat, charcoal trousers and a collarless grey-white shirt. The rest of the crew were, in large part, young enthusiastic writers and – though ready to give constructive criticism – unfailingly polite.

"Look," I said, "I'm doing a bit of scene setting and I'm establishing the somewhat pompous nature of the narrator, alright? And actually I'm showing, not telling. So there. Now, can you just hold your comments until I've read the rest of the piece?"

"Ppphh," he sprayed, then muttered: "Three hundred and sixty-eight."

"Please, Eric, let Richard finish his reading and then we can all talk about it."

It was Tilly. Always smartly dressed and endlessly creative with the way she wore her multi-coloured neck scarves, Tilly was the reliably sensible member of the group. Her organisational skills were recognised and exploited by everyone. That any of the group's occasional peripatetic activities happened at all depended in large part on Tilly, let alone that the room above the lounge bar of the Hangman's Arms was regularly booked and paid for.

We had been meeting there every month for about a year. Before that we'd workshopped for a while in one another's homes, but numbers had grown and we'd moved to these premises. Some evenings our sessions were intense – everyone bought something to read. There was wacky science fiction, often fabulous fantasy, occasional crime and a soupçon of horror. Literary tales, even biography got a fairly regular look in, but it was genre stuff that really excited this lot the most.

As my reading reached the end of the previous paragraph, my eyes caught Eric's. He raised his hand to his mouth, hamming a small yawn. I felt like telling him that I was building to set up the Wilful Misunderstanding word in this story, but decided it was better to press on.

Some nights, though, were slacker. There'd perhaps be just one or two readings and much of the time we'd sit and chat – about writing sometimes, other times anything that took our fancy. It was at one of these sessions that someone asked Del whether he was working on anything at the moment. Del read rarely, but when he did bring something it was usually pretty impressive. Sometimes, in smaller groups, we'd speculate on which of us would be most likely to write a bestseller. The betting was usually on Del.

A man of few words, he answered the question saying: "Oh, I'm just nibbling away at something now. Got to research it. Could take a while."

At that point, Dave Combes – whose work almost invariably had us all falling about laughing – declared exultantly: "Hey! 'Nibbling', that's such a great word. I like it. All of us here, nibbling away at stories. Little bit of plot here, little bit of dialogue there – and then, hopefully, it all comes together. So long as you haven't bitten off more than you can chew, I guess."

"Ah!" said Aneira. A specialist in well researched medieval romances, she had long blonde hair, an elegant frame, and was fancied by most of the men in the group. "That could be like one of the words in Richard's 'Wilful Misunderstandings' stories. A special word that writers use, like when they're talking amongst themselves."

All eyes turned to me. I didn't say anything. I was too busy writing the word 'nibble' down in my notebook, followed by 'word that writers use'. I could see the potential. Nibbling was a way of chasing a story out of nowhere, or poking around until you plucked it out of the ether. Nibbling was finding your way, when the route map was buried somewhere in your mind and you couldn't quite get at it.

My thoughts dissolved as I became conscious of a familiar sound.
"Ppphh."

Eric had joined the writing group about six months before and had already been the topic of some heated arguments. We'd always had an unwritten rule that critiques of other people's work should be constructive. We were here to help one another, not slag each other off. Eric did not appear to get this at all. More than once we'd been on the point of asking him to leave. The trouble was we were all too polite. 'Well, when he reads his own stuff, it's pretty damn good,' we'd say, when discussing him in his absence. This was true. He wrote dark, dark horror stories that more often than not got right under your skin and creeped you out. 'And when he's critiquing, he's often right on the ball,' is another thing we'd say. And: 'He does hold back a bit when there's someone new or clearly unconfident.'

So Eric got to stay on. He was our wild card.

"Ppphh. Look at him," he was saying, "writing it all down in his notebook. He's going to pass that 'nibble' thing off as one of his own ideas now, you wait and see."

"So what if I do?" I retorted. "We exchange ideas freely here. I've probably given you one or two since you've been coming."

Eric shook his head firmly. "No, no, no... There's a difference. You were talking about my story at the time, throwing in your ideas about what I'd come up with. But when Del came up with that word, and Dave picked up on it, they weren't talking about any story of yours, were they? I reckon they should have first dibs on it." He looked over at Del and Dave Combes. "What do you say? It's your idea. Ideas are gold dust in this malarkey."

They looked at Eric. They looked at me. "No, it's okay. We don't mind if Richard wants to use that as one of his words," Del said. Politely.

At this point I stopped my reading. "That's as far as I've got," I said. "The next bit is where everyone critiques the story so far. So, what do you think?"

There was absolute silence. Seconds slowed to a near halt. Everyone was looking down, studiously, at any notes they had or hadn't made while I'd been reading. 'Oh shit,' I thought, 'They all hate it. I knew it. I've just written a load of crap.'

Tilly broke the silence. "Well, I liked it. I liked the way you sketched in all the characters, just enough to differentiate them for the story without any unnecessary detail. And yet they all felt like people I know, somehow."

"Though in fact," added Del, thoughtfully, "you've only set up half a dozen characters. Aren't there any more people than that in this writing group?"

It was true. There were. But the others just sat at the table looking like showroom dummies. I hadn't given them any life. Dealing with that issue was going to be tricky. I made a note in my notebook. "Yeah, good point, Del. Thanks."

Dave Combes broke in. "I don't know. I'm not sure about all this kind of post-modernist self-referential stuff. And I kept losing track of where you were – in the present, like, reading the story – and then what bits were actually in the story that you were reading."

I nodded. "Yeah, I did wonder about that. But I think if you were actually reading it on the page, you'd be able to figure it out. The bits in the past are sort of in context, and I've used phrases like 'I stopped reading' or whatever to snap us back to the present."

"Mmm..." Dave was still dubious.

"No, that Eric character," said Eric. "He's pants, frankly. I mean he starts off all sweary and confrontational, but by this point he's sounding almost as polite as the rest of 'em."

"I see what you mean, Eric. I'll have to do something about that."

"Sodding right, you will. You're one thousand five hundred and eighty-four words into this so-called story by now and I'm buggered if I can see where it's going."

I had another moment of supreme smugness. "That's called 'keeping you in suspense', Eric."

"Sod off."

"Eric, please..." moaned Tilly.

I looked over at Aneira. She'd sat quietly so far, but as my eye caught hers, she spoke. "Richard, I'd like to know something."

"Wouldn't we all?" muttered Eric. Tilly glared at him. Chastened, he looked down at the table.

"I'd like to know whether your story is really set in this writing group, or whether we... all of us... are actually fictional characters that you've created."

"Well..." I said. I knew I was heading into dangerous territory. I'd been hoping that none of them would notice. I'd have to pick my words carefully. Fortunately I had time to do that, given that I was the one who was creating the story. If I could just keep them talking for another two hundred words or so, and then bring it to a close, I could maybe get away with it before anything really nasty happened.

It wouldn't be the first time that a writer had been a victim of his own characters.

"Oh," said Eric loudly. "So we are all just your sodding characters!"

Damn! That bit of narrative... They were still listening.

Even Tilly was giving me a shocked expression. "Richard... That's really rather unfair, isn't it? To create us all, and then stuff us into a story that has to end in no more than two thousand words."

"Yeah," said Dave Combes. "Why couldn't you put us all into a novel? Or a bloody trilogy come to that. Then we could have had a bit more dimension. Other interests. Lives outside this room. Subplots."

Though not generally a writer of violent scenes, it was looking like I'd be getting some practice. Eric was on his feet, nudging Del to join him. "Come on. Let's sort Mr Smartarse out before he writes us off." Eric I could perhaps have handled, but Del – although I'd not previously described his appearance – was looking beefy and mean. The dummies too began to appear threatening.

"I really am sorry, guys," I said lamely. "Look, maybe I could do some sort of sequel. A really thick novel. Could be a series. You could all have your own solo books."

But by then I was safe. One thousand nine hundred and ninety-three words. I'd nibbled my way to...

The End

Acknowledgements

One story in this collection dates back to sometime in the 1990s. It sat in a file near-forgotten until sometime in 2009 when I dug it out of its hidey-hole, conceived the possibility that I could wilfully misunderstand words or phrases to create some more stories of a similar nature and began the work that has led to this book. Along the way, quite a few people have generously offered time to read my work and assist me with its development.

So first a huge thank-you to Tish Oakwood who read every one of the stories, offering an always helpful critical perspective, a good many ideas and continual encouragement. The same goes for the late Steve Moore, who read the majority of them and offered the same. A man much missed since his departure to the lunar realms.

For help with specific tales, advice, reference and further encouragement, thanks go to: Alan Moore, Sally Spedding, John Billingsley, Deb Delano, Tim Cutting, Malcolm Green, Emily Hinshelwood, RG Gregory and Shaftesbury's excellent 'Storyslingers' writers' group.

I also acknowledge here those who saw fit to publish individual stories. They are 'The View from Here' website which featured 'Beast' (no longer active as a site but an archive remains); 'Brautigan Free Press' who took an enthusiastic dive into 'Frank's Cocoon'; 'Jupiter' who were up for 'Encounters' and 'Confingo' who took 'Friendly Smiles and Calm Voices'. My thanks too go to a number of small magazine editors who offered favourable comments and useful suggestions. Knowing such mags – labours of love – are deluged with submissions, I appreciate greatly the time taken to respond.

And finally massive thanks to Jamie Delano for taking this book into the Lepus fold and uncounted but plentiful hours of work on the final edits of these stories. Not to mention advice, technical and design assistance, suggestions, patience and good humour. There is not a comma or a dash in this book which has not been carefully assessed by Jamie.

Having completed a BA in literature at Essex University in 1973, Richard Foreman took on a variety of occupations including community arts and theatre work. In the late 1980s, writing as 'Dick Foreman', he became a full time scriptwriter of comic strips, progressing from one-off stories to a monthly series for US publisher DC comics. 'Black Orchid' ran for two years. Richard's working life then switched to other interests, but for twenty years he continued writing quarterly scripts for photo-stories/comic strips in 'Who Cares?', a national magazine for children in care. Since 2009 he has returned full time to writing. Following a series of well-received articles for Alan Moore's 'Dodgem Logic' magazine, he began work on 'Wilful Misunderstandings'. He has recently contributed to the magazines 'Roundyhouse' and 'Tears in the Fence' and is currently writing a novel.

Comic book scripts (writing as 'Dick Foreman')

1988: stories for 2000AD, Blaam!
1990: 1 issue 'Hellblazer' (DC Comics)
1991: story for 'Taboo' magazine (Tundra)
1992: 2 issues 'Swamp Thing' (DC Comics)
1993-96: 23 issues 'Black Orchid' (DC Comics)
1990-2010: quarterly photostories and comic strips for UK children's magazine 'Who Cares'

Prose/poetry

2010-11: contributed articles to Alan Moore's 'Dodgem Logic' magazine (Knockabout)
2012: Contributed to Welsh poetry anthology 'And This Global Warming' (Roynetree Press)
2012-2015: contributions to Welsh poetry magazine 'Roundyhouse'
2016: poem and short story to appear in 'Tears in the Fence' magazine.

Also Available from Lepus Books:

"Book Thirteen"
A novel by A. William James (aka Jamie Delano)

"Kiss My ASBO"
A novel by Alistair Fruish

"Leepus | DIZZY"
A novel by Jamie Delano

"The Things You Do"
A memoir by Deborah Delano

"The Saddest Sound"
A novel by Deborah Delano

And coming in 2016:

"Leepus | THE RIVER"
A second 'Leepus' novel by Jamie Delano

9 780993 390104